As I crossed the ridge, I saw the cairn. Ortali had dislodged many of the boulders and an unholy radiance rose from the aperture he had made—and I saw there the helmeted figure of Odin on the stones where I had placed it so many centuries ago in another life.

As Ortali leaned forward to examine his find, a gasping cry broke from my lips—for the sprig of holly worn in his lapel slipped from its place and fell on the mailed breast of the figure, where it blazed suddenly with a brightness too dazzling for human eyes. The figure moved; the mighty limbs flexed, tumbling the stones aside. A new gleam lighted the terrible eye and animated the carven features.

Out of the cairn the Gray Man rose, and the northern lights played terribly about him as he changed and altered in horrific transmutation. The human features faded and the armor crumbled to dust, and the fiendish spirit of ice and frost and darkness that the sons of the North deified as Odin stood nakedly and terribly in the stars. About his grisly head played lightnings.

Ortali cowered, screaming wordlessly, as the taloned malformed hands reached for him. I heard Ortali scream once as a blinding blue glare burst about him, then his body was dashed earthward—shriveled and blackened, like a man blasted by a thunderbolt. Then the slavering monster lumbered toward me, shadowy tentacle-like arms outspread, the pale starlight making a luminous pool of his great inhuman eye. . . .

—from "The Cairn on the Headland"

THE ROBERT E. HOWARD LIBRARY

Cormac Mac Art
Kull
Solomon Kane
Bran Mak Morn
Eons of the Night
Trails in Darkness
Beyond the Borders

BEYOND THE BORDERS

ROBERT E. HOWARD

BEYOND THE BORDERS

This is a work of fiction. All the characters and events portrayed in this book are fictional, and any resemblance to real people or incidents is purely coincidental.

A Baen Books Original

Baen Publishing Enterprises
PO Box 1403
Riverdale, NY 10471

ISBN: 0-671-87742-9

Cover art by C.W. Kelly

First printing, October 1996

Distributed by Simon & Schuster
1230 Avenue of the Americas
New York, NY 10020

Printed in the United States of America

CONTENTS

Introduction by T.K.F. Weisskopf..... vii

The Voice of El-Lil................................. 1

The Cairn on the Headland............... 34

Casonetto's Last Song 61

The Cobra in the Dream.................... 67

Dig Me No Grave................................. 76

The Haunter of the Ring.................... 95

Dermod's Bane.................................. 117

King of the Forgotten People.......... 125

The Children of the Night 152

The Dream Snake 173

The Hyena 182

People of the Black Coast 200

The Fire of Asshurbanipal............... 213

ACKNOWLEDGMENTS

INTRODUCTION

WELCOME TO THE CLUB

To those of you who are familiar with Robert E. Howard through his great archetypal hero, Conan the Barbarian, welcome. You are in for a treat. You are about to meet some of Conan's brothers and sisters. To those who are reading Howard for the first time, welcome beyond the borders of what you once knew of the world.

Though they are not part of a strictly defined series, the stories in this volume all come from the same place. One gets the impression that the men who are telling these stories, acting in them, and listening to them, all know one another—or could at some future time, in some smoke-filled room in a men's club somewhere, say, or on a wind-swept beach, meet and raise a glass. And such is the charm of Robert E. Howard, for a short time, while you are reading the stories, you are part of that club, too.

Beyond the Borders is volume seven of Baen's Robert E. Howard library, a series of collections of Howard's best short stories, *sans* Conan. It seems appropriate to end the series with a group of traveling stories; even if Howard never left Texas, you can.

These stories illustrate the absolute fallacy of that trite maxim, beloved of creative writing teachers, to "write what you know." Howard transports his readers to the sands of the Middle East, to darkest Africa, to mist-shrouded Ireland, to desert islands, lost cities, and haunted swamps without ever once going beyond the borders of the Southwest. But writing mimetic fiction about small-town life during the Depression was not what Howard wanted to do.

Which is not to say that Howard was weaving the background for these fantastic adventures out of whole cloth. A voracious reader who thought about what he read, Howard probably did know all there was to know about ancient civilizations, about the explorers and their discoveries of his time—and this was the time of "Indiana Jones"-style archaeologists. Men of science who were also men of adventure. Kirowan and O'Donnell easily could have been colleagues of Flinders Petrie, the wild British Egyptologist mentioned in "The Children of the Night."

Howard is clearly interested in what makes heroes tick. He finds them objects of study, contemplation, and for this reason his heroes are not mere muscle-bound caricatures. While partaking of all that science and the organization that employing its method brings to the universe, Howard was exploring the borders of what science could explain. He plays with this in "Dig Me No Grave," where the mystery at first seems to be explained by a modern understanding of the nature of epilepsy—but that explanation only goes so far.

Another way Howard strengthens his reader's belief in the story and in the veracity of his narrators was to lard his tales with real historical references, real literary references, and modern scientific theory. Most of the time, Howard's exotic terms will be accurate. For instance, "Kara-Shehr" does indeed mean "Black City" in Turkish, and "Beledel-Djinn" does translate to "City of Devils" in Arabic, just as he states in "The Fire of Asshurbanipal." But, like his friend and contemporary H.P. Lovecraft, he wasn't above sneaking in a fictional reference along with the fact. I've learned a great deal attempting to separate the fiction from the fact of the stories in this volume. The cult of Malik Tous, mentioned in several stories, is—so far as my research can tell me—one that only existed in the pages of *Weird Tales*. Fans of Lovecraft will, of course, notice references to the Necronomicon, the works of Von Junzt, and to the mad Arab

Alhazred. Experienced readers of Howard will recognize Bran Mak Morn the Pict, a character about whom Howard wrote many stories (see Volume IV of this series). But I expect that only true Howard fanatics will be familiar with the work of the poet Tevis Clyde Smith, quoted in an offhand manner in "People of the Black Coast." He was a friend of Howard's from Texas whose work was entirely self-published, and that, years after Howard's death—with the exception of several pieces that appeared in a fanzine called *The Howard Collector*.

To describe his heroes, Howard used time honored means of writing about them. The lists of literary works mentioned above are reminiscent of those found in all epic poetry. At its best, Howard's prose sings. It is vigorous, masculine; like Homer, there is rhythm in his prose, like the author of "Beowulf," he uses alliteration to powerful effect. It is clear on reading just a few of his stories that while Howard certainly had not one iota of racial political correctness in him, he felt that it was what one did with one's life that counted. Whether one was male or female, white or black, yellow or brown, Christian or pagan. (A typically American attitude, I should add.)

Because the prose matters, we have chosen in the Baen Robert E. Howard Library to publish the stories as Howard wrote them or as they were first published in *Weird Tales* in the 1930s. These texts have had later editorial additions deleted and excisions restored—they have been "un-Bowdlerized," if you will. I believe that an intelligent reader will not be shocked by reading Howard as he presented himself.

Even though Howard's themes and prose style are virile, this is not to say that Howard appeals only to macho men. Howard wrote about all kinds of people, strong men and weak, and women who were their equals in both. Certainly when I was a teenager, encountering Howard for the first time I was nothing but enthralled. I owe a debt to Jerry Page, Hank Reinhardt, and John Maddox Roberts, Southern writers whose strong interest in Howard's works and the very idea of "heroic fantasy" was catching.

In fact, countless writers have been influenced by Robert E. Howard. There's no denying that his works have shaped the field, that his words have a power even beyond the grave, not the least of which is the power to inspire faithful readers. I'd like to take this opportunity, in this, the last volume of Baen's Robert E. Howard Library, to thank some of those faithful without whom this project would never have happened. David Drake, Glenn Lord, and Rusty Burke were incredible and invaluable resources during the entire process. Kudos also go to artist Ken Kelly—his enthusiasm for the works came through in the excellent paintings for the covers. Kirby McCauley was a tireless Howard advocate. Hank Davis's efforts in-house were beyond the borders of duty. Deane Fetrow, our typist, was extremely helpful—and another Howard fan from way back. David Weber, Ramsey Campbell, and Steve Stirling all did wonderful introductions to earlier volumes. And, of course, without Jim Baen nothing could have been accomplished. They are all definitely members of the club. I hope after reading this volume, you'll feel you are, too.

—Toni Weisskopf
Riverdale, NY 1996

The story of a lost city, a love triangle, and a terrible magic—or is it all just a wanderer's tall tale?

THE VOICE OF EL-LIL

Muskat, like many another port, is a haven for the drifters of many nations who bring their tribal customs and peculiarities with them. Turk rubs shoulders with Greek and Arab squabbles with Hindoo. The tongues of half the Orient resound in the loud smelly bazaar. Therefore it did not seem particularly incongruous to hear, as I leaned on a bar tended by a smirking Eurasian, the musical notes of a Chinese gong sound clearly through the lazy hum of native traffic. There was certainly nothing so startling in those mellow tones that the big Englishman next to me should start and swear and spill his whiskey-and-soda on my sleeve.

He apologized and berated his clumsiness with honest profanity, but I saw he was shaken. He interested me as his type always does—a fine upstanding fellow he was, over six feet tall, broad-shouldered, narrow-hipped, heavy-limbed, the perfect fighting man, brown-faced, blue-eyed and tawny-haired. His breed is old as Europe, and the man himself brought to mind vague legendary characters—Hengist, Hereward, Cedrik—born rovers and fighters of the original barbarian stock.

I saw, furthermore, that he was in a mood to talk. I introduced myself, ordered drinks and waited. My specimen thanked me, muttered to himself, quaffed his liquor hastily and spoke abruptly:

"You're wondering why a grown man should be so suddenly upset by such a small thing—well, I admit that damned gong gave me a start. It's that fool Yotai Lao, bringing his nasty joss sticks and Buddhas into a decent town—for a half-penny I'd bribe some Moslem fanatic to cut his yellow throat and sink his confounded gong into the gulf. And I'll tell you why I hate the thing.

"My name," he said, "is Bill Kirby. It was in Jibuti on the Gulf of Aden that I met John Conrad. A slim, keen-eyed young New Englander he was— professor too, for all his youth. Victim of obsession also, like most of his kind. He was a student of bugs, and it was a particular bug that had brought him to the East Coast; or rather, the hope of the blooming beast, for he never found it. It was almost uncanny to see the chap work himself into a blaze of enthusiasm when speaking on his favorite subject. No doubt he could have taught me much I should know, but insects are not among my enthusiasms, and he talked, dreamed and thought of little else at first. . . .

"Well, we paired off well from the start. He had money and ambitions and I had a bit of experience and a roving foot. We got together a small, modest but efficient safari and wandered down into the back country of Somaliland. Now you'll hear it spoken today that this country has been exhaustively explored and I can prove that statement to be a lie. We found things that no white man has ever dreamed of.

"We had trekked for the best part of a month and had gotten into a part of the country I knew was unknown to the average explorer. The veldt and thorn forests gave way to what approached real jungle and what natives we saw were a thick-lipped, low browed, dog-tooth breed—not like the Somali at all. We wandered on though, and our porters and askari began muttering among themselves. Some of the black fellows had been hobnobbing with them and telling them tales that frightened them from going on. Our men wouldn't talk to me or Conrad about it, but we had a camp servant, a half-caste named Selim, and I told him to see what he could learn. That night he came to my tent. We had pitched a camp in a sort of big glade and had built a thorn boma; for the lions were raising merry Cain in the bush.

" 'Master,' he said in the mongrel English he was so proud of, 'them black fella he is scaring the porters and askari with bad ju-ju talk. They be tell about a might ju-ju curse on the country in which we go to, and—'

"He stopped short, turned ashy, and my head jerked up. Out of the dim, jungle-haunted mazes of the south whispered a haunting voice. Like the echo of an echo it was, yet strangely distinct, deep, vibrant, melodious. I stepped from my tent and saw Conrad standing before fire, taut and tense as a hunting hound.

" 'Did you hear that?' he asked. 'What was it?'

" 'A native drum,' I answered—but we both knew
I lied. The noise and chatter of our natives about
their cooking-fires had ceased as if they had all
died suddenly.

"We heard nothing more of it that night, but the
next morning we found ourselves deserted. The
black boys had decamped with all the luggage they
could lay hand to. We held a council of war, Conrad, Selim and I. The half-caste was scared pink,
but the pride of his white blood kept him carrying
on.

" 'What now?' I asked Conrad. 'We've our guns
and enough supplies to give us a sporting chance
of reaching the coast.'

" 'Listen!' he raised his hand. Out across the
bush-country throbbed again that haunting whisper.
'We'll go on. I'll never rest until I know what makes
that sound. I never heard anything like it in the
world before.'

" 'The jungle will pick our bally bones,' I said.
He shook his head.

" 'Listen!' he said.

"It was like a call. It got into your blood. It drew
you as a fakir's music draws a cobra. I knew it was
madness. But I didn't argue. We cached most of
our duffle and started on. Each night we built a
thorn boma and sat inside it while the big cats
yowled and grunted outside. And ever clearer as we
worked deeper and deeper in the jungle mazes, we
heard that voice. It was deep, mellow, musical. It
made you dream strange things; it was pregnant
with vast age. The first glories of antiquity whispered in its blooming. It centered in its resonance
all the yearning and mystery of life; all the magic

soul of the East. I awoke in the middle of night to listen to its whispering echoes, and slept to dream of sky-towering minarets, of long ranks of bowing, brown-skinned worshippers, of purple-canopied peacock thrones and thundering golden chariots.

"Conrad had found something at last that rivalled his infernal bugs in his interest. He didn't talk much; he hunted insects in an absent-minded way. All day he would seem to be in an attitude of listening, and when the deep golden notes would roll out across the jungle, he would tense like a hunting dog on the scent, while into his eyes would steal a look strange for a civilized professor. By Jove, it's curious to see some ancient primal influence steal through the veneer of a cold-blooded scientist's soul and touch the red flow of life beneath! It was new and strange to Conrad; here was something he couldn't explain away with his new-fangled, bloodless psychology.

"Well, we wandered on in that mad search—for it's the white man's curse to go into Hell to satisfy his curiosity. Then in the gray light of an early dawn the camp was rushed. There was no fight. We were simply flooded and submerged by numbers. They must have stolen up and surrounded us on all sides; for the first thing I knew, the camp was full of fantastic figures and there were a half dozen spears at my throat. It rasped me terribly to give up without a shot fired, but there was no bettering it, and I cursed myself for not having kept a better lookout. We should have expected something of the kind, with that devilish chiming in the south.

"There were at least a hundred of them, and I got a chill when I looked at them closely. They weren't black boys and they weren't Arabs. They were lean men of middle height, light yellowish, with dark eyes and big noses. They wore no beards and their heads were close-shaven. They were clad in a sort of tunic, belted at the waist with a wide leather girdle, and sandals. They also wore a queer kind of iron helmet, peaked at the top, open in front and coming down nearly to their shoulders behind and at the sides. They carried big metal-braced shields, nearly square and were armed with narrow-bladed spears, strangely made bows and arrows, and short straight swords as I had never seen before—or since.

"They bound Conrad and me hand and foot and they butchered Selim then and there—cut his throat like à pig while he kicked and howled. A sickening sight—Conrad nearly fainted and I dare say I looked a bit pale myself. Then they set out in the direction we had been heading, making us walk between them, with our hands tied behind our backs and their spears threatening us. They brought along our scanty dunnage, but from the way they carried the guns I didn't believe they knew what those were for. Scarcely a word had been spoken between them and when I essayed various dialects I only got the prod of a spear-point. Their silence was a bit ghostly and altogether ghastly. I felt as we'd been captured by a band of spooks.

"I didn't know what to make of them. They had the look of the Orient about them but not the Orient with which I was familiar, if you understand me. Africa is of the East, but not one with it. They looked no more African than a Chinaman does. This is hard to explain. But I'll say this: Tokyo is Eastern, and Benares is equally so, but Benares symbolizes a different, older phase of the Orient, while Pekin represents still another, and older one. These men were of an Orient I had never known; they were part of an East older than Persia—older than Assyria—older than Babylon! I felt it about them like an aura and I shuddered from the gulfs of time they symbolized. Yet it fascinated me, too. Beneath the Gothic arches of an age-old jungle, speared along by silent Orientals whose type has been forgotten for God knows how many eons, a man can have fantastic thoughts. I almost wondered if these fellows were real, or but the ghosts of warriors dead four thousand years!

"The trees began to thin, and the ground sloped upward. At last we came out upon a sort of cliff and saw a sight that made us gasp. We were looking into a big valley surrounded entirely by high, steep cliffs, through which various streams had cut narrow canyons to feed a good-sized lake in the center of the valley. In the center of the lake was an island and on that island was a temple and at the farther end of the lake was a city! No native village of mud and bamboo, either. This seemed to be of stone, yellowish-brown in color.

"The city was walled and consisted of square-built, flat-topped houses, some apparentlly three or four stories high. All the shores of the lake were in cultivation and the fields were green and flourishing, fed by artificial ditches. They had a system of irrigation that amazed me. But the most astonishing thing was the temple on the island.

"I gasped, gaped and blinked. It was the Tower of Babel true to life! Not as tall or as big as I'd imagined it, but some ten tiers high and sullen and massive just like the pictures, with that same intangible impression of evil hovering over it.

"Then as we stood there, from that vast pile of masonry there floated out across the lake that deep resonant booming—close and clear now—and the very cliffs seemed to quiver with the vibrations of that music-laden air. I stole a glance at Conrad; he looked all at sea. He was of that class of scientists who have the universe classified and pigeonholed and everything in it proper little nook. By Jove! It knocks them in a heap to be confronted with the paradoxical-unexplainable-shouldn't-be more than it does common chaps like you and me, who haven't many preconceived ideas of things in general.

"The soldiers took us down a stairway cut into the solid rock of the cliffs and we went through irrigated fields were shaven-headed men and dark-eyed women paused in their work to stare curiously at us. They took us to a big, iron-braced gate where a small body of soldiers, equipped like our captors, challenged them, and after a short parley we were escorted into the city. It was much like any other Eastern city—men, women and children going to and fro, arguing, buying and selling. But all in all, it had that same effect of apartness—of vast antiquity. I couldn't classify the architecture any more than I could understand the language. The only things I could think of as I stared at those squat, square buildings was the huts of certain low-caste, mongrel people still built in the valley of the Euphrates in Mesopotamia. Those huts might be a degraded evolution from the architecture in that strange African city.

"Our captors took us straight to the largest building in the city, and while we marched along the streets, we discovered that the houses and walls were not of stone after all, but a sort of brick. We

were taken into a huge-columned hall before which
stood ranks of silent soldiery, and taken before a
dais up which led broad steps. Armed warriors
stood behind and on either side of a throne, a scribe
stood beside it, girls clad in ostrich-plumes lounged
on the broad steps, and on the throne sat a grim-
eyed devil who alone of all the men of that fantastic
city wore his hair long. He was black-bearded, wore
a sort of crown and had the haughtiest, cruelest face
I ever saw on any man. An Arab sheikh or Turkish
shah was a lamb beside him. He reminded me of
some artist's conception of Belshazzar or the Pha-
raohs—a king who was more than a king in his own
mind and the eyes of his people—a king who was
at once a king and high priest and god.

"Our escort promptly prostrated themselves
before him and knocked their heads on the matting
until he spoke a languid word to the scribe and this
personage signed for them to rise. They rose, and
the leader began a long rigmarole to the king, while
the scribe scratched away like mad on a clay tablet
and Conrad and I stood there like a pair of blooming gaping jackasses, wondering what it was all
about. Then I heard a word repeated continually,
and each time he spoke it, he indicated us. The
word sounded like 'Akkadian," and suddenly my
brain reeled with the possibilities it betokened. It
couldn't be—yet it had to be!

"Not wanting to break in on the conversation and
maybe lose my bally head, I said nothing, and at
last the king gestured and spoke, the soldiers bowed
again and seizing us, hustled us roughly from the
royal presence into a columned corridor, across a
huge chamber and into a small cell where they

thrust us and locked the door. There was only a heavy bench and one window, closely barred.

"'My heavens, Bill,' exclaimed Conrad, 'who could have imagined anything equal to this? It's like a nightmare—or a tale from *The Arabian Nights!* Where are we? Who are these people?'

"'You won't believe me,' I said, 'but—you've heard of the ancient empire of Sumeria?'

"'Certainly; it flourished in Mesopotamia some four thousand years ago. But what—by Jove!' he broke off, staring at me wide-eyed as the connection struck him.

"'I leave it to you what the descendants of an Asia-Minor kingdom are doing in East Africa,' I said, feeling for my pipe, 'but it must be—the Sumerians built their cities of sun-dried brick. I saw men making bricks and stacking them up to dry along the lake shore. The mud is remarkably like that you find in the Tigris and Euphrates valley. Likely that's why these chaps settled here. The Sumerians wrote on clay tablets by scratching the surface with a sharp point just as the chap was doing in the throne room.

"'Then look at their arms, dress and physiognomy. I've seen their art carved on stone and pottery and wondered if those big noses were part of their faces or part of their helmets. And look at that temple in the lake! A small counterpart of the temple reared to the god El-Lil in Nippur—which probably started the myth of the Tower of Babel.

"'But the thing that clinches it is the fact that they referred to us as Akkadians. Their empire was conquered and subjugated by Sargon of Akkad in 2750 B.C. If these are descendants of a band who fled their conqueror, it's natural that, pent in these hinterlands and separated from the rest of the world, they'd come to call all outlanders Akkadians, much as secluded Oriental nations call all Europeans Franks in memory of Martel's warriors who scuttled them at Tours.'

" 'Why do you suppose they haven't been discovered before now?'

" 'Well, if any white man's been here before, they took good care he didn't get out to tell his tale. I doubt if they wander much; probably think the outside world's overrun with blood-thirsty Akkadians.'

"At this moment the door of our cell opened to admit a slim young girl, clad only in a girdle of silk and golden breastplates. She brought us food and wine, and I noted how lingeringly she gazed at Conrad. And to my surprise she spoke to us in fair Somali.

" 'Where are we?' I asked. 'What are they going to do? Who are you?'

" 'I am Naluna, the dancer of El-Lil,' she answered—and she looked it—lithe as a she-panther she was. 'I am sorry to see you in this place; no Akkadian goes forth from here alive.'

" 'Nice friendly sort of chaps,' I grunted, but glad to find someone I could talk to and understand. 'And what's the name of the city?'

" 'This is Eridu,' she said. 'Our ancestors came here many ages ago from ancient Sumer, many moons to the East. They were driven by a great and powerful king, Sargon of the Akkadians—desert people. But our ancestors would not be slaves like their kin, so they fled, thousands of them in one great band, and traversed many strange, savage countries before they came to this land.'

"Beyond that her knowledge was very vague and

mixed up with myths and improbable legends. Conrad and I discussed it afterward, wondering if the old Sumerians came down the west coast of Arabia and crossed the Red Sea about where Mocha is now, or if they went over the Isthmus of Suez and came down on the African side. I'm inclined to the last opinion. Likely the Egyptians met them as they came out of Asia Minor and chased them south. Conrad thought they might have made most of the trip by water, because, as he said, the Persian Gulf ran up something like a hundred and thirty miles farther than it does now, and Old Eridu was a seaport town. But just at the moment something else was on my mind.

" 'Where did you learn to speak Somali?' I asked Naluna.

" 'When I was little,' she answered, 'I wandered out of the valley and into the jungle where a band of raiding black men caught me. They sold me to a tribe who lived near the coast and I spent my childhood among them. But when I had grown into girlhood I remembered Eridu and one day I stole a camel and rode across many leagues of veldt and jungle and so came again to the city of my birth. In all Eridu I alone can speak a tongue not mine own, except for the black slaves—and they speak not at all, for we cut out their tongues when we capture them. The people of Eridu go not forth beyond the jungles and they traffic not with the black peoples who sometimes come against us, except as they take a few slaves.'

"I asked her why they killed our camp servant and she said that it was forbidden for blacks and whites to mate in Eridu and the offspring of such union was not allowed to live. They didn't like the poor beggar's color.

"Naluna could tell us little of the history of the city since its founding, outside the events that had happened in her own memory—which dealt mainly with scattered raids by a cannibalistic tribe living in the jungles to the south, petty intrigues of court and temple, crop failures and the like—the scope of a woman's life in the East is much the same, whether in the palace of Akbar, Cyrus or Asshurbanipal. But I learned that the ruler's name was Sostoras and that he was both high priest and king—just as the rulers were in old Sumer, four thousand years ago. El-Lil was their god, who abode in the temple in the lake, and the deep booming we had heard was, Naluna said, the voice of the god.

"At last she rose to go, casting a wistful look at Conrad, who sat like a man in a trance—for once his confounded bugs were clean out of his mind.

" 'Well,' said I, 'what d'you think of it, young fella-me-lad?'

" 'It's incredible,' said he, shaking his head. 'It's absurd—an intelligent tribe living here four thousand years and never advancing beyond their ancestors.'

" 'You're stung with the bug of progress,' I told him cynically, cramming my pipe bowl full of weed. 'You're thinking of the mushroom growth of your own country. You can't generalize on an Oriental from a Western viewpoint. What about China's famous long sleep? As for these chaps, you forget they're no tribe but the tag-end of a civilization that lasted longer than any has lasted since. They passed the peak of their progress thousands of years ago. With no intercourse with the outside world and no

new blood to stir them up, these people are slowly
sinking in the scale. I'd wager their culture and art
are far inferior to that of their ancestors.'

" 'Then why haven't they lapsed into complete
barbarism?'

" 'Maybe they have, to all practical purposes,' I
answered, beginning to draw on my old pipe. 'They
don't strike me as being quite the proper thing for
offsprings of an ancient and honorable civilization.
But remember they grew slowly and their retrogression is bound to be equally slow. Sumerian culture
was unusually virile. Its influence is felt in Asia
Minor today. The Sumerians had their civilization
when our bloomin' ancestors were scrapping with
cave bears and saber-tooth tigers, so to speak. At
least the Europeans hadn't passed the first mile-
stones on the road to progress, whoever their animal
neighbors were. Old Eridu was a seaport of conse-
quence as early as 6500 B.C. From then to 2750
B.C. is a bit of time for any empire. What other
empire stood as long as the Sumerian? The Akkadian dynasty established by Sargon stood two hundred years before it was overthrown by another
Semitic people, the Babylonians, who borrowed
their culture from Akkadian Sumer just as Rome
later stole hers from Greece; the Elamitish Kassite
dynasty supplanted the original Babylonian, the
Assyrian and the Chaldean followed—well, you
know the rapid succession of dynasty on dynasty in
Asia Minor, one Semitic people overthrowing
another, until the real conquerors hove in view of
the Eastern horizon—the Medes and Persians—
who were destined to last scarcely longer than
their victims.

" 'Compare each fleeting kingdom with the long

dream reign of the ancient pre-Semitic Sumerians! We think the Minoan Age of Crete is a long time back, but the Sumerian empire of Erech was already beginning to decay before the rising power of Sumerian Nippur, before the ancestors of the Cretans had emerged from the Neolithic Age. The Sumerians had something the succeeding Hamites, Semites and Aryans lacked. They were stable. They grew slowly and if left alone would have decayed as slowly as these fellows are decaying. Still and all, I note these chaps have made one advancement— notice their weapons?

" 'Old Sumer was in Bronze Age. The Assyrians were the first to use iron for anything besides ornaments. But these lads have learned to work iron ore, I daresay.'

" 'But the mystery of Sumer still remains," Conrad broke in. 'Who are they? Whence did they come? Some authorities maintain they were of Dravidian origin, akin to the Basques—'

" 'It won't stick, me lad,' said I. 'Even allowing for possible admixture of Aryan or Turanian blood in the Dravidian descendants, you can see at a glance these people are not of the same race.'

" 'But their language—' Conrad began arguing, which is a fair way to pass the time while you're waiting to be put in the cooking-pot, but doesn't prove much except to strengthen your own original ideas.

"Naluna came again about sunset with food, and this time she sat down by Conrad and watched him eat. Seeing her sitting thus, elbows on knees and chin on hands, devouring him with her large, lustrous dark eyes, I said to the professor in English, so she wouldn't understand: 'The girl's badly smitten with you; play up to her. She's our only chance.'

"He blushed like a blooming school girl. 'I've a fiancee back in the States.'

" 'Blast your fiancee,' I said. 'Is it she that's going to keep the bally heads on our blightin' shoulders? I tell you this girl's silly over you. Ask her what they're going to do with us.'

"He did so and Naluna said: 'Your fate lies in the lap of El-Lil.'"

" 'And the brain of Sostoras,' I muttered. 'Naluna, what was done with the guns that were taken from us?'

"She replied that they were hung in the temple of El-Lil as trophies of victory. None of the Sumerians was aware of their purpose. I asked her if the natives they sometimes fought had never used guns and she said no. I could easily believe that, seeing that there are many wild tribes in those hinterlands who've scarcely seen a single white man. But it seemed incredible that some of the Arabs who've raided back and forth across Somaliland for a thousand years hadn't stumbled onto Eridu and shot it up. But it turned out to be true—just one of those peculiar quirks and back-eddies in events like the wolves and wildcats you still find in New York State, or those queer pre-Aryan peoples you come onto in small communities in the hills of Connaught and Galway. I'm certain that big slave raids had passed within a few miles of Eridu, yet the Arabs had never found it and impressed on them the meaning of firearms.

"So I told Conrad: 'Play up to her, you chump! If you can persuade her to slip us a gun, we've a sporting chance."

"So Conrad took heart and began talking to Naluna in a nervous sort of manner. Just how he'd have come out, I can't say, for he was little of the Don Juan, but Naluna snuggled up to him, much to his embarrassment, listening to his stumbling Somali with her soul in her eyes. Love blossoms suddenly and unexpectedly in the East.

"However, a peremptory voice outside our cell made Naluna jump half out of her skin and sent her scurrying, but as she went she pressed Conrad's hand and whispered something in his ear that we couldn't understand, but it sounded highly passionate.

"Shortly after she had left, the cell opened again and there stood a file of silent dark-skinned warriors. A sort of chief, whom the rest addressed as Gorat, motioned us to come out. Then down a long, dim colonnaded corridor we went, in perfect silence except for the soft scruff of their sandals and the tramp of our boots on the tiling. An occasional torch flaring on the walls or in a niche of the columns lighted the way vaguely. At last we came out into the empty streets of the silent city. No sentry paced the streets or the walls, no lights showed from inside the flat-topped houses. It was like walking a street in a ghost city. Whether every night in Eridu was like that or whether the people kept indoors because it was a special and awesome occasion, I haven't any idea.

"We went on down the streets toward the lake side of the town. There we passed through a small gate in the wall—over which, I noted with a slight shudder, a grinning skull was carved—and found ourselves outside the city. A broad flight of steps led down to the water's edge and the spears at our backs guided us down them. There a boat waited, a strange high-prowed affair whose prototype must have plied the Persian Gulf in the days of Old Eridu.

"Four black men rested on their oars, and when they opened their mouths I saw their tongues had been cut out. We were taken into the boat, our guards got in and we started a strange journey. Out on the silent lake we moved like a dream, whose silence was broken only by the low rippling of the long, slim, golden-worked oars through the water. The stars flecked the deep blue gulf of the lake with silver points. I looked back and saw the great dark bulk of the temple loom against the stars. The naked black mutes pulled the shining oars and the silent warriors sat before and behind us with their spears, helms and shields. It was like the dream of some fabulous city of Haround-al-Rashid's time, or of Sulieman-ben-Daoud's, and I thought how blooming incongruous Conrad and I looked in that setting, with our boots and dingy, tattered khakis.

"We landed on the island and I saw it was girdled with masonry—built up from the water's edge in broad flights of steps which circled the entire island. The whole seemed older, even, than the city—the Sumerians must have built it when they first found the valley, before they began on the city itself.

"We went up the steps, that were worn deep by countless feet, to a huge set of iron doors in the temple, and here Gorat laid down his spear and shield, dropped on his belly and knocked his helmeted head on the great sill. Someone must have been watching from a loophole, for from the top of the tower sounded one deep golden note and the doors swung silently open to disclose a dim, torch-lighted entrance. Gorat rose and led the way, we following with those confounded spears pricking our back.

"We mounted a flight of stairs and came onto a series of galleries built on the inside of each tier and winding around and up. Looking up, it seemed much higher and bigger than it had seemed from without, and the vague, half-lighted gloom, the silence and the mystery gave me the shudders. Conrad's face gleamed white in the semi-darkness. The shadows of past ages crowded in upon us, chaotic and horrific, and I felt as though the ghosts of all the priests and victims who had walked those galleries for four thousand years were keeping pace with us. The vast wings of dark, forgotten gods hovered over that hideous pile of antiquity.

"We came out on the highest tier. There were three circles of tall column, one inside the other—and I want to say that for columns built of sun-dried brick, these were curiously symmetrical. But there was none of the grace and open beauty of say, Greek architecture. This was grim, sullen, monstrous—something like the Egyptian, not quite so massive but even more formidable in starkness—an architecture symbolizing an age when men were still in the dawn-shadows of Creation and dreamed of monstrous gods.

"Over the inner circle of columns was a curving roof—almost a dome. How they built it, or how they came to anticipate the Roman builders by so many ages, I can't say, for it was a startling departure from the rest of their architectural style, but there it was. And from this domelike roof hung a great round shining thing that caught the starlight in a silver net. I knew then what we had been following for so many mad miles! It was a great gong—

the voice of El-Lil. It looked like jade but I'm not sure to this day. But whatever it was, it was the symbol on which the faith and cult of the Sumerians hung—the symbol of the god-head itself. And I know Naluna was right when she told us that her ancestors brought it with them on that long, gruelling trek, ages ago, when they fled before Sargon's wild riders. And how many eons before that dim time must it have hung in El-Lil's temple in Nippur, Erech or Old Eridu, booming out its mellow threat or promise over the dreamy valley of the Euphrates, or across the green foam of the Persian Gulf!

"They stood us just within the first ring of columns, and out of the shadows somewhere, looking like a shadow from the past himself, came old Sostoras, the priest-king of Eridu. He was clad in a long robe of green, covered with scales like a snake's hide, and it rippled and shimmered with every step he took. On his head he wore a head-piece of wavering plumes and in his hand he held a long-shafted golden mallet.

"He tapped the gong lightly and golden waves of sound flowed over us like a wave suffocating us in its exotic sweetness. And then Naluna came. I never knew if she came from behind the columns or up through some trap floor. One instant the space before the gong was bare, the next she was dancing like a moonbeam on a pool. She was clad in some light, shimmery stuff that barely veiled her sinuous body and lithe limbs. And she danced before Sostoras and El-Lil as women of her breed had danced in Old Sumer four thousand years ago.

"I can't begin to describe that dance. It made me freeze and tremble and burn inside. I heard Conrad's breath come in gasps and he shivered like a reed in the wind. From somewhere sounded music that was old when Babylon was young, music as elemental as the fire in a tigress's eyes, and as soulless as an African midnight. And Naluna danced. Her dancing was a whirl of fire and wind and passion and all elemental forces. From all basic, primal fundamentals she drew underlying principles and combined them in one pin-wheel motion. She narrowed the universe to a dagger-point of meaning and her flying feet and shimmering body wove out the mazes of that one central Thought. Her dancing stunned, exalted, maddened and hypnotized.

"As she whirled and spun, she was the elemental Essence, one and a part of all powerful impulses and moving or sleeping powers—the sun, the moon, the stars, the blind groping of hidden roots to light, the fire from the furnace, the sparks from the anvil, the breath of the fawn, the talons of the eagle. Naluna danced and her dancing was Time and Eternity, the urge of Creation and the urge of Death; birth and dissolution in one, age and infancy combined.

"My dazed mind refused to retain more impressions; the girl merged into a whirling flicker of white fire before my dizzy eyes; then Sostoras struck one light note on the Voice and she fell at his feet, a quivering white shadow. The moon was just beginning to glow over the cliffs to the East.

"The warriors seized Conrad and me, and bound me to one of the outer columns. Him they dragged to the inner circle and bound to a column directly in front of the great gong. And I saw Naluna, white in the growing glow, gaze drawnly at him, then shoot a glance full of meaning at me, as she faded from sight among the dark sullen columns.

"Old Sostoras made a motion and from the shadows came a wizened black slave who looked incredibly old. He had the withered features and vacant stare of a deaf-mute, and the priest-king handed the golden mallet to him. Then Sostoras fell back and stood beside me, while Gorat bowed and stepped back a pace and the warriors likewise bowed and backed still farther away. In fact they seemed most blooming anxious to get as far away from that sinister ring of columns as they could.

"There was a tense moment of waiting. I looked out across the lake at the high, sullen cliffs that girt the valley, at the silent city lying beneath the rising moon. It was like a dead city. The whole scene was most unreal, as if Conrad and I had been transported to another planet or back into a dead and forgotten age. Then the black mute struck the gong.

"At first it was a low, mellow whisper that flowed from under the black man's steady mallet. But it swiftly grew in intensity. The sustained, increasing sound became nerve-racking—it grew unbearable. It was more than mere sound. The mute evoked a quality of vibration that entered into every nerve and racked it apart. It grew louder and louder until I felt that the most desirable thing in the world was complete deafness, to be like that blank-eyed mute who neither heard nor felt the perdition of sound he was creating. And yet I saw sweat beading his ape-like brow. Surely some thunder of that brain-shattering cataclysm re-echoed in his own soul. El-Lil spoke to us and death was in his voice. Surely, if one of the terrible, black gods of past ages could speak, he would speak in just such tongue! There was neither mercy, pity nor weakness in its roar. It was the assurance of a cannibal god to whom mankind was but a plaything and a puppet to dance on his string.

"Sound can grow too deep, too shrill or too loud for the human ear to record. Not so with the Voice of El-Lil, which had its creation in some inhuman age when dark wizards knew how to rack brain, body and soul apart. Its depth was unbearable, its volume was unbearable, yet ear and soul were keenly alive to its resonance and did not grow mercifully numb and dulled. And its terrible sweetness was beyond human endurance; it suffocated us in a smothering wave of sound that yet was barbed with golden fangs. I gasped and struggled in physical agony. Behind me I was aware that even old Sostoras had his hands over his ears, and Gorat groveled on the floor, grinding his face into the bricks.

"And if it so affected me, who was just within the magic circle of columns, and those Sumerians who were just outside the circle, what was it doing to Conrad, who was inside the inner ring and beneath that domed roof that intensified every note?

"Till the day he dies Conrad will never be closer to madness and death than he was then. He writhed in his bonds like a snake with a broken back; his face was horribly contorted, his eyes distended, and foam flecked his livid lips. But in that hell of golden, agonizing sound I could hear nothing—I could only see his gaping mouth and his frothy, flaccid lips, open and writhing like an imbecile's. But I sensed he was howling like a dying dog.

"Oh, the sacrificial daggers of the Semites were merciful. Even Moloch's lurid furnace was easier than the death promised by this rending and ripping vibration that armed sound-waves with venomed talons. I felt my own brain was brittle as frozen glass. I knew that a few seconds more of that torture and Conrad's brain would shatter like a crystal goblet and he would die in the black raving of utter madness. And then something snapped me back from the mazes I'd gotten into. It was the fierce grasp of a small hand on mine, behind the column to which I was bound. I felt a tug at my cords as if a knife edge was being passed along them, and my hands were free. I felt something pressed into my hand and a fierce exultation surged through me. I'd recognize the familiar checkered grip of my Webley .44 in a thousand!

"I acted in a flash that took the whole gang off guard. I lunged away from the column and dropped the black mute with a bullet through his brain, wheeled and shot old Sostoras through the belly. He went down, spewing blood, and I crashed a volley square into the stunned ranks of the soldiers. At that range I couldn't miss. Three of them dropped and the rest woke up and scattered like a flock of birds. In a second the place was empty except for Conrad, Naluna and me, and the men on the floor. It was like a dream, the echoes from the shots still crashing, and the acrid scent of powder and blood knifing the air.

"The girl cut Conrad loose and he fell on the floor and yammered like a dying imbecile. I shook him but he had a wild glare in his eyes and was frothing like a mad dog, so I dragged him up, shoved an arm under him and started for the stairs. We weren't out of the mess yet, by a long shot. Down those wide, winding, dark galleries we went expecting any minute to be ambushed but the chaps must have still been in a bad funk, because we got out of that hellish temple without any interference. Outside the iron portals Conrad collapsed and I tried to talk to him, but he could neither hear nor speak. I turned to Naluna.

" 'Can you do anything for him?'

"Her eyes flashed in the moonlight. 'I have not defied my people and my god and betrayed my cult and my race for naught! I stole the weapon of smoke and flame, and freed you, did I not? I love him and I will not lose him now!'

"She darted into the temple and was out almost instantly with a jug of wine. She claimed it had magical powers. I don't believe it. I think Conrad simply was suffering from a sort of shell-shock from close proximity to that fearful noise and that lake water would have done as well as the wine. But Naluna poured some wine between his lips and emptied some over his head, and soon he groaned and cursed.

" 'See!' she cried triumphantly, 'the magic wine has lifted the spell El-Lil put on him!' And she flung her arms around his neck and kissed him vigorously.

" 'My God, Bill,' he groaned, sitting up and holding his head, 'what kind of a nightmare is this?'

" 'Can you walk, old chap?' I asked, 'I think we've stirred up a bloomin' hornet's nest and we'd best leg it out of here.'

" 'I'll try.' He staggered up, Naluna helping him. I heard a sinister rustle and whispering in the black mouth of the temple and I judged the warriors and priests inside were working up their nerve to rush us. We made it down the steps in a great hurry to where lay the boat that had brought us to the island. Not even the black rowers were there. An ax and shield lay in it and I seized the ax and knocked holes in the bottoms of the other boats which were tied near it.

"Meanwhile the big gong had begun to boom out again and Conrad groaned and writhed as every intonation rasped his raw nerves. It was a warning note this time and I saw lights flare up in the city and heard a sudden hum of shouts float out across the lake. Something hissed softly by my head and slashed into the water. A quick look showed me Gorat standing in the door of the temple bending his heavy bow. I leaped in, Naluna helped Conrad in, and we shoved off in a hurry to the accompaniment of several more shafts from the charming Gorat, one of which took a lock of hair from Naluna's pretty head.

"I laid to the oars while Naluna steered and Conrad lay on the bottom of the boat and was violently sick. We saw a fleet of boats put out from the city, and as they saw us by the gleam of the moon, a yell of concentrated rage went up that froze the blood in my veins. We were heading for the opposite end of the lake and had a long start on them, but in this way we were forced to round the island and we'd scarcely left it astern when out of some nook leaped a long boat with six warriors—I saw Gorat in the bows with that confounded boy of his.

"I had no spare cartridges so I laid to it with all my might, and Conrad, somewhat green in the face, took the shield and rigged it up in the stern, which was the saving of us, because Gorat hung within bowshot of us all the way across the lake and he filled that shield so full of arrows it resembled a blooming porcupine. You'd have thought they'd had plenty after the slaughter I made among them on the roof, but they were after us like hounds after a hare.

"We'd a fair start on them but Gorat's five rowers shot his boat through the water like a racehorse, and when we grounded on the shore, they weren't half a dozen jumps behind us. As we scrambled out I saw it was either make a fight of it there and be cut down from the front, or else be shot like rabbits as we ran. I called to Naluna to run but she laughed and drew a dagger—she was a man's woman, that girl!

"Gorat and his merry men came surging up to the landing with a clamor of yells and a swirl of oars—they swarmed over the side like a gang of bloody pirates and the battle was on! Luck was with Gorat at the first pass, for I missed him and killed the man behind him. The hammer snapped on an empty shell and I dropped the Webley and snatched up the ax just as they closed with us. By Jove! It stirs my blood now to think of the touch-and-go fury of that fight! Knee-deep in water we met them, hand to hand, chest to chest!

"Conrad brained one with a stone he picked from the water, and out of the tail of my eye, as I swung for Gorat's head, I saw Naluna spring like a she-panther on another, and they went down together in a swirl of limbs and a flash of steel. Gorat's sword was thrusting for my life, but I knocked it aside with the ax and he lost his footing and went down— for the lake bottom was solid stone there, and treacherous as sin.

"One of the warriors lunged in with a spear, but he tripped over the fellow Conrad had killed, his helmet went off and I crushed his skull before he could recover his balance. Gorat was up and coming for me, and the other was swinging his sword in both hands for a death blow, but he never struck, for Conrad caught up the spear that had been dropped, and spitted him from behind, neat as a whistle.

"Gorat's point raked my ribs as he thrust for my heart and I twisted to one side, and his up-flung arm broke like a rotten stick beneath my stroke but saved his life. He was game—they were all game or they'd never have rushed my gun. He sprang in like a blood-mad tiger, hacking for my head. I ducked and avoided the full force of the blow but couldn't get away from it altogether and it laid my scalp open in a three-inch gash, clear to the bone— here's the scar to prove it. Blood blinded me and I struck back like a wounded lion, blind and terrible, and by sheer chance I landed squarely. I felt the ax crunch through metal and bone, the haft splintered in my hand, and there was Gorat dead at my feet in a horrid welter of blood and brains.

"I shook the blood out of my eyes and looked about for my companions. Conrad was helping Naluna up and it seemed to me she swayed a little. There was blood on her bosom but it might have come from the red dagger she gripped in a hand stained to the waist. God! it *was* a bit sickening, to think of it now. The water we stood in was choked with corpses and ghastly red. Naluna pointed out across the lake as we saw Eridu's boats sweeping down on us—a good way off as yet, but coming swiftly. She led us at a run away from the lake's edge. My wound was bleeding as only a scalp wound can bleed, but I wasn't weakened as yet. I shook the blood out of my eyes, saw Naluna stagger as she ran and tried to put my arm about her to steady her, but she shook me off.

"She was making for the cliffs and we reached them out of breath. Naluna leaned against Conrad and pointed upward with a shaky hand, breathing in great, sobbing gasps. I caught her meaning. A rope ladder led upward. I made her go first with Conrad following. I came after him, drawing the ladder up behind me. We'd gotten some half-way up when the boats landed and the warriors raced up the shore, loosing their arrows as they ran. But we were in the shadow of the cliffs, which made aim uncertain, and most of the shafts fell short or broke on the face of the cliff. One stuck in my left arm, but I shook it out and didn't stop to congratulate the marksman on his eye.

"Once over the cliff's edge, I jerked the ladder up and tore it loose, and then turned to see Naluna sway and collapse in Conrad's arms. We laid her gently on the grass, but a man with half an eye could tell she was going fast. I wiped the blood from her bosom and stared aghast. Only a woman with a great love could have made that run and that climb with such a wound as that girl had under her heart.

"Conrad cradled her head in his lap and tried to falter a few words, but she weakly put her arms around his neck and drew his face down to hers.

" 'Weep not for me, my lover,' she said, as her voice weakened to a whisper. 'Thou has been mine aforetime, as thou shalt be again. In the mud huts of the Old River, before Sumer was, when we tended the flocks, we were as one. In the palaces of Old Eridu, before the barbarians came out of the

East, we loved each other. Aye, on this very lake have we floated in past ages, living and loving, thou and I. So weep not, my lover, for what is one little life when we have known so many and shall know so many more? And in each of them, thou are mine, and I am thine.

" 'But thou must not linger. Hark! They clamor for thy blood below. But since the ladder is destroyed there is but one other way by which they may come upon the cliffs—the place by which they brought thee into the valley. Haste! They will return across the lake, scale the cliffs there and pursue thee, but thou may'st escape them if thou be'st swift. And when thou hearest the Voice of El-Lil, remember, living or dead, Naluna loves thee with a greater love than any god.

" 'But one boon I beg of thee,' she whispered, her heavy lids drooping like a sleepy child's. 'Press, I beg thee, thy lips on mine, my master, before the shadows utterly enfold me; then leave me here and go, and weep not, oh my lover, for what is—one— little—life—to—us—who—have—loved—in—so— many—'

"Conrad wept like a blithering baby and so did I, by Judas, and I'll stamp the lousy brains out of the jackass who twists me for it! We left her with her arms folded on her bosom and a smile on her lovely face, and if there's a heaven for Christian folk, she's there with the best of them, on my oath.

"Well, we reeled away in the moonlight and my wounds were still bleeding and I was about done in. All that kept me going was a sort of wild beast instinct to live, I fancy, for if I was ever near to lying down and dying, it was then. We'd gone perhaps a mile when the Sumerians played their last ace. I

think they'd realized we'd slipped out of their grasp
and had too much start to be caught.

"At any rate, all at once that damnable gong
began booming. I felt like howling like a dog with
rabies. This time it was a different sound. I never
saw or heard a gong before or since whose notes
could convey so many different meanings. This was
an insidious call—a luring urge, yet a peremptory
command for us to return. It threatened and promised; if its attraction had been great before we stood
on that Babel tower and felt its full power, now it
was almost irresistible. It was hypnotic. I know now
how a bird feels when charmed by a snake and how
the snake himself feels when the fakirs play on their
pipes. I can't begin to make you understand the
overpowering magnetism of that call. It made you
want to writhe and tear at the air and run back,
blind and screaming, as a hare runs into a python's
jaw. I had to fight it as a man fights for his soul.

"As for Conrad, it had him in its grip. He halted
and rocked like a drunken man.

" 'It's no use,' he mumbled thickly. 'It drags at
my heart-strings; it's fettered my brain and my soul;
it embraces all the evil lure of all the universe. I
must go back.'

"And he started staggering back the way we had
come—toward the golden lie floating to us over the
jungle. But I thought of the girl Naluna that had
given up her life to save us from that abomination,
and a strange fury gripped me.

" 'See here!' I shouted. 'This won't do, you bloody
fool! You're off your bally bean! I won't have it,
d'you hear?'

"But he paid no heed, shoving by me with eyes
like a man in a trance, so I let him have it—an

honest right hook to the jaw that stretched him out
dead to the world. I slung him over my shoulder
and reeled on my way, and it was nearly an hour
before he came to, quite sane and grateful to me.

"Well, we saw no more of the people of Eridu.
Whether they trailed us at all or not, I haven't any
idea. We would have fled no faster than we did,
for we were fleeing the haunting, horrible mellow
whisper that dogged us from the south. We finally
made it back to the spot where we'd cached our
dunnage, and then, armed and scantily equipped,
we started the long trek for the coast. Maybe you
read or heard something about two emaciated wanderers being picked up by an elephant-hunting
expedition in the Somaliland back country, dazed
and incoherent from suffering. Well, we were about
done for, I'll admit, but we were perfectly sane.
The incoherent part was when we tried to tell our
tale and the blasted idiots wouldn't believe it. They
patted our backs and talked in soothing tones and
poured whiskey-and-sodas down us. We soon shut
up, seeing we'd only be branded as liars or lunatics.
They got us back to Jibuti, and both of us had had
enough of Africa for a spell. I took ship for India
and Conrad went the other way—couldn't get back
to New England quick enough, where I hope he
married that little American girl and is living hap-
pily. A wonderful chap, for all his damnable bugs.

"As for me, I can't hear any sort of a gong today
without starting. On that long, gruelling trek I never
breathed easily until we were beyond the sound of
that ghastly Voice. You can't tell what a thing like
that may do your mind. It plays the very deuce with
all rational ideas.

"I still hear that hellish gong in my dreams, some-times, and see that silent, hideously ancient Tower of Babel city in that nightmare valley. Sometimes I wonder if it's still calling to me across the years. But that's nonsense. Anyway, there's the yarn as it stands and if you don't believe me, I won't blame you at all."

But I prefer to believe Bill Kirby, for I know his breed from Hengist down, and know him to be like all the rest—truthful, aggressive, profane, restless, sentimental and straightforward, a true brother of the roving, fighting, adventuring Sons of Man.

The Dark Continent is not the only one to hold ancient mysteries. Ireland continues to replay old enmities even unto the present day. The one described in this story, though, is older than most. . . .

THE CAIRN ON THE HEADLAND

"And the next instant this great red loon was shaking me like a dog shaking a rat. 'Where is Meve MacDonnal?' he was screaming. By the saints, it's a grisly thing to hear a madman in a lonely place at midnight screaming the name of a woman dead three hundred years."

—The Longshoreman's Tale

"This is the cairn you seek," I said, laying my hand gingerly on one of the rough stones which composed the strangely symmetrical heap.

An avid interest burned in Ortali's dark eyes. His gaze swept the landscape and came back to rest on the great pile of massive weather-worn boulders.

"What a wild, weird, desolate place!" he said. "Who would have thought to find such a spot in this vicinity? Except for the smoke rising yonder,

34

one would scarcely dream that beyond that headland lies a great city! Here there is scarcely even a fisherman's hut within sight."

"The people shun the cairn as they have shunned it for centuries," I replied.

"Why?"

"You've asked me that before," I replied impatiently. "I can only answer that they now avoid by habit what their ancestors avoided through knowledge."

"Knowledge!" he laughed derisively. "Superstition!"

I looked at him somberly with unveiled hate. Two men could scarcely have been of more opposite types. He was slender, self-possessed, unmistakably Latin with his dark eyes and sophisticated air. I am massive, clumsy and bear-like, with cold blue eyes and tousled red hair. We were countrymen in that we were born in the same land; but the homelands of our ancestors were as far apart as South from North.

"Nordic superstition," he repeated. "I cannot imagine a Latin people allowing such a mystery as this to go unexplored all these years. The Latins are too practical—too prosaic, if you will. Are you sure of the date of this pile?"

"I find no mention of it in any manuscript prior to 1014 A.D.," I growled, "and I've read all such manuscripts extant, in the original. MacLiag, King Brian Boru's poet speaks of the rearing of the cairn immediately after the battle, and there can be little doubt that this is the pile referred to. It is mentioned briefly in the later chronicles of the Four Masters, also in the Book of Leinster, compiled in the late 1150's, and again in the Book of Lecan, compiled by the MacFirbis about 1416. All connect it with the battle of Clontarf, without mentioning why it was built."

"Well, what is the mystery about it?" he queried. "What more natural than that the defeated Norseman should rear a cairn above the body of some great chief who had fallen in the battle?"

"In the first place," I answered, "there is a mystery concerning the existence of it. The building of cairns above the dead was a Norse, not an Irish, custom. Yet according to the chroniclers, it was not Norsemen who reared this heap. How could they have built it immediately after the battle, in which they had been cut to pieces and driven in headlong flight through the gates of Dublin? Their chieftains lay where they had fallen and the ravens picked their bones. It was Irish hands that heaped these stones."

"Well, was that so strange?" persisted Ortali. "In old times the Irish heaped up stones before they went into battle, each man putting a stone in place; after the battle the living removed their stones, leaving in that manner a simple tally of the slain for any who wished to count the remaining stones."

I shook my head.

"That was in more ancient times; not in the battle of Clontarf. In the first place, there were more than twenty thousand warriors, and four thousand fell here; this cairn is not large enough to have served as a tally of the men killed in battle. And it is too symmetrically built. Hardly a stone has fallen away in all these centuries. No, it was reared to cover something."

"Nordic superstitions!" the man sneered again.

"Aye, superstitions if you will!" fired by his scorn, I exclaimed so savagely that he involuntarily stepped back, his hand slipping inside his coat. "We of North Europe had gods and demons before which the pallid mythologies of the South fade to childishness. At a time when your ancestors were lolling on silken cushions among the crumbling marble pillars of a decaying civilization, my ancestors were building their own civilization in hardships and gigantic battles against foes human and inhuman.

"Here on this very plain the Dark Ages came to an end and the light of a new era dawned on a world of hate and anarchy. Here, as even you know, in the year 1014, Brian Boru and his Dalcassian ax wielders broke the power of the heathen Norsemen forever—those grim anarchistic plunderers who had held back the progress of civilization for centuries.

"It was more than a struggle between Gael and Dane for the crown of Ireland. It was a war between the White Christ and Odin, between Christian and pagan. It was the last stand of the heathen—of the people of the old, grim ways. For three hundred years the world had writhed beneath the heel of the Viking, and here on Clontarf that scourge was lifted forever.

"Then, as now, the importance of that battle was underestimated by polite Latin and Latinized writers and historians. The polished sophisticates of the civilized cities of the South were not interested in the battles of barbarians in the remote northwestern corner of the world—a place and peoples of whose very names they were only vaguely aware. They only knew that suddenly the terrible raids of the sea kings ceased to sweep along their coasts, and in another century the wild age of plunder and slaughter had almost been forgotten—all because a rude, half-civilized people who scantily covered their nakedness with wolf hides rose up against the conquerors.

"Here was Ragnarok, the fall of the Gods! Here in very truth Odin fell, for his religion was given its death blow. He was last of all the heathen gods to stand before Christianity, and it looked for a time as if his children might prevail and plunge the world back into darkness and savagery. Before Clontarf, legends say, he often appeared on earth to his worshipers, dimly seen in the smoke of the sacrifices where naked human victims died screaming, or riding the wind-torn clouds, his wild locks flying in the gale, or, appareled like a Norse warrior, dealing thunderous blows in the forefront of nameless battles. But after Clontarf he was seen no more; his worshipers called on him in vain with wild chants and grim sacrifices. They lost faith in him, who had failed them in their wildest hour; his altars crumbled, his priests turned gray and died, and men turned to his conqueror, the White Christ. The reign of blood and iron was forgotten; the age of the red-handed sea kings passed. The rising sun slowly, dimly, lighted the night of the Dark Ages, and men forgot Odin, who came no more on earth.

"Aye, laugh if you will! But who knows what shapes of horror have had birth in the darkness, the cold gloom, and the whistling black gulfs of the North? In the southern lands the sun shines and flowers blow; under the soft skies men laugh at demons. But in the North who can say what elemental spirits of evil dwell in the fierce storms and the darkness? Well may it be that from such fiends of the night men evolved the worship of the grim ones, Odin and Thor, and their terrible kin."

Ortali was silent for an instant, as if taken aback

by my vehemence; then he laughed. "Well said, my Northern philosopher! We will argue these questions another time. I could hardly expect a descendant of Nordic barbarians to escape some trace of the dreams and mysticism of his race. But you cannot expect me to be moved by your imaginings, either. I still believe that this cairn covers no grimmer secret than a Norse chief who fell in the battle—and really your ravings concerning Nordic devils have no bearing on the matter. Will you help me tear into this cairn?"

"No," I answered shortly.

"A few hours' work will suffice to lay bare whatever it may hide," he continued as if he had not heard. "By the way, speaking of superstitions, is there not some wild tale concerning holly connected with this heap?"

"An old legend says that all trees bearing holly were cut down for a league in all directions, for some mysterious reason," I answered sullenly. "That's another mystery. Holly was an important part of Norse magic-making. The Four Masters tell of a Norseman—a white-bearded ancient of wild aspect, and apparently a priest of Odin—who was slain by the natives while attempting to lay a branch of holly on the cairn, a year after the battle."

"Well," he laughed, "I have procured a sprig of holly—see?—and shall wear it in my lapel; perhaps it will protect me against your Nordic devils. I feel more certain than ever that the cairn covers a sea king—and they were always laid to rest with all their riches: golden cups and jewel-set sword hilts and silver corselets. I feel that this cairn holds wealth, wealth over which clumsy-footed Irish peasants have been stumbling for centuries, living in want and dying in hunger. Bah! We shall return here at about midnight, when we may be fairly certain that we will not be interrupted—and you will aid me at the excavations."

The last sentence was rapped out in a tone that sent a red surge of blood-lust through my brain. Ortali turned and began examining the cairn as he spoke, and almost involuntarily my hand reached out stealthily and closed on a wicked bit of jagged stone that had become detached from one of the boulders. In that instant I was a potential murderer if ever one walked the earth. One blow, quick, silent and savage, and I would be free forever from a slavery bitter as my Celtic ancestors knew beneath the heels of the Vikings.

As if sensing my thoughts, Ortali wheeled to face me. I quickly slipped the stone into my pocket, not knowing whether he noted the action. But he must have seen the red killing instinct burning in my eyes, for again he recoiled and again his hand sought the hidden revolver.

But he only said: "I've changed my mind. We will not uncover the cairn tonight. Tomorrow night perhaps. We may be spied upon. Just now I am going back to the hotel."

I made no reply, but turned my back upon him and stalked moodily away in the direction of the shore. He started up the slope of the headland beyond which lay the city, and when I turned to look at him, he was just crossing the ridge, etched clearly against the hazy sky. If hate could kill, he would have dropped dead. I saw him in a red-tinged haze, and the pulses in my temples throbbed like hammers.

I turned back toward the shore, and stopped suddenly. Engrossed with my own dark thoughts, I had approached within a few feet of a woman before seeing her. She was tall and strongly made, with a strong stern face, deeply lined and weather-worn as the hills. She was dressed in a manner strange to me, but I thought little of it, knowing the curious styles of clothing worn by certain backward types of our people.

"What would you be doing at the cairn?" she asked in a deep, powerful voice. I looked at her in surprise; she spoke in Gaelic, which was not strange of itself, but the Gaelic she used I had supposed was extinct as a spoken language: it was the Gaelic of scholars, pure, and with a distinctly archaic flavor. A woman from some secluded hill country, I thought, where the people still spoke the unadulterated tongue of their ancestors.

"We were speculating on its mystery," I answered in the same tongue, hesitantly, however, for though skilled in the more modern form taught in the schools, to match her use of the language was a strain on my knowledge of it. She shook her head slowly. "I like not the dark man who was with you," she said somberly. "Who are you?"

"I am an American, though born and raised here," I answered. "My name is James O'Brien."

A strange light gleamed in her cold eyes.

"O'Brien? You are of my clan. I was born an O'Brien. I married a man of the MacDonnals, but my heart was ever with the folk of my blood."

"You live hereabouts?" I queried, my mind on her unusual accent.

"Aye, I lived here upon a time," she answered, "but I have been far away for a long time. All is changed—changed. I would not have returned, but I was drawn back by a call you would not understand. Tell me, would you open the cairn?"

I started and gazed at her closely, deciding that she had somehow overheard our conversation.

"It is not mine to say," I answered bitterly. "Ortali—my companion—he will doubtless open it and I am constrained to aid him. Of my own will I would not molest it."

Her cold eyes bored into my soul.

"Fools rush blind to their doom," she said somberly. "What does this man know of the mysteries of this ancient land? Deeds have been done here whereof the world reechoed. Yonder, in the long ago, when Tomar's Wood rose dark and rustling against the plain of Clontarf, and the Danish walls of Dublin loomed south of the river Liffey, the ravens fed on the slain and the setting sun lighted lakes of crimson. There King Brian, your ancestor and mine, broke the spears of the North. From all lands they came, and from the isles of the sea; they came in gleaming mail and their horned helmets cast long shadows across the land. Their dragon-prows thronged the waves and the sound of their oars was as the beat of a storm.

"On yonder plain the heroes fell like ripe wheat before the reaper. There fell Jarl Sigurd of the Orkneys, and Brodir of Man, last of the sea kings, and all their chiefs. There fell, too, Prince Murrogh and his son Turlogh, and many chieftains of the Gael, and King Brian Boru himself, Erin's mightiest monarch."

"True!" My imagination was always fired by the epic tales of the land of my birth. "Blood of mine was spilled here, and, though I have passed the best part of my life in a far land, there are ties of blood to bind my soul to this shore."

She nodded slowly, and from beneath her robes drew forth something that sparkled dully in the setting sun.

"Take this," she said. "As a token of blood tie, I give it to you. I feel strange and monstrous happenings—but this will keep you safe from evil and the people of the night. Beyond reckoning of man, it is holy."

I took it, wonderingly. It was a crucifix of curiously worked gold, set with tiny jewels. The workmanship was extremely archaic and unmistakably Celtic. And vaguely within me stirred a memory of a long-lost relic described by forgotten monks in dim manuscripts.

"Great heavens!" I exclaimed. "This is—must be—this *can* be nothing less than the lost crucifix of Saint Brandon the Blessed!"

"Aye." She inclined her grim head. "Saint Brandon's cross, fashioned by the hands of the holy man in long ago, before the Norse barbarians made Erin a red hell—in the days when a golden peace and holiness ruled the land."

"But, woman!" I exclaimed wildly, "I cannot accept this as a gift from you! You cannot know its value! Its intrinsic worth alone is equal to a fortune; as a relic it is priceless—"

"Enough!" Her deep voice struck me suddenly silent. "Have done with such talk, which is sacrilege. The cross of Saint Brandon is beyond price. It was never stained with gold; only as a free gift has it ever changed hands. I give it to you to shield you against the powers of evil. Say no more."

"But it has been lost for three hundred years!" I exclaimed. "How—where . . . ?"

"A holy man gave it to me long ago," she answered. "I hid it in my bosom—long it lay in my bosom. But now I give it to you; I have come from a far country to give it to you, for there are monstrous happenings in the wind, and it is sword and shield against the people of the night. An ancient evil stirs in its prison, which blind hands of folly may break open; but stronger than any evil is the cross of Saint Brandon which has gathered power and strength through the long, long ages since that forgotten evil fell to the earth."

"But who are you?" I exclaimed.

"I am Meve MacDonnal," she answered.

Then, turning without a word, she strode away in the deepening twilight while I stood bewildered and watched her cross the headland and pass from sight, turning inland as she topped the ridge. Then I, too, shaking myself like a man waking from a dream, went slowly up the slope and across the headland. When I crossed the ridge it was as if I had passed out of one world into another: behind me lay the wilderness and desolation of a weird mediaeval age; before me pulsed the lights and the roar of modern Dublin. Only one archaic touch was lent to the scene before me: some distance inland loomed the straggling and broken lines of an ancient graveyard, long deserted and grown up in weeds, barely discernible in the dusk. As I looked I saw a tall figure moving ghostily among the crumbling tombs, and I shook my head bewilderedly. Surely Meve Mac-Donnal was touched with madness, living in the past, like one seeking to stir to flame the ashes of dead yesterdays. I set out toward where, in the near distance, began the straggling window-gleams that grew into the swarming ocean of lights that was Dublin.

Back at the suburban hotel where Ortali and I had our rooms, I did not speak to him of the cross the woman had given me. In that at least he should not share. I intended keeping it until she requested its return, which I felt sure she would do. Now as I recall her appearance, the strangeness of her costume returned to me, with one item which had impressed itself on my subconscious mind at the time, but which I had not consciously realized. Meve MacDonnal had been wearing sandals of a type not worn in Ireland for centuries. Well, it was perhaps natural that with her retrospective nature she should imitate the apparel of the past ages which seemed to claim all her thoughts.

I turned the cross reverently in my hands. There was no doubt that it was the very cross for which antiquarians had searched so long in vain, and at last in despair had denied the existence of. The priestly scholar, Michael O'Rourke, in a treatise written about 1690, described the relic at length, chronicled its history exhaustively and maintained that it was last heard of in the possession of Bishop Liam O'Brien, who, dying in 1595, gave it into the keeping of a kinswoman; but who this woman was, it was never known, and O'Rourke maintained that she kept her possession of the cross a secret, and that it was laid away with her in her tomb.

At another time my elation at discovering this relic would have been extreme, but, at the time, my mind was too filled with hate and smoldering fury. Replacing the cross in my pocket, I fell moodily to reviewing my connections with Ortali, connections which puzzled my friends, but which were simple enough.

Some years before I had been connected with a certain large university in a humble way. One of the professors with whom I worked—a man named Reynolds—was of intolerably overbearing disposition toward those whom he considered his inferiors. I was a poverty-ridden student striving for life in a system which makes the very existence of a scholar precarious. I bore Professor Reynolds' abuse as long as I could, but one day we clashed. The reason does not matter; it was trivial enough in itself. Because I dared reply to his insults, Reynolds struck me and I knocked him senseless.

That very day he caused my dismissal from the university. Facing not only an abrupt termination of my work and studies, but actual starvation, I was reduced to desperation and I went to Reynolds' study late that night intending to thrash him within an inch of his life. I found him alone in his study, but the moment I entered, he sprang up and rushed at me like a wild beast, with a dagger he used for a paperweight. I did not strike; I did not even touch him. As I stepped aside to avoid his rush, a small rug slipped beneath his charging feet. He fell headlong and, to my horror, in his fall the dagger in his hand was driven into his heart. He died instantly. I was at once aware of my position. I was known to have quarreled, and even exchanged blows with the man. I had every reason to hate him. If I were found in the study with the dead man, no jury in the world would not believe that I had murdered him. I hurriedly left by the way I had come, thinking that I had been unobserved. But Ortali, the dead man's secretary, had seen me. Returning from

The Cairn on the Headland

a dance, he had observed me entering the premises, and, following me, had seen the whole affair through the window. But this I did not know until later.

The body was found by the professor's housekeeper, and naturally there was a great stir. Suspicion pointed to me, but lack of evidence kept me from being indicted, and this same lack of evidence brought about a verdict of suicide. All this time Ortali had kept quiet. Now he came to me and disclosed what he knew. He knew, of course, that I had not killed Reynolds, but he could prove that I was in the study when the professor met his death, and I knew Ortali was capable of carrying out his threat of swearing that he had seen me murder Reynolds in cold blood. And thus began a systematic blackmail.

I venture to say that a stranger blackmail was never levied. I had no money then; Ortali was gambling on my future, for he was assured of my abilities. He advanced me money, and, by clever wirepulling, got me an appointment in a large college. Then he sat back to reap the benefits of his scheming, and he reaped full fold of the seed he sowed. In my line I became eminently successful. I soon commanded an enormous salary in my regular work, and I received rich prizes and awards for researches of various difficult nature, and of these Ortali took the lion's share—in money at least. I seemed to have the Midas touch. Yet of the wine of my success tasted only the dregs.

I scarcely had a cent to my name. The money that had flowed through my hands had gone to enrich my slaver, unknown to the world. A man of remarkable gifts, he could have gone to the heights in any line, but for a queer streak in him, which, coupled with an inordinately avaricious nature, made him a parasite, a blood-sucking leech.

This trip to Dublin had been in the nature of a vacation for me. I was worn out with study and labor. But he had somehow heard of Grimmin's Cairn, as it was called, and, like a vulture that scents dead flesh, he conceived himself on the track of hidden gold. A golden wine cup would have been, to him, sufficient reward for the labor of tearing into the pile, and reason enough for desecrating or even destroying the ancient landmark. He was a swine whose only god was gold.

Well, I thought grimly, as I disrobed for bed, all things end, both good and bad. Such a life as I had lived was unbearable. Ortali had dangled the gallows before my eyes until it had lost its terrors. I had staggered beneath the load I carried because of my love for my work. But all human endurance has its limits. My hands turned to iron as I thought of Ortali, working beside me at midnight at the lonely cairn. One stroke, with such a stone as I had caught up that day, and my agony would be ended. That life and hopes and career and ambitions would be ended as well, could not be helped. Ah, what a sorry, sorry end to all my high dreams! When a rope and the long drop through the black trap should cut short an honorable career and a useful life! And all because of a human vampire who feasted his rotten lust on my soul, and drove me to murder and ruin.

But I knew my fate was written in the iron books of doom. Sooner or later I would turn on Ortali and kill him, be the consequences what they might. And I had reached the end of my road. Continual torture had rendered me, I believe, partly insane. I knew that at Grimmin's Cairn, when we toiled at midnight, Ortali's life would end beneath my hands, and my own life would be cast away.

Something fell out of my pocket and I picked it up. It was the piece of sharp stone I had caught up off the cairn. Looking at it moodily, I wondered what strange hands had touched it in old times, and what grim secret it helped to hide on the bare headland of Grimmin. I switched out the light and lay in the darkness, the stone still in my hand, forgotten, occupied with my own dark broodings. And I glided gradually into deep slumber.

At first I was aware that I was dreaming, as people often are. All was dim and vague, and connected in some strange way, I realized, with the bit of stone still grasped in my sleeping hand. Gigantic, chaotic scenes and landscapes and events shifted before me, like clouds that rolled and tumbled before a gale. Slowly these settled and crystallized into one distinct landscape, familiar and yet wildly strange. I saw a broad bare plain, fringed by the gray sea on one side, and a dark, rustling forest on the other; this plain was cut by a winding river, and beyond this river I saw a city—such a city as my waking eyes had never seen: bare, stark, massive, with the grim architecture of an earlier, wilder age. On the plain I saw, as in a mist, a mighty battle. Serried ranks rolled backward and forward, steel flashed like a sunlit sea, and men fell like ripe wheat beneath the blades. I saw men in wolfskins, wild and shockheaded, wielding dripping axes, and tall men in horned helmets and glittering mail, whose eyes were cold and blue as the sea. And I saw myself.

Yes, in my dream I saw and recognized, in a semi-detached way, myself. I was tall and rangily powerful; I was shock-headed and naked but for a wolf hide girt about my loins. I ran among the ranks yelling and smiting with a red ax, and blood ran down my flanks from wounds I scarcely felt. My eyes were cold blue and my shaggy hair and beard were red.

Now for an instant I was cognizant of my dual personality, aware that I was at once the wild man who ran and smote with the gory ax, and the man who slumbered and dreamed across the centuries. But this sensation quickly faded. I was no longer aware of any personality other than that of the barbarian who ran and smote. James O'Brien had no existence; I was Red Cumal, kern of Brian Boru, and my ax was dripping with the blood of my foes.

The roar of conflict was dying away, though here and there struggling clumps of warriors still dotted the plain. Down along the river half-naked tribesmen, waist-deep in reddening water, tore and slashed with helmeted warriors whose mail could not save them from the stroke of the Dalcassian ax. Across the river a bloody, disorderly horde was staggering through the gates of Dublin.

The sun was sinking low toward the horizon. All day I had fought beside the chiefs. I had seen Jarl Sigurd fall beneath Prince Murrogh's sword. I had seen Murrogh himself die in the moment of victory, by the hand of a grim mailed giant whose name none knew. I had seen, in the flight of the enemy, Brodir and King Brian fall together at the door of the great king's tent.

Aye, it had been a feasting of ravens, a red flood of slaughter, and I knew that no more would the dragon-prowed fleets sweep from the blue North with torch and destruction. Far and wide the Vikings lay in their glittering mail, as the ripe wheat lies after the reaping. Among them lay thousands of bodies clad in the wolf hides of the tribes, but the dead of the Northern people far outnumbered the dead of Erin. I was weary and sick of the stench of raw blood. I had glutted my soul with slaughter; now I sought plunder. And I found it—on the corpse of a richly-clad Norse chief which lay close to the seashore. I tore off the silver-scaled corselet, the horned helmet. They fitted as if made for me, and I swaggered among the dead, calling on my wild comrades to admire my appearance, though the harness felt strange to me, for the Gaels scorned armor and fought half-naked.

In my search for loot I had wandered far out on the plain, away from the river, but still the mail-clad bodies lay thickly strewn, for the bursting of the ranks had scattered fugitives and pursuers all over the countryside, from the dark waving Wood of Tomar, to the river and the seashore. And on the seaward slope of Drumna's headland, out of sight of the city and the plain of Clontarf, I came suddenly upon a dying warrior. He was tall and massive, clad in gray mail. He lay partly in the folds of a great dark cloak, and his sword lay broken near his mighty right hand. His horned helmet had fallen from his head and his elf-locks blew in the wind that swept out of the west.

Where one eye should have been was an empty socket and the other eye glittered cold and grim as the North Sea, though it was glazing with approach of death. Blood oozed from a rent in his corselet. I approached him warily, a strange cold fear, that I could not understand, gripping me. Ax ready to dash out his brains, I bent over him, and recognized him as the chief who had slain Prince Murrogh, and who had mown down the warriors of the Gael like a harvest. Wherever he had fought, the Norsemen had prevailed, but in all other parts of the field, the Gaels had been irresistible.

And now he spoke to me in Norse and I understood, for had I not toiled as slave among the sea people for long bitter years?

"The Christians have overcome," he gasped in a voice whose timbre, though low-pitched, sent a curious shiver of fear through me; there was in it an undertone as of icy waves sweeping along a Northern shore, as of freezing winds whispering among the pine trees. "Doom and shadows stalk on Asgaard and here has fallen Ragnarok. I could not be in all parts of the field at once, and now I am wounded unto death. A spear—a spear with a cross carved in the blade; no other weapon could wound me."

I realized that the chief, seeing mistily my red beard and the Norse armor I wore, supposed me to be one of his own race. But crawling horror surged darkly in the depths of my soul.

"White Christ, thou has not yet conquered," he muttered deliriously. "Lift me up, man, and let me speak to you."

Now for some reason I complied, and as I lifted him to a sitting posture, I shuddered and my flesh crawled at the feel of him, for his flesh was like ivory—smoother and harder than is natural for human flesh, and colder than even a dying man should be.

"I die as men die," he muttered. "Fool, to assume the attributes of mankind, even though it was to aid the people who deify me. The gods are immortal, but flesh can perish, even when it clothes a god. Haste and bring a sprig of the magic plant—even holly—and lay it on my bosom. Aye, though it be no larger than a dagger point, it will free me from this fleshly prison I put on when I came to war with men with their own weapons. And I will shake off this flesh and stalk once more among the thundering clouds. Woe, then, to all men who bend not the knee to me! Haste; I will await your coming."

His lionlike head fell back, and feeling shudderingly under his corselet, I could distinguish no heartbeat. He was dead, as men die, but I knew that locked in that semblance of a human body, there but slumbered the spirit of a fiend of the frost and darkness.

Aye, I knew him: Odin, the Gray Man, the One-eyed, the god of the North who had taken the form of a warrior to fight for his people. Assuming the form of a human he was subject to many of the limitations of humanity. All men knew this of the gods, who often walked the earth in the guise of men. Odin, clothed in human semblance, could be wounded by certain weapons, and even slain, but a touch of the mysterious holly would rouse him in grisly resurrection. This task he had set me, not knowing me for an enemy; in human form he could only use human faculties, and these had been impaired by onstriding death.

My hair stood up and my flesh crawled. I tore from my body the Norse armor, and fought a wild panic that prompted me to run blind and screaming with terror across the plain. Nauseated with fear, I gathered boulders and heaped them for a rude couch, and on it, shaking with horror, I lifted the body of the Norse god. And as the sun set and the stars came silently out, I was working with fierce energy, piling huge rocks above the corpse. Other tribesmen came up and I told them of what I was sealing up—I hoped forever. And they, shivering with horror, fell to aiding me. No sprig of magic holly should be laid on Odin's terrible bosom. Beneath these rude stones the Northern demon should slumber until the thunder of Judgment Day, forgotten by the world which had once cried out beneath his iron heel. Yet not wholly forgot, for, as we labored, one of my comrades said: "This shall be no longer Drumna's Headland, but the Headland of the Gray Man."

That phrase established a connection between my dream-self and my sleeping self. I started up from sleep exclaiming: "Gray Man's Headland!"

I looked about dazedly, the furnishings of the room, faintly lighted by the starlight in the windows, seeming strange and unfamiliar until I slowly oriented myself with time and space.

"Gray Man's Headland," I repeated, "Gray Man—Graymin—Grimmin—*Grimmin's Headland!* Great God, the thing under the cairn!"

Shaken, I sprang up, and realized that I still gripped the piece of stone from the cairn. It is well known that inanimate objects retain psychic associations. A round stone from the plain of Jericho had been placed in the hand of a hypnotized medium, and she has at once reconstructed in her mind the battle and siege of the city, and the shattering of the walls. I did not doubt that this bit of stone had acted as a magnet to drag my modern mind through the mists of the centuries into a life I had known before.

I was more shaken than I can describe, for the whole fantastic affair fitted in too well with certain formless vague sensations concerning the cairn which had already lingered at the back of my mind, to be dismissed as an unusually vivid dream. I felt the need of a glass of wine, and remembered that Ortali always had wine in his room. I hurriedly donned my clothes, opened my door, crossed the corridor and was about to knock at Ortali's door, when I noticed that it was partly open, as if some one had neglected to close it carefully. I entered, switching on a light. The room was empty.

I realized what had occurred. Ortali mistrusted me; he feared to risk himself alone with me in a lonely spot at midnight. He had postponed the visit to the cairn, merely to trick me, to give him a chance to slip away alone.

My hatred for Ortali was for the moment completely submerged by a wild panic of horror at the thought of what the opening of the cairn might result in. For I did not doubt the authenticity of my dream. It was no dream; it was a fragmentary bit of memory, in which I had relived that other life of mine. Gray Man's Headland—Grimmin's Headland, and under those rough stones that grisly corpse in its semblance of humanity—I could not hope that, imbued with the imperishable essence of an elemental spirit, that corpse had crumbled to dust in the ages.

Of my race out of the city and across those semi-desolate reaches, I remember little. The night was a cloak of horror through which peered red stars like the gloating eyes of uncanny beasts, and my footfalls echoed hollowly so that repeatedly I thought some monster loped at my heels.

The straggling lights fell away behind me and I entered the region of mystery and horror. No wonder that progress had passed to the right and to the left of this spot, leaving it untouched, a blind back-eddy given over to goblin-dreams and nightmare memories. Well that so few suspected its very existence.

Dimly I saw that headland, but fear gripped me and held me aloof. I had a vague, incoherent idea of finding the ancient woman, Meve MacDonnal. She was grown old in the mysteries and traditions of the mysterious land. She could aid me, if indeed the blind fool Ortali loosed on the world the forgotten demon men once worshiped in the North.

A figure loomed suddenly in the starlight and I caromed against him, almost upsetting him. A stammering voice in a thick brogue protested with the petulancy of intoxication. It was a burly longshoreman returning to his cottage, no doubt, from some late revel in a tavern. I seized him and shook him, my eyes glaring wildly in the starlight.

"I am looking for Meve MacDonnal! Do you know her? Tell me, you fool! Do you know old Meve MacDonnal?"

It was as if my words sobered him as suddenly as a dash of icy water in his face. In the starlight I saw his face glimmer whitely and a catch of fear was at his throat. He sought to cross himself with an uncertain hand.

"Meve MacDonnal? Are ye mad? What would ye be doin" with *her*?"

"Tell me!" I shrieked, shaking him savagely. "Where is Meve MacDonnal?"

"There!" he gasped, pointing with a shaking hand where dimly in the night something loomed against the shadows. "In the name of the holy saints, begone, be ye madman or devil, and l'ave an honest man alone! There—there ye'll find Meve MacDonnal—where they laid her, full three hundred years ago!"

Half heeding his words I flung him aside with a fierce exclamation, and, as I raced across the weed-grown plain, I heard the sounds of his lumbering flight. Half blind with panic, I came to the low structure the man had pointed out. And floundering deep in weeds, my feet sinking into musty mold, I realized with a shock that I was in the ancient graveyard on the inland side of Grimmin's Headland, into which I had seen Meve MacDonnal disappear the evening before. I was close by the door of the largest tomb, and with an eery premonition I leaned close, seeking to make out the deeply-carven inscription. And partly by the dim light of the stars and partly by the touch of my tracing fingers, I made out the words and figures, in the half-forgotten Gaelic of three centuries ago: "Meve MacDonnal—1565-1640."

With a cry of horror I recoiled and, snatching out the crucifix she had given me, made to hurl it into the darkness—but it was as if an invisible hand caught my wrist. Madness and insanity—but I could not doubt: Meve MacDonnal had come to me from the tomb wherein she had rested for three hundred years to give me the ancient, ancient relic entrusted to her so long ago by her priestly kin. The memory of her words came to me, and the memory of Ortali and the Gray man. From a lesser horror I turned squarely to a greater, and ran swiftly toward the headland which loomed dimly against the stars toward the sea.

As I crossed the ridge I saw, in the starlight, the cairn, and the figure that toiled gnomelike above it. Ortali, with his accustomed, almost superhuman energy, had dislodged many of the boulders; and as I approached, shaking with horrified anticipation, I saw him tear aside the last layer, and I heard his savage cry of triumph, that froze me in my tracks some yards behind him, looking down from the slope. An unholy radiance rose from the cairn, and I saw, in the north, the aurora flame up suddenly with terrible beauty, paling the starlight. All about the cairn pulsed a weird light, turning the rough stones to a cold shimmering silver, and in this glow I saw Ortali, all heedless, cast aside his pick and lean gloatingly over the aperture he had made— and I saw there the helmeted head, reposing on the couch of stones where I, Red Cumal, placed it so long ago. I saw the inhuman terror and beauty of that awesome carven face, in which was neither human weakness, pity nor mercy. I saw the soul-freezing glitter of the one eye, which stared wide open in a fearful semblance of life. All up and down the tall mailed figure shimmered and sparkled cold darts and gleams of icy light, like the northern lights that blazed in the shuddering skies. Aye, the Gray Man lay as I had left him more than nine hundred years before, without a trace of rust or rot or decay.

And now as Ortali leaned forward to examine his find, a gasping cry broke from my lips—for the sprig of holly, worn in his lapel in defiance of "Nordic superstition," slipped from its place, and in the weird glow I plainly saw it fall upon the mighty mailed breast of the figure, where it blazed suddenly with a brightness to dazzling for human eyes. My cry was echoed by Ortali. The figure moved;

the mighty limbs flexed, tumbling the shining stones aside. A new gleam lighted the terrible eye and a tide of life flooded and animated the carven features.

Out of the cairn he rose, and the northern lights played terribly about him. And the Gray Man changed and altered in horrific transmutation. The human features faded like a fading mask; the armor fell from his body and crumbled to dust as it fell; and the fiendish spirit of ice and frost and darkness that the sons of the North deified as Odin, stood nakedly and terribly in the stars. About his grisly head played lightnings and the shuddering gleams of the aurora. His towering anthropomorphic form was dark as shadow and gleaming as ice; his horrible crest reared colossally against the vaulting arch of the sky.

Ortali cowered, screaming wordlessly, as the taloned malformed hands reached for him. In the shadowy indescribable features of the Thing there was no tinge of gratitude toward the man who had released it—only a demoniac gloating and a demoniac hate for all the sons of men. I saw the shadowy arms shoot out and strike. I heard Ortali scream once—a single unbearable screech that broke out at the shrillest pitch. A single instant a blinding blue glare burst about him, lighting his convulsed features and his upward-rolling eyes; then his body was dashed earthward as by an electric shock, so savagely that I distinctly heard the splintering of his bones. But Ortali was dead before he touched the ground—dead, shriveled and blackened, exactly like a man blasted by a thunderbolt, to which cause, indeed, men later ascribed his death.

The slavering monster that had slain him lumbered now toward me, shadowy tentacle-like arms outspread, the pale starlight making a luminous pool of his great inhuman eye, his frightful talons dripping with I know not what elemental forces to blast the bodies and souls of men.

But I flinched not, and in that instant I feared him not, neither the horror of his countenance nor the threat of his thunderbolt dooms. For in a blinding white flame had come to me the realization of why Meve MacDonnal had come from her tomb to bring me the ancient cross which had lain in her bosom for three hundred years, gathering unto itself unseen forces of good and light, which war forever against the shapes of lunacy and shadow.

As I plucked from my garments the ancient cross, I felt the play of gigantic unseen forces in the air about me. I was but a pawn in the game—merely the hand that held the relic of holiness, that was the symbol of the powers opposed forever against the fiends of darkness. As I held it high, from it shot a single shaft of white light, unbearably pure, unbearably white, as if all the awesome forces of Light were combined in the symbol and loosed in one concentrated arrow of wrath against the monster of darkness. And with a hideous shriek the demon reeled back, shriveling before my eyes. Then with a great rush of vulture-like wings, he soared into the stars, dwindling, dwindling among the play of the flaming fires and the lights of the haunted skies, fleeing back into the dark limbo which gave him birth, God only knows how many grisly eons ago.

The poet William Congreve said, approximately, that music hath charms to soothe the savage breast. Its opposite is also true.

The glorious tenor Enrico Caruso died in 1921, when Howard was a young man, but his preternaturally fine voice lives on in recordings.

CASONETTO'S LAST SONG

I eyed the package curiously. It was thin and flat and the address was written clearly in the curving elegant hand I had learned to hate—the hand I knew to now be cold in death.

"You had better be careful, Gordon," said my friend Costigan. "Sure, why should that black devil be sending you anything but something to do you harm?"

"I had thought of a bomb or something similar," I answered, "but this is too thin a package to contain anything like that. I'll open it."

In spite of my words, I was nervous enough until I had unfastened the cords and bared the contents.

"By the powers!" Costigan laughed shortly. " 'Tis one of his songs he's sending you!"

An ordinary talking machine record lay before us.

Ordinary did I say? I might say the most extraordinary record in the world. For to the best of our

knowledge, it was the only one which held impris-
oned in its flat bosom the golden voice of Giovanni
Casonetto, that great and evil genius whose operatic
singing had thrilled the world, and whose dark and
mysterious crimes had shocked that same world.

"The death cell where Casonetto lay awaits the
next doomed one, and the black singer lies dead,"
said Costigan. "What then, is the spell of this disc
that he sends it to the man whose testimony sent
him to the gallows?"

I shrugged my shoulders. By no art of mine but
purely through accident I stumbled upon Casonetto's monstrous secret. By no wish of mine had
I come to the cavern where he practiced ancient
abominations and offered up human sacrifices to
the Devil he worshipped. But what I had seen I
told in court and before the hangman adjusted the
noose, Casonetto had promised me such a fate as
no one had ever experienced before.

All the world knew now of the atrocities practiced
by the inhuman cult of which Casonetto had been
high priest, and now that he was dead, records
made of his voice were sought by wealthy collectors,
but according to the terms of his last wish, all of
these had been destroyed.

At least I had thought so, but the thin round disc
in my hand proved that at least one had escaped
the general destruction. I gazed at it, but the record
in the center was blank and without title.

"Read the note," suggested Costigan.

A small slip of white paper had been contained
in the package also. I scanned it. The letters were
in Casonetto's handwriting.

"To my friend Stephen Gordon, to be listened to
alone in his study."

"That's all," I said after reading this curious request aloud.

"Sure, and 'tis more than enough. Is it not black magic he's trying to make on you? Else why should he wish you to listen to his caterwauling alone?"

"I don't know. But I think I'll do it."

"You're a fool," said Costigan frankly. "If ye will not be taking my advice and throwing the thing into the sea, it's myself will be with you when you put it on your talking machine. And that's final!"

I did not try to argue. Truly, I was somewhat apprehensive of Casonetto's promised vengeance, though I could not see how this was to be accomplished by the mere rendition of a song heard on a talking machine.

Costigan and I repaired to my study and there placed on the machine the last record of Giovanni Casonetto's golden voice. I saw Costigan's jaw muscles bulge belligerently as the disc began to whirl and the diamond point to spin down the circling grooves. I involuntarily tensed myself as if for a coming struggle. Clear and loud a voice spoke.

"Stephen Gordon!"

I started in spite of myself and almost answered! How strange and fearful it is to hear your name spoken in the voice of a man you know to be dead.

"Stephen Gordon," the clear, golden and hated voice went on, "if you hear this I shall be dead, for if I live I shall dispose of you in another manner. The police will soon be here and they have cut off every avenue of escape. There is nothing for me to do but stand my trial and your words will put a noose about my neck. But there is time for one last song!

"This song I shall imprison in the disc which now

rests upon my recording machine and before the police arrive I shall send it to you by one who will not fail me. You will receive it through the mails the day after I am hanged.

"My friend, this is a suitable setting for the last song of the high priest of Satan! I am standing in the black chapel where you first surprised me when you came blundering into my secret cavern and my clumsy neophytes let you escape.

"Before me stands the shrine of the Unnameable and before it the red-stained altar where many a virgin soul has gone winging up to the dark stars. On all sides hover dark mysterious things and I hear the swish of mighty wings in the gloom.

"Satan, lover of darkness, gird my soul with evil and strike chords of horror in my golden song.

"Stephen Gordon, harken ye!"

Full, deep and triumphant the golden voice surged up, lifted in a strange rhythmic chant, indescribably haunting and weird.

"Great God!" whispered Costigan. "He's singing the invocation from the Black Mass!"

I did not reply. The uncanny notes of that song seemed to stir my very heart within me. In the darksome caverns of my soul, some blind and monstrous thing moved and stirred like a dragon waking from slumber. The room faded and grew indistinct as I fell under the mesmeric power of the chant. About me inhuman forces seemed to glide and I could almost sense the touch of bat-like wings brushing my face in their flight—as though by virtue of his singing, the dead man had summoned up ancient and horrible demons to haunt me.

I saw again the sombre chapel, lit by a single small fire that flickered and leaped on the altar behind and above which brooded the Horror, the Unnameable—a horned and winged thing to which the devil worshippers bowed. I saw again the red-dyed altar, the long sacrificial dagger raised in the hands of the black-clad acolyte, the swaying, robed forms of the worshippers.

The voice rose and rose, swinging into a triumphant booming. It filled the room—the world, the sky, the universe! It blotted out the stars with a tangible veil of darkness! I staggered from it as from a physical force.

If ever hate and evil were incarnated in *sound* I heard and felt it then. That voice bore me down to deeps of Hell undreamed. Abysses loathsome and endless yawned before me. I had hints and glimpses of inhuman voids and unholy dimensions outside of all human experience. All the concentrated essence of Purgatory flowed out at me from that whirling disc, on the wings of that wonderful and terrible voice.

Cold sweat stood out on my body as I realized the feelings of a victim bound for sacrifice. I *was* the victim. I lay on the altar and the hand of the slayer hovered above me, gripping the dagger.

From the whirling disc the voice surged on, sweeping on irresistibly to my doom, swinging higher and higher, deeper and deeper, tinged with insanity as it approached the climax.

I realized my danger. I felt my brain crumbling before the onslaught of those spears of sound. I sought to speak, to scream! But my mouth gaped without sound. I tried to step forward, to shut off the machine, to break the record. But I could not move.

Now the chant rose to heights unnameable and

unbearable. A hideous triumph swept its notes; a million mocking devils screamed and bellowed at me, taunting me through that flood of demon-music, as if the chant were a gate through which the hordes of Hell came streaming, red-handed and roaring.

Now it swept with dizzy speed toward the point where, in the Black Mass, the dagger drinks the life of the sacrifice, and with one last effort that strained fading soul and dimming brain, I broke the mesmeric chains—I screamed! An inhuman, unearthly shriek, the shriek of a soul being dragged into Hell—of a mind being hurled into insanity.

And echoing my screech came the shout of Costigan as he lunged forward and crashed his sledgehammer fist down on the top of the machine, smashing into oblivion that terrible, golden voice forever.

Another Costigan story, revealing that "The Dark Continent [is] not Africa, but the brain of man."

THE COBRA IN THE DREAM

"I dare not sleep!"

I gazed at the speaker in amazement. I had known John Murken for years, and knew that he was a man of steely nerves. An explorer and adventurer, he had travelled all over the world, had faced all manner of perils in the waste places of the earth; and while I could not condone many of his acts, I had always admired his ruthless courage.

But now, as he stood in my apartments, I read real terror in his eyes. He was a tall rangy fellow, athletic and hard as steel and whalebone, but now he seemed trembling on the verge of a mental and physical collapse. His face seemed wasted away, and his sunken eyes gleamed unnaturally. His fingers worked incessantly as he talked.

"Yes, I am threatened with danger—terrible danger! But not from without! *It is in my own brain!*"

"Murken, what do you mean? Are you insane?"

He laughed jerkily and almost fiercely. "I don't know. I will be if this keeps on. I have walked the streets for the past two nights, keeping myself awake by the force of motion. Yesterday I had to shoot myself full of dope to keep from going to sleep, and tonight that's failing me. I am in a terrible predicament. If I don't get some sleep, I'll die; and if I do sleep—" he broke off with a shudder.

I gazed at him in a kind of horror. It is an eery thing to be awakened at two o'clock in the morning and listen to a tale like that. My gaze wandered to his jerking fingers. They were bloody, and I saw innumerable small cuts on them. His gaze followed mine.

"When I have had to stop and rest a few moments, I've fastened my penknife beneath my hands so that when I began to sink into sleep against my will, my relaxing hands would be cut by the blade and so spur my drugged senses into wakefulness."

"For the love of heaven, Murken," I exclaimed, "give me some idea of what this is all about! Are you being haunted by some crime you have committed, are you afraid of being murdered in your sleep, or what?"

He sank down in a chair. For the moment he seemed wakeful enough, but the lids drooped wearily over his eyes in the manner of a man who is swiftly approaching nervous exhaustion.

"I'll tell you the whole story, and if it sounds like the ravings of a maniac, remember there are many dark regions of the brain which are unexplored, and anything may be possible! The Dark Continent! Not

Africa, but the brain of man!" he laughed wildly, and then continued more calmly:

"Several years ago I was in a portion of India which is little frequented by white man. My reason for being there has nothing to do with my story. But while there I learned of a treasure which the great bandit Alam Singh was purported to have concealed in a cavern in the foothills. A Hindu renegade swore that he had been one of the outlaw's men, and that he knew the cavern wherein the treasure had been hidden some twenty years before. As events proved, he was not lying. I think he intended getting the treasure with my aid and then murdering me and taking all of it himself.

"At any rate, the two of us went up into the low, densely-treed hills where the gayly plumed birds flew through the intertwining branches, and the monkeys kept up an incessant chatter; and after considerable searching we came upon the cavern which my companion swore was the one we sought. It was a large affair, opening out on the hillside, but the entrance was partly screened by vines. The Hindu did not think that anyone knew of it but himself, for most of Alam Singh's men had been hung long ago, and the chief himself killed in a border raid; so we went boldly in.

"Instantly we found we had made a mistake. As we pushed through the clinging vines, dark forms leaped on us from every side. There was no opportunity for resistance. The Hindu they stabbed to death instantly, and me they bound hand and foot; and they carried me back into the cave, where they lit an oil lamp. Its light flung eery shadows on the bare walls and dusty floor of the cave, and on the bearded faces leering over me.

" 'We are the sons of the men that rode with Alam Singh,' they said. 'We have watched this treasure for twenty years, and will guard it for twenty years more, if necessary. We hold it for Alam's sister's son, who will take his great uncle's place someday and free us from the English swine.'

" 'You will be hanged like Alam Singh's men if you kill me,' I answered.

" 'No one will know,' they replied. 'Many men have vanished in these hills, and even their bones are never found. You came at a good time, sahib; we had already decided to move the treasure elsewhere. You can have the cave to yourself!' They laughed meaningly.

"I knew my doom was sealed. But the consummation of my fate was more horrible than I imagined—" a shudder shook my friend's powerful frame.

"They bound me hand and foot to pegs driven in the floor. I could not move, I could not stir; I could only turn my head. Then they brought in the largest cobra I have ever seen in my life, handling him with prongs—you know how snake tamers use them, so the snakes cannot strike the men.

"They fastened a thin noose of uncured hide about the hideous hood of the thing, and made the other end of the thong fast to a niche in the wall. Of course the reptile began striking at me instantly, but I was several inches out of reach. They hung a jar over the thong which held the snake, and the jar was filled with water. A small hole in the bottom allowed the water to escape, a drop at a time. Each drop fell on the stiff hide. As you know, when uncured hide is dry, it is hard and inflexible, but when it is wet, it will stretch a great deal. Dry, the thong was too short to allow the cobra to reach me, but as the water dropped on it, it slowly became saturated with moisture, and each time the snake struck at me, he stretched it slightly. There they left me, bearing with them a heavy chest—the treasure, no doubt.

"How long I lay there, I have no idea. Seconds melted into minutes, minutes into hours, hours into Eternities. The entire Universe faded, narrowed, and centered to a pinpoint which was the cave wherein I lay. I gazed in terrible fascination at the long sinuous body which rippled toward me and receded in almost rhythmic regularity—at the evil head with its burning eyes, and the broad marked hood just below. I struggled, I screamed. But my bonds held me firm, and my cries echoed emptily through the cavern. It was hot, but cold sweat stood out on my brow. In my agony I cursed the dead Hindu and my torturers alike; cursed my own avariciousness, and in a burst of senseless frenzy cursed all things and all men.

"Then I lay exhausted and silent, watching the captive snake with eyes as unwinking as his own. I sought to turn my head, to refuse to look at my fate, but always my gaze was drawn back and held there. I decided upon the exact place where he would strike me when he finally reached me; my left wrist was nearest to him, and he would strike there, on the outer side, just above the hand.

"Time passed; the great snake kept striking on with a persistence and endurance that amazed me. He did not strike so often now, but he struck regularly. Little by little, very slowly but very surely, the hide thong was stretching. Now he was within a few inches of my wrist. My flesh crawled and shrank, my blood seemed to freeze at the nearness of my approaching doom. A violent nausea seized me. Suddenly the oil lamp guttered and went out.

"A new horror took hold of me; death in the dark is worse than death in the light, even in the light of an oil lamp. I screamed again and again, until my voice failed me. Now I could hear the creaking of the thong as it stretched—stretched—now I could feel the loathsome fetid breath against my wrist. Yet he still could not reach me! A few more strokes—then suddenly the cavern was flooded with light, men shouted, a pistol cracked, and I sank into a dead faint.

"I lay raving in delirium for days afterward, living over again my hideous experience. My hair had turned white at the temples. My escape was so narrow that I could not believe it, and during my delirium I thought that I was going through the hallucinations which sometime accompany death.

"A party of tiger hunters—white men, whom I did not even know were in the country—had heard my last burst of screaming and had arrived just in time. They swept the cave with electric torches, and one of them shot the cobra which I verily believe would have reached me with one more stroke.

"I left India as soon as I could, and even today the sight of a snake nauseates me. But it was not over. After several months I began to dream at irregular intervals, several months apart, and always the dream would be vague and chaotic. I would awake in a cold sweat and often be unable to sleep for the rest of the night.

"Then the dreams began to grow in clarity. They became extraordinarily vivid; they began to recur more often. They shadowed my whole life. In each dream, every small detail stood out amazingly clear.

"Since that time, I have dreamed that same dream hundreds of times, and each time it is the same. The dream starts abruptly; once more I am lying alone on the dusty floor of Alam Singh's cave, with the oil lamp flickering and guttering above me, and that scaly fiend darting his frightful length at me again and again. Until recently, however, the dream breaks abruptly just before the oil lamp goes out. But I can see the thong stretching—and I tell you, it stretches more with each dream! The first few times I dreamed it, the snake was a fairly good distance from me; the thong had not stretched at all. Then it began to give slowly, but it took thirty or forty dreams for the serpent to get an inch nearer me. But of late it has been stretching with fearful speed.

"The other night I dreamed it last—and for the first time I felt, as I felt in reality, the cold fetid breath of the monster against my wrist. The lamp on the wall flickered—I awoke with a scream and a realization of my doom. Costigan, in my dream that snake will strike me, and I will die in reality!"

I shuddered in spite of myself.

"Murken, this is insanity! You were rescued in reality, in the event of which you dream—why should you not dream of your rescue?"

"I don't know. I'm no psychologist. But I've never dreamed of either the events leading up to the point of my being struck at, nor the events which really follow. Always it is the snake and I, alone. I believe that the affair was grooved so deeply into my brain that it struck into some of those dark corners of which I told you, implanting into my subconscious mind or whatever it is, the cognizance of impending doom. They say—some of the psychologists say—that certain parts of your brain work out thoughts transmitted them by the higher brain. All except fear and the certainty of death was crowded out of my mind. When the hunters burst in and saved me, I was delirious; I do not believe that my lower brain even recognized the rescue, for it was filled with the thoughts of my coming death. That explanation is hazy and vague; I cannot explain why I know it, but I know that if I dream that dream again, I'll die! That dark subconscious mind which works only when the higher mind is at rest will work out the terrible drama as it would have worked out in reality had not those men chanced along, and the culmination of it will blot out my physical life!"

"On the other hand," said I, "I believe that if you will dream the dream through, you will rid yourself forever of the hallucination. The hunters will rush in, the dream snake will die, and you will find yourself again."

He shook his head, letting his hands drop in a hopeless manner.

"I am marked by death," he said, and I could not move him from his fatalistic mood.

"Telling this tale has resigned me somewhat," he said. "I will sleep; if you are right, I will awake, myself again, freed of this curse. But if I am right, I will not awake in this world."

He then bid me leave the light burning, and lay down on my couch. He did not fall instantly into slumber. He seemed unconsciously to fight against sleeping, but at last his lids sank and he lay still. His face in the light looked horribly like a skull, with its sunken cheeks and sallow parchment-like skin. The nightmare had evidently taken a terrific toll of mind and body. Time dragged on. I, too, grew sleepy. I found it almost impossible to hold my eyes open and wondered at the endurance which had kept John Murken awake for nearly three days and nights.

Murken muttered in his sleep, and moved restlessly. The light shone full in his eyes, and I decided that it was disturbing his slumber. I glanced at the clock on the mantel. The hands stood at five. I turned the light off and took a single step toward my bed.

There in the darkness, I do not know whether or not John Murken's eyes opened in his last moment, but he gave one ghastly cry: "Oh God, the lamp has gone out!" And there followed a scream which froze the blood in my veins.

Cold sweat standing on each trembling limb, I turned on the light. John Murken lay dead, and the distortion of his face was hideous to see. There was no wound on him, but his right hand was clenched in a desperate death-grip about his left wrist.

This story introduces Kirowan. He is clearly kin to Costigan but with perhaps more nerve. Kirowan is an explorer, going not only to strange lands, but beyond the borders of evil itself.

DIG ME NO GRAVE

The thunder of my old-fashioned door-knocker, reverberating eerily through the house, roused me from a restless and nightmare-haunted sleep. I looked out the window. In the last light of the sinking moon, the white face of my friend John Conrad looked up at me.

"May I come up, Kirowan?" His voice was shaky and strained.

"Certainly!" I sprang out of bed and pulled on a bathrobe as I heard him enter the front door and ascend the stairs.

A moment later he stood before me, and in the light which I had turned on I saw his hands tremble and noticed the unnatural pallor of his face.

"Old John Grimlan died an hour ago," he said abruptly.

"Indeed? I had not known that he was ill."

"It was a sudden, virulent attack of peculiar nature, a sort of seizure somewhat akin to epilepsy. He had been subject to such spells of late years, you know."

I nodded. I knew something of the old hermit-like man who had lived in his great dark house on the hill; indeed, I had once witnessed one of his strange seizures, and I had been appalled at the writhings, howlings and yammerings of the wretch, who had groveled on the earth like a wounded snake gibbering terrible curses and black blasphemies until his voice broke in a wordless screaming which spattered his lips with foam. Seeing this, I understood why people in old times looked on such victims as men possessed by demons.

"—some hereditary trait," Conrad was saying. "Old John doubtless fell heir to some ingrown weakness brought on by some loathsome disease, which was his heritage from perhaps a remote ancestor—such things occasionally happen. Or else—well, you know old John himself pried about in the mysterious parts of the earth, and wandered all over the East in his younger days. It is quite possible that he was infected with some obscure malady in his wanderings. There are still many unclassified diseases in Africa and the Orient."

"But," said I, "you have not told me the reason for this sudden visit at this unearthly hour—for I notice that it is past midnight."

My friend seemed rather confused.

"Well, the fact is that John Grimlan died alone, except for myself. He refused to receive any medical aid of any sort, and in the last few moments when it was evident that he was dying, and I was prepared to go for some sort of help in spite of him, he set up such a howling and screaming that I could not refuse his passionate pleas—which were that he should not be left to die alone.

"I have seen men die," added Conrad, wiping the perspiration from his pale brow, "but the death of John Grimlan was the most fearful I have ever seen."

"He suffered a great deal?"

"He appeared to be in much physical agony, but this was mostly submerged by some monstrous mental or psychic suffering. The fear in his distended eyes and his screams transcended any conceivable earthly terror. I tell you, Kirowan, Grimlan's fright was greater and deeper than the ordinary fear of the Beyond shown by a man of ordinarily evil life."

I shifted restlessly. The dark implications of this statement sent a chill of nameless apprehension trickling down my spine.

"I know the country people always claimed that in his youth he sold his soul to the Devil, and that his sudden epileptic attacks were merely a visible sign of the Fiend's power over him; but such talk is foolish, of course, and belongs in the Dark Ages. We all know that John Grimlan's life was a peculiarly evil and vicious one, even toward his last days. With good reason he was universally detested and feared, for I never heard of his doing a single good act. You were his only friend."

"And that was a strange friendship," said Conrad. "I was attracted to him by his unusual powers, for despite his bestial nature, John Grimlan was a highly educated man, a deeply cultured man. He had dipped deep into occult studies, and I first met him in this manner; for as you know, I have always been strongly interested in these lines of research myself.

"But, in this as in all things, Grimlan was evil and perverse. He had ignored the white side of the occult and delved into the darker, grimmer phases of it—into devil-worship and voodoo and Shintoism. His knowledge of these foul arts and sciences was immense and unholy. And to hear him tell of his researches and experiments was to know such horror and repulsion as a venomous reptile might inspire. For there had been no depths to which he had not sunk, and some things he only hinted at, even to me. I tell you, Kirowan, it is easy to laugh at tales of the black world of the unknown, when one is in pleasant company under the bright sunlight, but had you sat at ungodly hours in the silent bizarre library of John Grimlan and looked on the ancient musty volumes and listened to his grisly talk as I did, your tongue would have cloven to your palate with sheer horror as mine did, and the supernatural would have seemed very real and near to you—as it seemed to me!"

"But in God's name, man!" I cried, for the tension was growing unbearable; "come to the point and tell me what you want of me."

"I want you to come with me to John Grimlan's house and help carry out his outlandish instructions in regard to his body."

I had no liking for the adventure, but I dressed hurriedly, an occasional shudder of premonition shaking me. Once fully clad, I followed Conrad out of the house and up the silent road which led to the house of John Grimlan. The road wound uphill, and all the way, looking upward and forward, I could see that great grim house perched like a bird of evil on the crest of the hill, bulking black and stark against the stars. In the west pulsed a single dull red smear where the young moon had just sunk from view behind the low black hills. The whole night seemed full of brooding evil, and the persistent swishing of a bat's wings somewhere overhead caused my taut nerves to jerk and thrum. To drown the quick pounding of my own heart, I said:

"Do you share the belief so many hold, that John Grimlan was mad?"

We strode on several paces before Conrad answered, seemingly with a strange reluctance, "But of one incident, I would say no man was ever saner. But one night in his study, he seemed suddenly to break all bonds of reason.

"He had discoursed for hours on his favorite subject—black magic—when suddenly he cried, as his face lit with a weird unholy glow: 'Why should I sit here babbling such child's prattle to you? These voodoo rituals—these Shinto sacrifices—feathered snakes—goats without horns—black leopard cults— bah! Filth and dust that the wind blows away! Dregs of the real Unknown—the deep mysteries! Mere echoes from the Abyss!

" 'I could tell you things that would shatter your paltry brain! I could breathe into your ear names that would wither you like a burnt weed! What do you know of Yog-Sathoth, of Kathulos and the sunken cities? None of these names is even included in your mythologies. Not even in your dreams have you glimpsed the black cyclopean walls of Koth, or shriveled before the noxious winds that blow from Yuggoth!

" 'But I will not blast you lifeless with my black wisdom! I cannot expect your infantile brain to bear

what mine holds. Were you as old as I—had you
seen, as I have see, kingdoms crumble and generations pass away—had you gathered as ripe grain the
dark secrets of the centuries—'

"He was raving away, his wildly lit face scarcely
human in appearance, and suddenly, noting my evident bewilderment, he burst into a horrible cack-
ling laugh.

"'Gad!' he cried in a voice and accent strange to
me, 'methinks I've frighted ye, and certes, it is not
to be marveled at, sith ye be but a naked savage in
the arts of life, after all. Ye think I be old, eh? Why,
ye gaping lout, ye'd drop dead were I to divulge
the generations of men I've known—'

"But at this point such horror overcame me that
I fled from him as from an adder, and his high-
pitched, diabolical laughter followed me out of the
shadowy house. Some day later I received a letter
apologizing for his manner and ascribing it candidly—too candidly—to drugs. I did not believe it,
but I renewed our relations, after some hesitation."

"It sounds like utter madness," I muttered.

"Yes," admitted Conrad, hesitantly. "But—Kirowan, have you ever seen anyone who knew John
Grimlan in his youth?"

I shook my head.

"I have been at pains to inquire about him dis-
creetly," said Conrad. "He has lived here—with the
exception of mysterious absences often for months
at a time—for twenty years. The older villagers
remember distinctly when he first came and took
over that old house on the hill, and they all say that
in the intervening years he seems not to have aged
perceptibly. When he came here he looked just as

he does now—or did, up to the moment of his death—of the appearance of a man about fifty.

"I met old Von Boehnk in Vienna, who said he knew Grimlan when a very young man studying in Berlin, fifty years ago, and he expressed astonishment that the old man was still living; for he said at that time Grimlan seemed to be about fifty years of age."

I gave an incredulous exclamation, seeing the implication toward which the conversation was trending.

"Nonsense! Professor Von Boehnk is past eighty himself, and liable to the errors of extreme age. He confused this man with another." Yet as I spoke, my flesh crawled unpleasantly and the hairs on my neck prickled.

"Well," shrugged Conrad, "here we are at the house."

The huge pile reared up menacingly before us, and as we reached the front door a vagrant wind moaned through the nearby trees and I started foolishly as I again heard the ghostly beat of the bat's wings. Conrad turned a large key in the antique lock, and as we entered, a cold draft swept across us like a breath from the grave—moldy and cold. I shuddered.

We groped our way through a black hallway and into a study, and here Conrad lighted a candle, for no gas lights or electric lights were to be found in the house. I looked about me, dreading what the light might disclose, but the room, heavily tapestried and bizarrely furnished, was empty save for us two.

"Where—where is—*It?*" I asked in a husky whispered, from a throat gone dry.

"Upstairs," answered Conrad in a low voice, showing that the silence and mystery of the house had laid a spell on him also. "Upstairs, in the library where he died."

I glanced up involuntarily. Somewhere above our head, the lone master of this grim house was stretched out in his last sleep—silent, his white face set in a grinning mask of death. Panic swept over me and I fought for control. After all, it was merely the corpse of a wicked old man, who was past harming anyone—this argument rang hollowly in my brain like the words of a frightened child who is trying to reassure himself.

I turned to Conrad. He had taken a time-yellowed envelope from an inside pocket.

"This," he said, removing from the envelope several pages of closely written, time-yellowed parchment, "is, in effect, the last word of John Grimlan, though God alone knows how many years ago it was written. He gave it to me ten years ago, immediately after his return from Mongolia. It was shortly after this that he had his first seizure.

"This envelope he gave me, sealed, and he made me swear that I would hide it carefully, and that I would not open it until he was dead, when I was to read the contents and follow their directions exactly. More, he made me swear that no matter what he said or did after giving me the envelope, I would go ahead as first directed. 'For,' he said with a fearful smile, 'the flesh is weak but I am a man of my word, and though I might, in a moment of weakness, wish to retract, it is far, far too late now. You may never understand the matter, but you are to do as I have said.' "

"Well?"

"Well," again Conrad wiped his brow, "tonight as he lay writhing in his death-agonies, his wordless howls were mingled with frantic admonitions to me to bring him the envelope and destroy it before his eyes! As he yammered this, he forced himself up on his elbows and with eyes staring and hair standing straight up on his head, he screamed at me in a manner to chill the blood. And he was shrieking for me to destroy the envelope, not to open it; and once he howled in his delirium for me to hew his body into pieces and scatter the bits to the four winds of heaven!"

An uncontrollable exclamation of horror escaped my dry lips.

"At last," went on Conrad, "I gave in. Remembering his commands ten years ago, I at first stood firm, but at last, as his screeches grew unbearably desperate, I turned to go for the envelope, even though that meant leaving him alone. But as I turned, with one last fearful convulsion in which blood-flecked foam flew from his writhing lips, the life went from his twisted body in a single great wrench."

He fumbled at the parchment.

"I am going to carry out my promise. The directions herein seem fantastic and may be the whims of a disordered mind, but I gave my word. They are, briefly, that I place his corpse on the great black ebony table in his library, with seven black candles burning about him. The doors and windows are to be firmly closed and fastened. Then, in the darkness which precedes dawn, I am to read the formula, charm or spell which is contained in a smaller, sealed envelope inside the first, and which I have not yet opened."

"But is that all?" I cried. "No provisions as to the disposition of his fortune, his estate—or his corpse?"

"Nothing. In his will, which I have seen elsewhere, he leaves estate and fortune to a certain Oriental gentleman named in the document as—Malik Tous!"

"What!" I cried, shaken to my soul. "Conrad, this is madness heaped on madness! Malik Tous—good God! No mortal man was ever so named! That is the title of the foul god worshipped by the mysterious Yezidees—they of Mount Alamout the Accursed—whose Eight Brazen Towers rise in the mysterious wastes of deep Asia. His idolatrous symbol is the brazen peacock. And the Muhammadans, who hate his demon-worshipping devotees, say he is the essence of the evil of all the universe—the Prince of Darkness—Ahriman—the Old Serpent—the veritable Satan! And you say Grimlan names this mythical demon in his will?"

"It is the truth," Conrad's throat was dry. "And look—he has scribbled a strange line at the corner of his parchment: 'Dig me no grave; I shall not need one.'"

Again a chill wandered down my spine.

"In God's name," I cried in a kind of frenzy, "let us get this incredible business over with!"

"I think a drink might help," answered Conrad, moistening his lips. "It seems to me I've seen Grimlan go into this cabinet for wine—" He bent to the door of an ornately carved mahogany cabinet, and after some difficulty opened it.

"No wine here," he said disappointedly, "and if ever I felt the need of stimulants—what's this?"

He drew out a roll of parchment, dusty, yellowed

and half covered with spiderwebs. Everything in that grim house seemed, to my nervously excited senses, fraught with mysterious meaning and import, and I leaned over his shoulder as he unrolled it.

"It's a record of peerage," he said, "such a chronicle of births, deaths and so forth, as the old families used to keep, in the Sixteenth Century and earlier."

"What's the name?" I asked.

He scowled over the dim scrawls, striving to master the faded, archaic script.

"G-r-y-m—I've got it—Grymlann, of course. It's the records of old John's family—the Grymlanns of Toad's-heath manor, Suffolk—what an outlandish name for an estate! Look at the last entry."

Together we read, "John Grymlann, borne, march 10, 1630." And then we both cried out. Under this entry was freshly written, in a strange scrawling hand, "Died, March 10, 1930." Below this there was a seal of black wax, stamped with a strange design, something like a peacock with a spreading tail.

Conrad stared at me speechless, all the color ebbed from his face. I shook myself with the rage engendered by fear.

"It's the hoax of a madman!" I shouted. "The stage has been set with such great care that the actors have overstepped themselves. Whoever they are, they have heaped up so many incredible effects as to nullify them. It's all a very stupid, very dull drama of illusion."

And even as I spoke, icy sweat stood out on my body and I shook as with an ague. With a wordless motion Conrad turned toward the stairs, taking up a large candle from a mahogany table.

"It was understood, I suppose," he whispered, "that I should go through with this ghastly matter alone; but I had not the moral courage, and now I'm glad I had not."

A still horror brooded over the silent house as we went up the stairs. A faint breeze stole in from somewhere and set the heavy velvet hangings rustling and I visualized stealthy taloned fingers drawing aside the tapestries, to fix red gloating eyes upon us. Once I thought I heard the indistinct clumping of monstrous feet somewhere above us, but it must have been the heavy pounding of my own heart.

The stairs debouched into a wide dark corridor, in which our feeble candle cast a faint gleam which but illuminated our pale faces and made the shadows seem darker by comparison. We stopped at a heavy door, and I heard Conrad's breath draw in sharply as a man's will when he braces himself physically or mentally. I involuntarily clenched my fists until the nails bit into the palms; then Conrad thrust the door open.

A sharp cry escaped his lips. The candle dropped from his nerveless fingers and went out. The library of John Grimlan was ablaze with light, though the whole house had been in darkness when we entered it.

This light came from seven black candles placed at regular intervals about the great ebony table. On this table, between the candles—I had braced myself against the sight. Now in the face of the mysterious illumination and the sight of the thing on the table, my resolution nearly gave way. John Grimlan had been unlovely in life; in death he was hideous. Yes, he was hideous even though his face was mercifully covered with the same curious silken robe, which, worked in fantastic bird-like designs, covered his whole body except the crooked claw-like hands and the bare withered feet.

A strangling sound came from Conrad. "My God!" he whispered; "what is this? I laid his body out on the table and placed the candles about it, but I did not light them, nor did I place that robe over the body! And there were bedroom slippers on his feet when I left—"

He halted suddenly. We were not alone in the deathroom.

At first we had not seen him, as he sat in the great armchair in a farther nook of a corner, so still that he seemed a part of the shadows cast by the heavy tapestries. As my eyes fell upon him, a violent shuddering shook me and a feeling akin to nausea racked the pit of my stomach. My first impression was of vivid, oblique yellow eyes which gazed unwinkingly at us. Then the man rose and made a deep salaam, and we saw that he was an Oriental. Now when I strive to etch him clearly in my mind, I can resurrect no plain image of him. I only remember those piercing eyes and the yellow, fantastic robe he wore.

We returned his salute mechanically and he spoke in a low, refined voice, "Gentlemen, I crave your pardon! I have made so free as to light the candles—shall we not proceed with the business pertaining to our mutual friend."

He made a slight gesture toward the silent bulk on the table. Conrad nodded, evidently unable to speak. The thought flashed through our minds at the same time, that this man had also been given a sealed envelope—but how had he come to the Grimlan house so quickly? John Grimlan had been dead scarcely two hours and to the best of our knowledge no one knew of his demise but ourselves. And how had he got into the locked and bolted house?

The whole affair was grotesque and unreal in the extreme. We did not even introduce ourselves or ask the stranger his name. He took charge in a matter-of-fact way, and so under the spell of horror and illusion were we that we moved dazedly, involuntarily obeying his suggestions, given us in a low, respectful tone.

I found myself standing on the left side of the table, looking across its grisly burden at Conrad. The Oriental stood with arms folded and head bowed at the head of the table, nor did it then strike me as being strange that he should stand there, instead of Conrad who was to read what Grimlan had written. I found my gaze drawn to the figure worked on the breast of the stranger's robe, in black silk—a curious figure, somewhat resembling a peacock and somewhat resembling a bat, or a flying dragon. I noted with a start that the same design was worked on the robe covering the corpse.

The doors had been locked, the windows fastened down.

Conrad, with a shaky hand, opened the inner envelope and fluttered open the parchment sheets contained therein. These sheets seemed much older than those containing the instructions to Conrad, in the larger envelope. Conrad began to read in a monotonous drone which had the effect of hypnosis on the hearer; so at times the candles grew dim in my gaze and the room and its occupants swam strange and monstrous, veiled and distorted like an hallucination. Most of what he read was gibberish;

it meant nothing; yet the sound of it and the archaic style of it filled me with an intolerable horror.

"To ye contract elsewhere recorded, I, John Grymlann, herebye sweare by ye Name of ye Nameless One to keep goode faithe. Wherefore do I now write in blood these wordes spoken to me in thys grim and silent chamber in ye dedde citie of Koth, whereto no mortal manne hath attained but mee. These same wordes now writ down by mee to be rede over my bodie at ye appointed tyme to fulfill my parte of ye bargain which I entered intoe of mine own free will & knowlege beinge of rite mynd & fiftie years of age this yeare of 1680, A.D. Here begynneth ye incantation:

"Before manne was, ye Elder ones were, & even yet their lord dweleth amonge ye shadows to which if a manne sette his foote he maye not turn vpon his track."

The words merged into a barbaric gibberish as Conrad stumbled through an unfamiliar language— a language faintly suggesting the Phoenician, but shuddery with the touch of a hideous antiquity beyond any remembered earthly tongue. One of the candles flickered and went out. I made a move to relight it, but a motion from the silent Oriental stayed me. His eyes burned into mine, then shifted back to the still form on the table.

The manuscript had shifted back into its archaic English.

"—And ye mortal which gaineth to ye black citadels of Koth & speaks with ye Darke Lord whose face is hidden, for a price may he gain hys heartes desire, ryches & knowledge beyond countinge & lyffe beyond mortal span even two hundred and fiftie yeares."

Again Conrad's voice trailed off into unfamiliar gutturals. Another candle went out.

"—Let not ye mortals flynche as ye tyme draweth nigh for payement & ye fires of Hel laye hold vpon ye vytals as the sign of reckoninge. For ye Prince of Darkness taketh hys due in ye endde & he is not to bee cozened. What ye have promised, that shall ye deliver. *Augantha ne shuba*—"

At the first sound of those barbaric accents, a cold hand of terror locked about my throat. My frantic eyes shot to the candles and I was not surprised to see another flicker out. Yet there was no hint of any draft to stir the heavy black hangings. Conrad's voice wavered; he drew his hand across his throat, gagging momentarily. The eyes of the Oriental never altered.

"—Amonge ye sonnes of men glide strange shadows for ever. Men see ye tracks of ye talones but not ye feete that make them. Over ye souls of men sprad great black wingges. There is but one Black Master though men calle hym Sathanas & Beelzebub & Apolleon & Ahriman & Malik Tous—"

Mists of horror engulfed me. I was dimly aware of Conrad's voice droning on and on, both in English and in that other fearsome tongue whose horrific import I scarcely dared try to guess. And with stark fear clutching at my heart, I saw the candles go out, one by one. And with each flicker, as the gathering gloom darkened about us, my horror mounted. I could not speak, I could not move; my distended eyes were fixed with agonized intensity on the remaining candle. The silent Oriental at the head of that ghastly table was included in my fear. He had not moved nor spoken, but under his drooping lids, his eyes burned with devilish triumph; I knew that beneath his inscrutable exterior he was gloating fiendishly—but why—*why?*

But I *knew* that the moment the extinguishing of the last candle plunged the room into utter darkness, some nameless, abominable thing would take place. Conrad was approaching the end. His voice rose to the climax in gathering crescendo.

"Approacheth now ye moment of payement. Ye ravens are flying. Ye bats winge against ye skye. There are skulls in ye starres. Ye soul & ye bodie are promised and shall bee delivered uppe. Not to ye dust agayne nor ye elements from which springe lyfe—"

The candle flickered slightly. I tried to scream, but my mouth gaped to a soundless yammering. I tried to flee, but I stood frozen, unable even to close my eyes.

"—Ye abysse yawns & ye debt is to paye. Ye light fayles, ye shadows gather. There is no god but evil; no lite but darkness; no hope but doom—"

A hollow groan resounded through the room. *It seemed to come from the robe-covered thing on the table!* The robe twitched fitfully.

"Oh winges in ye black darke!"

I started violently; a faint swish sounded in the gathering shadows. The stir of the dark hangings? It sounded like the rustle of gigantic wings.

"Oh redde eyes in ye shadows! What is promised, what is writ in bloode is fulfilled! Ye lite is gulfed in blackness! Ya—Koth!"

The last candle went out suddenly and a ghastly unhuman cry that came not from my lips or from Conrad's burst unbearably forth. Horror swept over me like a black icy wave; in the blind dark I heard myself screaming terribly. Then with a swirl and a great rush of wind something swept the room, flinging the hangings aloft and dashing chairs and tables crashing to the floor. For an instant an intolerable odor burned our nostrils, a low hideous tittering mocked us in the blackness; then silence fell like a shroud.

Somehow, Conrad found a candle and lighted it. The faint glow showed us the room in fearful disarray—showed us each other's ghastly faces—and showed us the black ebony table—empty! The doors and windows were locked as they had been, but the Oriental was gone—and so was the corpse of John Grimlan.

Shrieking like damned men we broke down the door and fled frenziedly down the well-like staircase where the darkness seemed to clutch at us with clammy black fingers. As we tumbled down into the lower hallway, a lurid glow cut the darkness and the scent of burning wood filled our nostrils.

The outer doorway held momentarily against our frantic assault, then gave way and we hurtled into the outer starlight. Behind us the flames leaped up with a crackling roar as we fled down the hill. Conrad, glancing over his shoulder, halted suddenly, wheeled and flung up his arms like a madman, and screamed, "Soul and body he sold to Malik Tous, who is Satan, two hundred and fifty years ago! This was the night of payment—and my God—look! *Look!* The Fiend has claimed his own!

I looked, frozen with horror. Flames had enveloped the whole house with appalling swiftness, and now the great mass was etched against the shadowed sky, a crimson inferno. And above the holocaust hovered a gigantic black shadow like a monstrous bat, and from its dark clutch dangled a small white thing, like the body of a man, dangling limply. Then, even as we cried out in horror, it was gone and our dazed gaze met only the shuddering walls and blazing roof which crumpled into the flames with an earth-shaking roar.

Kirowan is too close to the action to tell this story. Instead another member of The Wanderers' Club gives us his interpretation of this tale of prey and those who hunt the hunters.

THE HAUNTER OF THE RING

As I entered John Kirowan's study I was too much engrossed in my own thoughts to notice, at fist, the haggard appearance of his visitor, a big, handsome young fellow well known to me.

"Hello, Kirowan," I greeted. "Hello, Gordon. Haven't seen you for quite a while. How's Evelyn?" And before he could answer, still on the crest of the enthusiasm which had brought me there, I exclaimed: "Look here, you fellows, I've got something that will make you stare! I got it from that robber Ahmed Mektub, and I paid high for it, but it's worth it. Look!" From under my coat I drew the jewel-hilted Afghan dagger which had fascinated me as a collector of rare weapons.

Kirowan, familiar with my passion, showed only polite interest, but the effect on Gordon was shocking.

With a strangled cry he sprang up and backward, knocking the chair clattering to the floor. Fists clenched and countenance livid he faced me, crying: "Keep back! Get away from me, or—"

I was frozen in my tracks.

"What in the—" I began bewilderedly, when Gordon, with another amazing change of attitude, dropped into a chair and sank his head in his hands. I saw his heavy shoulders quiver. I stared helplessly from him to Kirowan, who seemed equally dumbfounded.

"Is he drunk?" I asked.

Kirowan shook his head, and filling a brandy glass, offered it to the man. Gordon looked up with haggard eyes, seized the drink and gulped it down like a man half famished. Then he straightened up and looked at us shamefacedly.

"I'm sorry I went off my handle, O'Donnel," he said. "It was the unexpected shock of you drawing that knife."

"Well," I retorted, with some disgust, "I suppose you thought I was going to stab you with it!"

"Yes, I did!" Then, at the utterly blank expression on my face, he added. "Oh, I didn't actually *think* that, at least, I didn't reach that conclusion by any process of reasoning. It was just the blind primitive instinct of a hunted man, against whom anyone's hand may be turned."

His strange words and the despairing way he said them sent a queer shiver of nameless apprehension down my spine.

"What are you talking about?" I demanded uneasily. "Hunted? For what? You never committed a crime in your life."

"Not in this life, perhaps," he muttered.

"What do you mean?"

"What if retribution for a black crime committed in a previous life were hounding me?" he muttered.

"That's nonsense," I snorted.

"Oh, is it?" he exclaimed, stung. "Did you ever hear of my great-grandfather, Sir Richard Gordon of Argyle?"

"Sure; but what's that got to do with—"

"You've seen his portrait: doesn't it resemble me?"

"Well, yes," I admitted, "Except that your expression is frank and wholesome whereas his is crafty and cruel."

"He murdered his wife," answered Gordon. "Suppose the theory of reincarnation were true? Why shouldn't a man suffer in one life for a crime committed in another?"

"You mean you think you are the reincarnation of your great-grandfather? Of all the fantastic—well, since he killed his wife, I suppose you'll be expecting Evelyn to murder you!" This last was delivered in searing sarcasm, as I thought of the sweet, gentle girl Gordon had married. His answer stunned me.

"My wife," he said slowly, "has tried to kill me three times in the past week."

There was no reply to that. I glanced helplessly at John Kirowan. He sat in his customary position, chin resting on his strong, slim hands; his white face was immobile, but his dark eyes gleamed with interest. In the silence I heard a clock ticking like a death-watch.

"Tell us the full story, Gordon," suggested Kirowan, and his calm, even voice was like a knife that cut a strangling, relieving the unreal tension.

*   *   *

"You know we've been married less than a year," Gordon began, plunging into the tale as though he were bursting for utterance; his words stumbled and tripped over one another. "All couples have spats, of course, but we've never had any real quarrels. Evelyn is the best-natured girl in the world.

"The first thing out of the ordinary occurred about a week ago. We had driven up in the mountains, left the car, and were wandering around picking wild flowers. At last we came to a steep slope, some thirty feet in height, and Evelyn called my attention to the flowers which grew thickly at the foot. I was looking over the edge and wondering if I could climb down without tearing my clothes to ribbons, when I felt a violent shove from behind that toppled me over.

"If it had been a sheer cliff, I'd have broken my neck. As it was, I went tumbling down, rolling and sliding, and brought up at at the bottom scratched and bruised, with my garments in rags. I looked up and saw Evelyn staring down, apparently frightened half out of her wits.

" 'Oh Jim!' she cried. 'Are you hurt? How came you to fall?'

"It was on the tip of my tongue to tell her that there was such a thing as carrying a joke too far, but these words checked me. I decided that she must have stumbled against me unintentionally, and actually didn't know it was she who precipitated me down the slope.

"So I laughed it off, and went home. She made a great fuss over me, insisted on swabbing my scratches with iodine, and lectured me for my carelessness! I hadn't the heart to tell her it was her fault.

"But four days later, the next thing happened. I was walking along our driveway, when I saw her coming up it in the automobile. I stepped out on the grass to let her by, as there isn't any curb along the driveway. She was smiling as she approached me, and slowed down the car, as if to speak to me. then, just before she reached me, a most horrible change came over her expression. Without warning the car leaped at me like a living thing as she drove her foot down on the accelerator. Only a frantic leap backward saved me from being ground under the wheels. The car shot across the lawn and crashed into a tree. I ran to it and found Evelyn dazed and hysterical, but unhurt. She sobbed of losing control of the machine.

"I carried her into the house and sent for Doctor Donnelly. He found nothing seriously wrong with her, and attributed her dazed condition to fright and shock. Within half an hour she regained her normal senses, but she's refused to touch the wheel since. Strange to say, she seemed less frightened on her own account than on mine. She seemed vaguely to know that she'd nearly run me down, and grew hysterical again when she spoke of it. Yet she seemed to take it for granted that I knew the machine had got out of her control. But I distinctly saw her wrench the wheel around, and I know she deliberately tried to hit me—why, God alone knows.

"Still I refused to let my mind follow the channel it was getting into. Evelyn had never given any evidence of any phychological weakness or 'nerves'; she's always been a level-headed girl, wholesome and natural. But I began to think she was subject to crazy impulses. Most of us have felt the impulse to leap from tall buildings. And sometimes a person feels a blind, childish and utterly reasonless urge to harm someone. We pick up a pistol, and the thought suddenly enters our mind how easy it would be to send our friend, who sits smiling and unaware, into eternity with a touch of the trigger. Of course we don't do it, but the impulse is there. So I thought perhaps some lack of mental discipline made Evelyn susceptible to these unguided impulses, and unable to control them."

"Nonsense," I broke in. "I've known her since she was a baby. If she has any such trait, she's developed it since she married you."

It was an unfortunate remark. Gordon caught it up with a despairing gleam in his eyes. "That's just it—since she married me! It's a curse—a black, ghastly curse, crawling like a serpent out of the past! I tell you, I was Richard Gordon and she—she was Lady Elizabeth, his murdered wife!" His voice ground to a blood-freezing whisper.

I shuddered; it is an awful thing to look upon the ruin of a keen clean brain, and such I was certain that I surveyed in James Gordon. Why or how, or by what grisly chance it had come about I could not way, but I was certain the man was mad.

"You spoke of three attempts." It was John Kirowan's voice again, calm and stable amid the gathering webs of horror and unreality.

"Look here!" Gordon lifted his arm, drew back the sleeve and displayed a bandage, the cryptic significance of which was intolerable.

"I came into the bathroom this morning looking for my razor," he said. "I found Evelyn just on the point of using my best shaving implement for some feminine purpose—to cut out a pattern, or something. Like many women she can't seem to realize the difference between a razor and a butcher-knife or a pair of shears.

"I was a bit irritated, and I said: 'Evelyn, how many times have I told you not to use my razors for such things? Bring it here; I'll give you my pocket-knife.'

" 'I'm sorry, Jim,' she said. 'I didn't know it would hurt the razor. Here it is.'

"She was advancing, holding the open razor toward me. I reached for it—then something warned me. It was the same look in her eyes, just as I had seen it the day she nearly ran over me. That was all that saved my life, for I instinctively threw up my hand just as she slashed at my throat with all her power. The blade gashed my arms as you see, before I caught her wrist. For an instant she fought me like a wild thing; her slender body was taut as steel beneath my hands. Then she went limp and the look in her eyes was replaced by a strange dazed expression. The razor slipped out of her fingers.

"I let go of her and she stood swaying as if about to faint. I went to the lavatory—my wound was bleeding in a beastly fashion—and the next thing I heard her cry out, and she was hovering over me.

" 'Jim!' she cried. 'How did you cut yourself so terribly?' "

Gordon shook his head and sighed heavily. "I guess I was a bit out of my head. My self control snapped.

" 'Don't keep up this pretense, Evelyn,' I said. 'God knows what's got into you, but you know as well as I that you've tried to kill me three times in the past week.'

"She recoiled as if I'd struck her, catching at her breast and staring at me as if at a ghost. She didn't say a word and just what I said I don't remember. But when I finished I left her standing there white and still as a marble statue. I got my arm bandaged at a drug store, and then came over here, not knowing what else to do.

"Kirowan—O'Donnel—it's damnable! Either my wife is subject to fits of insanity—" He choked on the word. "No, I can't believe it. Ordinarily her eyes are too clear and level—too utterly sane. But every time she has an opportunity to harm me, she seems to become a temporary maniac."

He beat his fists together in his impotence and agony.

"But it isn't insanity! I used to work in a psycho-pathic ward, and I've seen every form of mental unbalance. My wife is *not* insane!"

"Then what—" I began, but he turned haggard eyes on me.

"Only one alternative remains," he answered. "It is the old curse—from the days when I walked the earth with a heart as black as hell's darkest pits, and did evil in the sight of man and of God. *She* knows, in fleeting snatches of memory. People have *seen* before—have glimpsed forbidden things in momentary liftings of the veil, which bars life from life. She was Elizabeth Douglas, the ill-fated bride of Richard Gordon, whom he murdered in jealous frenzy, and the vengeance is hers. I shall die by her hands, as it was meant to be. And she—" he bowed his head in his hands.

"Just a moment." It was Kirowan again. "You

have mentioned a strange look in your wife's eyes. What sort of a look? Was it of maniacal frenzy?"

Gordon shook his head. "It was an utter blankness. All the life and intelligence simply vanished, leaving her eyes dark wells of emptiness."

Kirowan nodded, and asked a seemingly irrelevant question. "Have you any enemies?"

"Not that I know of."

"You forget Joseph Roelocke," I said. "I can't imagine that elegant sophisticate going to the trouble of doing you actual harm, but I have an idea that if he could discomfort you without any physical effort on his part, he'd do it with a right good will."

Kirowan turned on me an eye that had suddenly become piercing.

"And who is this Joseph Roelocke?"

"A young exquisite who came into Evelyn's life and nearly rushed her off her feet for a while. But in the end she came back to her first love—Gordon here. Roelocke took it pretty hard. For all his suaveness there's a streak of violence and passion in the man that might have cropped out but for his infernal indolence and blasé indifference."

"Oh, there's nothing to be said against Roelocke," interrupted Gordon impatiently. "He must know that Evelyn never really loved him. He merely fascinated her temporarily with his romantic Latin air."

"Not exactly Latin, Jim," I protested. "Roelocke does look foreign, but it isn't Latin. It's almost Oriental."

"Well, what has Roelocke to do with this matter?" Gordon snarled with the irascibility of frayed nerves. "He's been as friendly as a man could be since Evelyn and I were married. In fact, only a week ago he sent her a ring which he said was a peace-offering and a belated wedding gift; said that after all, her jilting him was a greater misfortune for her than it was for him—the conceited jackass!"

"A ring?" Kirowan had suddenly come to life; it was as if something hard and steely had been sounded in him. "What sort of a ring?"

"Oh, a fantastic thing—copper, made like a scaly snake coiled three times, with its tail in its mouth and yellow jewels for eyes. I gather he picked it up somewhere in Hungary."

"He has traveled a great deal in Hungary?"

Gordon looked surprised at this questioning, but answered: "Why, apparently the man's traveled everywhere. I put him down as the pampered son of a millionaire. He never did any work, so far as I know."

"He's a great student," I put in. "I've been up to his apartment several times, and I never saw such a collection of books—"

Gordon leaped to his feet with an oath, "Are we all crazy?" he cried. "I came up here hoping to get some help—and you fellows fall to talking of Joseph Roelocke. I'll go to Doctor Donnelly—"

"Wait!" Kirowan stretched out a detaining hand. "If you don't mind, we'll go over to your house. I'd like to talk to your wife."

Gordon dumbly acquiesced. Harried and haunted by grisly forebodings, he knew not which way to turn, and welcomed anything that promised aid.

We drove over in his car, and scarcely a word was spoken on the way. Gordon was sunk in moody ruminations, and Kirowan had withdrawn himself into some strange aloof domain of thought beyond my ken. He sat like a statue, his dark vital eyes

staring into space, not blankly, but as one who looks
with understanding into some far realm.

Though I counted the man as my best friend, I
knew but little of the past. He had come into my
life as abruptly and unannounced as Joseph Roelocke had come into the life of Evelyn Ash. I had
met him at the Wanderer's Club, which is composed of the drift of the world, travelers, eccentrics,
and all manner of men whose paths lie outside the
beaten tracks of life. I had been attracted to him,
and intrigued by his strange powers and deep
knowledge. I vaguely knew that he was the black
sheep younger son of a titled Irish family, and that
he had walked many strange ways. Gordon's mention of Hungary struck a chord in my memory; one
phase of his life Kirowan had once let drop, frag-
mentarily. I only knew that he had once suffered a
bitter grief and a savage wrong, and that it had been
in Hungary. but the nature of the episode I did
not know.

At Gordon's house Evelyn met us calmly, showing
inner agitation only by the over-restraint of her
manner. I saw the beseeching look she stole at her
husband. She was a slender, soft-spoken girl, whose
dark eyes were always vibrant and alight with emotion. That child try to murder her adored husband?
The idea was monstrous. Again I was convinced that
James Gordon himself was deranged.

Following Kirowan's lead, we made a pretense of
small talk, as if we had casually dropped in, but I
felt that Evelyn was not deceived. Our conversation
rang false and hollow, and presently Kirowan said:
"Mrs. Gordon, that is a remarkable ring you are
wearing. Do you mind if I look at it?"

"I'll have to give you my hand," she laughed. "I've been trying to get it off today, and it won't come off."

She held out her slim white hand for Kirowan's inspection, and his face was immobile as he looked at the metal snake that coiled about her slim finger. He did not touch it. I myself was aware of an unaccountable repulsion. There was something almost obscene about that dull copperish reptile wound about the girl's white finger.

"It's evil-looking, isn't it?" she involuntarily shivered. "At first I liked it, but now I can hardly bear to look at it. If I can get it off I intend to return it to Joseph—Mr. Roelocke."

Kirowan was about to make some reply, when the doorbell rang. Gordon jumped as if shot, and Evelyn rose quickly.

"I'll answer it, Jim—I know who it is."

She returned an instant later with two more mutual friends, those inseparable cronies, Doctor Donnelly, whose burly body, jovial manner and booming voice were combined with as keen a brain as any in the profession, and Bill Bain, elderly, lean, wiry, acidly witty. Both were old friends of the Ash family. Doctor Donnelly had ushered Evelyn into the world, and Bain was always Uncle Bill to her.

"Howdy, Jim! Howdy, Mr. Kirowan!" roared Donnelly. "Hey, O'Donnel, have you got any firearms with you? Last time you nearly blew my head off showing me an old flintlock pistol that wasn't supposed to be loaded—"

"Doctor Donnelly!"

We all turned. Evelyn was standing beside a wide table, holding it as if for support. Her face was white. Our badinage ceased instantly. A sudden tension was in the air.

"Doctor Donnelly," she repeated, holding her voice steady by an effort, "I sent for you and Uncle Bill—for the same reason for which I know Jim has brought Mr. Kirowan and Michael. There is a matter Jim and I can no longer deal with alone. There is something between us—something black and ghastly and terrible."

"What are you talking about, girl?" All the levity was gone from Donnelly's great voice.

"My husband—" She choked, then went blindly on: "My husband has accused me of trying to murder him."

The silence that fell was broken by Bain's sudden and energetic rise. His eyes blazed and his fists quivered.

"You young pup!" he shouted at Gordon. "I'll knock the living daylights—"

"Sit down, Bill!" Donnelly's huge hand crushed his smaller companion back into his chair. "No use goin' off half cocked. Go ahead, honey."

"We need help. We can not carry this thing alone." A shadow crossed her comely face. "This morning Jim's arm was badly cut. He said I did it. I don't know. I was handing him the razor. Then I must have fainted. At least, everything faded away. When I came to myself he was washing his arm in the lavatory—and—and he accused me of trying to kill him."

"Why, the young fool!" barked the belligerent Bain. "Hasn't he sense enough to know that if you did cut him, it was an accident?"

"Shut up, won't you?" snorted Donnelly. "Honey, did you say you fainted? That isn't like you."

"I've been having fainting spells," she answered. "The first time was when we were in the mountains and Jim fell down a cliff. We were standing on the edge—then everything went black, and when my sight cleared, he was rolling down the slope." She shuddered at the recollection.

"Then when I lost control of the car and it crashed into the tree. You remember—Jim called you over."

Doctor Donnelly nodded his head ponderously.

"I don't remember you ever having fainting spells before."

"But Jim says I pushed him over the cliff!" she cried hysterically. "He says I tried to run him down in the car! He says I purposely slashed him with the razor!"

Doctor Donnelly turned perplexedly, toward the wretched Gordon.

"How about it, son?"

"God help me," Gordon burst out in agony; "it's true!"

"Why, you lying hound!" It was Bain who gave tongue, leaping again to his feet. "If you want a divorce, why don't you get it in a decent way, instead of resorting to these despicable tactics—"

"Damn you!" roared Gordon, lunging up, and losing control of himself completely. "If you say that I'll tear your jugular out!"

Evelyn screamed; Donnelly grabbed Bain ponderously and banged him back into is chair with no overly gentle touch, and Kirowan laid a hand lightly on Gordon's shoulder. The man seemed to crumple into himself. He sank back into his chair and held out his hands gropingly toward his wife.

"Evelyn," he said, his voice thick with laboring

emotion, "you know I love you. I feel like a dog. But God help me, it's true. If we go on this way, I'll be a dead man, and you—"

"Don't say it!" she screamed. "I know you wouldn't lie to me, Jim. If you say I tried to kill you, I know I did. But I swear, Jim, I didn't do it consciously. Oh, I must be going mad! That's why my dreams have been so wild and terrifying lately—"

"Of what have you dreamed, Mrs. Gordon?" asked Kirowan gently.

She pressed her hands to her temples and stared dully at him, as if only half comprehending.

"A black thing," she muttered. "A horrible faceless black thing that mows and mumbles and paws over me with apish hands. I dream of it every night. And in the daytime I try to kill the only man I ever loved. I'm going mad! Maybe I'm already crazy and don't know it."

"Calm yourself, honey." To Doctor Donnelly, with all his science, it was only another case of feminine hysteria. His matter-of-fact voice seemed to soothe her, and she sighed and drew a weary hand through her damp locks.

"We'll talk this all over, and everything's goin' to be okay," he said, drawing a thick cigar from his vest pocket. "Gimme a match, honey."

She began mechanically to feel about the table, and just as mechanically Gordon said: "There are matches in the drawer, Evelyn."

She opened the drawer and began groping in it, when suddenly, as it struck by recollection and intuition, Gordon sprang up, white-faced, and shouted: "No, no! Don't open that drawer—don't—"

Even as he voiced that urgent cry, she stiffened,

as if at the feel of something in the drawer. Her change of expression held us all frozen, even Kirowan. The vital intelligence vanished from her eyes like a blown-out flame, and into them came the look Gordon had described as blank. The term was descriptive. Her beautiful eyes were dark wells of emptiness, as if the soul had been withdrawn from behind them.

Her hand came out of the drawer holding a pistol, and she fired point-blank. Gordon reeled with a groan and went down, blood starting from his head. For a flashing instant she looked down stupidly at the smoking gun in her hand, like one suddenly waking from a nightmare. Then her wild scream of agony smote our ears.

"Oh God, I've killed him! Jim! *Jim!*"

She reached him before any of us, throwing herself on her knees and cradling his bloody head in her arms, while she sobbed in an unbearable passion of horror and anguish. The emptiness was gone from her eyes; they were alive and dilated with grief and terror.

I was making toward my prostrate friend with Donnelly and Bain, but Kirowan caught my arm. His face was no longer immobile; his eyes glittered with a controlled savagery.

"Leave him to them!" he snarled. "We are hunters, not healers! Lead me to the house of Joseph Roelocke!"

I did not question him. We drove there in Gordon's car. I had the wheel, and something about the grim face of my companion caused me to hurl the machine recklessly through the traffic. I had the sensation of being part of a tragic drama which was hurtling with headlong speed toward a terrible climax.

I wrenched the car to a grinding halt at the curb before the building where Roelocke lived in a bizarre apartment high above the city. The very elevator that shot us skyward seemed imbued with something of Kirowan's driving urge for haste. I pointed out Roelocke's door, and he cast it open without knocking and shouldered his way in. I was close at his heels.

Roelocke, in a dressing-gown of chinese silk worked with dragons, was lounging on a divan, puffing quickly at a cigarette. He sat up, overturning a wine-glass which stood with a half-filled bottle at his elbow.

Before Kirowan could speak, I burst out with our news. "James Gordon has been shot!"

He sprang to his feet. "Shot? When? When did she kill him?"

"*She?*" I glared in bewilderment. "How did you know—"

With a steely hand Kirowan thrust me aside, and as the men faced each other, I saw recognition flare up in Roelocke's face. They made a strong contrast: Kirowan, tall, pale with some white-hot passion; Roelocke, slim, darkly handsome, with the saracenic arch of his slim brows above his black eyes. I realized that whatever else occurred; it lay between those two men. They were not strangers; I could sense like a tangible thing the hate that lay between them.

"John Kirowan!" softly whispered Roelocke.

"You remember me, Yosef Vrolok!" Only an iron

control kept Kirowan's voice steady. The other merely stared at him without speaking.

"Years ago," said Kirowan more deliberately, "when we delved in the dark mysteries together in Budapest, I saw whither you were drifting. I drew back; I would not descend to the foul depths of forbidden occultism and diabolism to which you sank. And because I would not, you despised me, and you robbed me of the only woman I ever loved; you turned her against me by means of your vile arts, and then you degraded and debauched her, sank her into your own foul slime. I had killed you with my hands then, Yosef Vrolok—vampire by nature as well as by name that you are—but your arts protected you from physical vengeance. But you have trapped yourself at last!"

Kirowan's voice rose in fierce exultation. All his cultured restraint had been swept away from him, leaving a primitive, elemental man, raging and gloating over a hated foe.

"You sought the destruction of James Gordon and his wife, because she unwittingly escaped your snare; you—"

Roelocke shrugged his shoulders and laughed. "You are mad. I have not seen the Gordons for weeks. Why blame for their family troubles?"

Kirowan snarled. "Liar as always. What did you say just now when O'Donnel told you Gordon had been shot? 'When did *she* kill him?' You were expecting to hear that the girl had killed her husband. Your psychic powers had told you that a climax was close at hand. You were nervously awaiting news of the success of your devilish scheme.

"But I did not need a slip of your tongue to recognize your handiwork. I knew as soon as I saw the ring on Evelyn Gordon's finger; the ring she could not remove; the ancient and accursed ring of Thoth-amon, handed down by foul cults of sorcerers since the days of forgotten Stygia. I knew that ring was yours, and I knew by what ghastly rites you came to possess it. And I knew its power. Once she put it on her finger, in her innocence and ignorance, she was in your power. By your black magic you summoned the black elemental spirit, *the haunter of the ring*, out of the gulfs of Night and the ages. Here in your accursed chamber you performed unspeakable rituals to drive Evelyn Gordon's soul and her body, and to cause that body to be possessed by that godless sprite from *outside* the human universe.

"She was too clean and wholesome, her love for her husband too strong, for the fiend to gain complete and permanent possession of her body; only for brief instants could it drive her own spirit into the void and animate her form. But that was enough for your purpose. But you have brought ruin upon yourself by your vengeance!"

Kirowan's voice rose to a feline screech.

"What was the price demanded by the fiend you drew from the Pits? Ha, you blench! Yosef Vrolok is not the only man to have learned forbidden secrets! After I left Hungary, a broken man, I took up again the study of the black arts, to trap you, you cringing serpent! I explored the ruins of Zimbabwe, the lost mountains of inner Mongolia, and the forgotten jungle islands of the southern seas. I learned what sickened my soul so that I forswore occultism for ever—but I learned of the black spirit that deals death by the hand of a beloved one, and is controlled by a master of magic.

"But, Yosef Vrolok, you are not an adept! You have not the power to control the fiend you have invoked. And you have sold your soul!"

The Hungarian tore at his collar as if it were a strangling noose. His face had changed, as if a mask had dropped away; he looked much older.

"You lie!" he panted. "I did not promise him *my* soul—"

"I do not lie!" Kirowan's shriek was shocking in its wild exultation. "I know the price a man must pay for calling forth the nameless shape that roams the gulf of Darkness. Look! There in the corner behind you! A nameless, sightless thing is laughing—is mocking you! It has fulfilled its bargain, and it has come for you, Yosef Vrolok!"

"No! No!" shrieked Vrolok, tearing his limp collar away from his sweating throat. His composure had crumpled, and his demoralization was sickening to see. "I tell you it was not *my* soul—I promised it a soul, but not *my* soul—he must take the soul of the girl, or of James Gordon—"

"Fool!" roared Kirowan. "Do you think *he* could take the souls of innocence? That he would not know they were beyond his reach? The girl and the youth he could kill; their souls were not his to take or yours to give. But *your* black soul is not beyond his reach, and he will have his wage. *Look!* He is materializing behind you! He is growing out of thin air!"

Was it the hypnosis inspired by Kirowan's burning words that caused me to shudder and grow cold, to feel an icy chill that was not of earth pervade the room? Was it a trick of light and shadow that seemed to produce the effect of a black anthropomorphic shadow on the wall behind the Hungarian?

No, by heaven! It grew, it swelled—Vrolok had not turned. He stared at Kirowan with eyes starting from his head, hair standing stiffly on his scalp, sweat dripping from his livid face.

Kirowan's cry started shudders down my spine.

"Look behind you, fool! *I see him!* He has come! He is here! His grisly mouth gapes in awful laughter! His misshapen paws reach for you!"

And then at last Vrolok wheeled, with an awful shriek, throwing his arms above his head in a gesture of wild despair. And for one brain-shattering instant he was *blotted out* by a great black shadow— Kirowan grasped my arm and we fled from that accursed chamber, blind with horror.

The same paper which bore a brief item telling of James Gordon having suffered a slight scalp-wound by the accidental discharge of a pistol in his home, headlined the sudden death of Joseph Roelocke, wealthy and eccentric clubman, in his sumptuous apartments—apparently from heart-failure.

I read it at breakfast, while I drank cup after cup of black coffee, from a hand that was not too steady, even after the lapse of a night. Across the table from me Kirowan likewise seemed to lack appetite. He brooded, as if he roamed again through bygone years.

"Gordon's fantastic theory of reincarnation was wild enough," I said at last. "But the actual facts were still more incredible. Tell me, Kirowan, was that last scene the result of hypnosis? Was it the power of your words that made me seem to see a black horror grow out of the air and rip Yosef Vrolok's soul from his living body?"

He shook his head. "No human hypnotism would strike that black-hearted devil dead on the floor. No; there are beings outside the ken of common humanity, foul shapes of transcosmic evil. Such a one it was with which Vrolok dealt."

"But how could it claim his soul?" I persisted. "If indeed such an awful bargain had been struck, it had not fulfilled its part, for James Gordon was not dead, but merely knocked senseless."

"Vrolok did not know it," answered Kirowan. "He thought that Gordon was dead, and I convinced him that he himself had been trapped, and was doomed. In his demoralization he fell easy prey to the thing he called forth. *It*, of course, was always watching for a moment of weakness on his part. The powers of Darkness never deal fairly with human beings; he who traffics with them is always cheated in the end."

"It's a mad nightmare," I muttered. "But it seems to me, then, that you as much as anything else brought about Vrolok's death."

"It is gratifying to think so," Kirowan answered. "Evelyn Gordon is safe now; and it is a small repayment for what he did to another girl, years ago, and in a far country."

Howard not only makes you feel as if he's been to the places he describes—in this case, Ireland again—but also makes you feel you should go there, too. Kirowan is back as narrator in this story of siblings, and a pure love conquering all.

DERMOD'S BANE

If your heart is sick in your breast and a blind black curtain of sorrow is between you and your brain and your eyes so that the very sunlight is pale and leprous—go to the city of Galway, in the county of the same name, in the province of Connaught, in the country of Ireland.

In the gray old City of Tribes as they call it, there is a dreamy soothing spell that is like enchantment, and if you are of Galway blood, no matter how far away, your grief will pass slowly from you like a dream, leaving only a sad sweet memory, like the scent of a dying rose. There is a mist of antiquity hovering over the old city which mingles with sorrow and makes one forget. Or you can go out into the blue Connaught hills and feel the salt sharp tang of the wind off the Atlantic, and life seems faint

117

and far away, with all its sharp joys and bitter sorrows, and no more real than the shadows of the clouds which pass.

I came to Galway as a wounded beast crawls back to his lair in the hills. The city of my people broke upon my gaze for the first time, but it did not seem strange or foreign. It seemed like a homecoming to me, and with each day passing the land of my birth seemed farther and farther away and the land of my ancestor closer.

I came to Galway with an aching heart. My twin sister, whom I loved as never I had loved anyone else, died; her going was swift and unexpected. It seemed to my 'mazed agony that one moment she was laughing beside me with her cheery smile and bright gray Irish eyes, and the next, the cold bitter grass was growing above her. Oh, my soul to God, not your Son alone endured crucifixion.

A black cloud like a shroud locked about me and in the dim borderland of madness I sat alone, tearless and speechless. My grandmother came to me at last, a great grim old woman, with hard haunted eyes that held all the woes of the Irish race.

"Let you go to Galway, lad. Let you go to the ould land. Maybe the sorrow of you will be drowned in the cold salt sea. Maybe the folk of Connaught can heal the wound that is on you. . . ."

I went to Galway.

Well, the people were kind there—all those great old families, the Martins, the Lynches, the Deanes, the Dorseys, the Blakes, the Kirowans—families of the fourteen great families who rule Galway.

Out on the hills and in the valleys I roved and talked with the kindly, quaint country folk, many of whom still spoke the good old Erse language which I could speak haltingly.

There, on a hill one night before a shepherd's fire I heard again the old legend of Dermod O'Connor. As the shepherd unfolded the terrible tale in his rich brogue, interlaced with many Gaelic phrases, I remembered that my grandmother had told me the tale when I was a child, but I had forgotten the most of it.

Briefly the story is this: there was a chief of the Clan na O'Connor and his name was Dermod, but people called him the Wolf. The O'Connors were kings in the old days, ruling Connaught with a hand of steel. They divided the rule of Ireland with the O'Briens in the South—Munster—and the O'Neills in the North—Ulster. With the O'Rourkes they fought the MacMurraughs of Leinster and it was Dermot MacMurraugh, driven out of Ireland by the O'Connors, who brought in Strongbow and his Norman adventurers. When Earl Pembroke (whom men called Strongbow) landed in Ireland, Roderick O'Connor was king of Ireland in name and claim at least. And the clan O'Connor, fierce Celtic warriors that they were, kept up their struggle for freedom until at last their power was broken by a terrible Norman invasion. All honor to the O'Connors. In the old times my people fought under their banners—but each tree has a rotten root. Each great house has its dark sheep. Dermod O'Cconnor was the black sheep of his clan and a blacker one never lived.

His hand was against all men, even his own house. He was no chieftain, fighting to regain the crown of Erin or to free his people; he was a red-handed reaver and he preyed alike on Norman and

Celt; he raided into The Pale and he carried torch
and steel into Munster and Leinster. The O'Briens
and the O'Carrolls had cause to curse him, and the
O'Neills hunted him like a wolf.

He left a trail of blood and devastation wherever
he rode and at last, his band dwindling from deser-
tions and constant fighting, he alone remained, hiding in caves and hills, butchering lone travelers for
the sheer lust of blood that was on him, and
descending on lonely farmer's houses or shepherd's
huts to commit atrocities on their women folk. He
was a giant of a man and the legends make of him
something inhuman and monstrous. It must be
truth that he was strange and terrible in appearance.

But his end came at last. He murdered a youth
of the Kirowan clan and the Kirowans rode out of
the city of Galway with vengeance in their hearts.
Sir Michael Kirowan met the marauder alone in the
hills—Sir Michael, a direct ancestor of mine, whose
very name I bear. Alone they fought with only the
shuddering hills to witness that terrible battle, till
the clash of steel reached the ears of the rest of the
clan who were riding hard and scouring the
countryside.

They found Sir Michael badly wounded and Dermod O'Connor dying with a cleft shoulder bone and
a ghastly wound in his breast. but such was their
fury and hatred, that they flung a noose about the
dying robber's neck and hanged him to a great tree
on the edge of a cliff overlooking the sea.

"And," said my friend, the shepherd, stirring the
fire, "the peasant folk still point out the tree and
call it Dermod's Bane, after the danish manner, and
men have seen the great outlaw o' nights, and him
gnashing his great tushes and spouting blood from

shoulder and breast and swearin' all manner o' ill on the Kirowans and their blood for all time to come.

"And so, sir, let you not walk in the cliffs over the sea by night for you are of the blood he hates and the same name of the man who felled him is on you. For let you laugh if so be you will, but the ghost of Dermod O'Connor the wolf is broad o' dark night and the moon out of the sky, and him with his great black beard and ghastly eyes and boar tushes."

They pointed me out the tree, Dermod's Bane, and strangely like a gallows it looked, standing there as it had stood for how many hundred years I do not know, for men live long in Ireland and trees live longer. There were no other trees near and the cliff rose sheer from the sea for four hundred feet. Below was only the deep sinister blue of the waves, deep and dark, breaking on the cruel rocks.

I walked much in the hills at night for when the silence of the darkness was on the world and no speech or noises of men to hold my thoughts, my sorrow was dark on my heart again and I walked on the hills where the stars seemed close and warm. And often my 'mazed brain wondered which star *she* was on, or if she had turned to a star.

One night the old, sharp agony returned unbearably. I rose from my bed—for I was staying at the time in a little mountain inn—and dressed and went into the hills. My temples throbbed and there was an unbearable weight about my heart. My dumb frozen soul shrieked up to God but I could not weep. I felt I must weep or go mad, for never a tear had passed my eyelids since . . .

Well, I walked on and on, how long or how far I do not know. The stars were hot and red and angry and gave me no comfort that night. At first I wanted to scream and howl and throw myself on the ground and tear the grass with my teeth. Then that passed and I wandered as in a trance. There was no moon and in the dim starlight the hills and their trees loomed dark and strange. Over the summits I could see the great Atlantic lying like a dusky silver monster and I heard her faint roaring.

Something flitted in front of me and I thought it was a wolf; but there have been no wolves in Ireland for many and many a year. Again I saw the thing, a long low shadowy shape. I followed it mechnically. Now in front of me I saw a cliff overlooking the sea. On the cliff's edge was a single great tree that loomed up like a gibbet. I approached this.

Then in front of me, as I neared the tree, a vague mist hovered. A strange fear spread over me as I watched stupidly. A form became evident. Dim and silky, like a shred of moon-mist, but with an undoubted human shape. A face—I cried out!

A vague, sweet face floated before me, indistinct, mist like—yet I made out the shimmery mass of dark hair, the high pure forehead, the red curving lips—the serious soft gray eyes.

"Moira!" I cried in agony and rushed forward, my aching arms spread wide, my heart bursting in my bosom.

She floated away from me like a mist blown by a breeze; now she seemed to waver in space—I felt myself staggering wildly on the very edge of the cliff, whither my blind rush had led me. As a man wakes from a dream I saw in one flashing instant the cruel rocks four hundred feet below. I heard the hungry lapping of the waves—as I felt myself falling forward I saw the vision, but now it was changed hideously. Great tusk-like teeth gleamed ghoulishly through a matted black beard. Terrible eyes blazed under penthouse brows; blood flowed from a wound in the shoulder and a ghastly gash in the broad breast . . .

"Dermod O'Connor!" I screamed, my hair bristling. "Avaunt, fiend out of hell . . ."

I swayed out for the fall I could not check, with death waiting four hundred feet below. Then a soft small hand closed on my wrist and I was drawn irresistably back. I fell, but back on the soft green grass at the lip of the cliff, not to the keen-edged rocks and waiting sea below. Oh, I knew—I could not be wrong. The small hand was gone from my wrist, the hideous face gone from the cliff edge— but that grasp on my wrist that drew me back from my doom—how could I fail to recognize it? A thousand times had I felt the dear touch of that soft hand on my arm or in my own hand. Oh, Moira, Moira, pulse of my heart, in life and in death you were ever at my side.

And now for the first time I wept and lying on my stomach with my face in my hands, Poured my racked heart out in scalding, blinding and soul easing tears, until the sun came up over the blue Galway hills and limned the branches of Dermod's Bane with a strange new radiance.

Now, did I dream or was I mad? Did in truth the ghost of that long dead outlaw lead me across the hills to the cliff under the death-tree, and there assume the shape of my dead sister to lure me to my doom? And did in truth the real hand of that dead sister, brought suddenly to my side by my peril, hold me back from death?

Believe or disbelieve as you will; to me it is a fact. I saw Dermod O'Connor that night and he led me over the cliff, and the soft hand of Moira Kirowan dragged me back and its touch loosened the frozen channels of my heart and brought me peace. For the wall that bars the living from the dead is but a thin veil, I know now, and so sure as a dead woman's love conquered a dead man's hate, so sure shall I some day in the world beyond, hold my sister in my arms again.

Lost Horizon, James Hilton's story of Shangri-La and a utopia in the mountains of Tibet, was published in 1933. Howard's story of a super-science utopia in the mountains of Mongolia is in no way romantic—and it wasn't published until 1966, thirty years after Howard's death.

KING OF THE FORGOTTEN PEOPLE

Jim Brill licked his parched lips, staring about him with bloodshot eyes. Behind him lay the sand, blown in curving ridges and long riffles; before him rose the stark outlines of the nameless mountains which were his goal. The sun hung above the western horizon, dull gold in the veil of dust which turned the sky a sickly yellow and lent its taste to the very air he breathed.

Yet he was thankful for it. But for the sand storm he would have shared the fate which had overtaken his guides and servants.

The attack had come at dawn. From behind a bare ridge which had concealed their approach, a swarm of squat riders on shaggy horses had rushed the camp, howling like devils, shooting and slashing. In the midst of the fight the storm had brought blinding clouds of dust rolling over the desert, and through it Jim Brill had fled, knowing that he alone remained alive of the expedition which had toiled so far on its strange quest.

Now, after a grind that had taxed to the uttermost the powers of himself and his steed, he saw nothing of his pursuers, though the dust which still hung over the desert limited the range of his vision considerably.

He had been the only white man in the expedition. His previous experiences with Mongol bandits told him that they would not let him escape if they could help it.

Brill's equipment consisted of the .45 at his hip, a canteen with a few drops of water remaining in it, and the weary horse which drooped under his weight after the long flight.

Mindful of this, the man swung down from the saddle and plodded on, leading the animal. He scanned the rugged slopes ahead of him without hope. Sure death awaited him in the desert; what the mountains held, he could not know. No man knew what lay in this unexplored region. If any white man had ever entered it, he had never come out alive to tell what he had found.

The horse snorted suddenly and threw up its head, pulling back on the rein. Brill swore wearily and tried to quiet it. Its eyes rolled and its haunches quivered. Uneasily he looked about him. They were entering the narrow mouth of a canyon, the rocky floor of which sloped upward. The sides were steep, broken by jutting ledges. On one of these ledges, that overhung the canyon mouth, *something* moved, scuttled behind a boulder. Brill had a vague impression of something bulky and hairy that moved in manner which suggested neither man nor beast.

He swung wide of that ledge, hugging the opposite wall. When they were even with it, the horse shied and snorted, but quieted after they had passed on. Whatever the animal feared was crouching up there among the boulders.

Brill was meditating on that matter as he went on up the canyon, when it was swept out of his mind by a sound that galvanized him—the drum of hoofs! He wheeled, the fear of a trapped wolf clutching him. Over the sands, heading for the canyon mouth, raced a cluster of riders—ten squat figures in wolf skins, flogging their horses and brandishing their sabers in exultation. The storm had not thrown them off his track. Now they had seen him, and they gave tongue stridently.

Brill let go the reins and dropped behind a rock, drawing his .45. They did not pull their rifles from the boots beneath their knees. They knew their prey was trapped, and their lust for slaughter with cold steel overcame their caution.

Brill sighted across the crest of the boulder at the foremost horseman. He mechanically judged the distance, intending to shoot just as the man came even with the overhanging ledge, under which his course was taking him. But that shot was never fired.

Just as the Mongol swept under the ledge, some sound or instinct caused him to look upward. As he did so, his yellow face went ashy; with a scream he threw up his arms. And simultaneously something black and hairy shot from the ledge and struck full on his breast, knocking him from his horse.

The men behind yelled in dismay and jerked their mounts back on their haunches. Above their clamor rose a scream of mortal agony. The horses wheeled and bolted, neighing shrilly.

The fallen Mongol writhed on the canyon floor, pinned beneath a shape that was like the figment of a nightmare. Brill glared at it, frozen with amazement. It was a spider, beyond the maddest dreams of spiders.

It was like a tarantula, with a gross body bristling with stiff hairs, and crouching black legs. But it was fully as big as a hog. Beneath it the shrieks of the Mongol ceased in a bubbling gurgle and his straining limbs went limp.

The other desert men had halted outside the canyon mouth, and one lifted a rifle and fired at the thing, but obviously his nerves were badly shaken. The bullet splatted harmlessly on a rock. As if disturbed by the sound, the monster turned in their direction, and with wild yells, the Mongols wheeled away and raced off across the sands in ignominious flight.

Brill watched them dwindle to black dots in the dust, then he rose gingerly from behind his rock. His horse had bolted away up the canyon. Twilight was approaching, and he was alone in the gorge with that hairy monstrosity which crouched like a black ogre over the man it had killed.

He hoped to steal away up the canyon without molestation. But the moment he rose into full view, the monster abandoned its prey and scuttled toward him at appalling speed.

Sweating with candid fright, Brill sighted at the oncoming black bulk and pulled the trigger. The impact of the big bullet knocked the thing sidewise, but it righted itself and came on, its eyes gleaming redly among its black bristles. Again and again the gun cracked, waking the echoes among the cliffs, before the monster tumbled over, working its hairy legs vainly. Then from all sides sounded a sinister rustling, and Brill shivered as he saw a grisly horde swarm down into the canyon. They seemed to emerge from every cranny, all converging on the stricken bulk quivering on the gorge floor. None were so large as it, but all were big enough and horrible enough to make a man doubt his sanity.

They ignored Brill, and fell on their mangled king as wolves fall on the wounded pack-leader. The giant was hidden in a writhing, working mass of black and grey-banded bodies, and Brill hurried up the canyon before they could finish their grisly repast and turn their attention to him.

He went up into the mountains because he dared not go down the gorge past that working hill of death; because only death by thirst lay in the desert beyond the canyon; and because it was to find these hills that he had plunged into the Gobi in the first place. Jim Brill was looking for a man; a man whom he hated more than anyone else on earth, yet for whom he was ready to risk his life.

It was certainly not love for Richard Barlow, eminent scientist and explorer, which had sent Brill on his quest; he had his own reasons and they were sufficient. Following dim clues and cryptic hints dropped by natives, he had concluded that the man he sought, if he still lived, was to be found in the mysterious hills which stood in an unmapped region of the Gobi. And he believed that these were the hills for which he had sought.

He emerged from the canyon into a wild tangle of cliffs and ravines. There was no vegetation, no water. The ridges rose grim and stark and black in the dusk about him. He thought of the great spiders, and strained his ears for the stealthy rustle of hairy legs. But the land lay desolate as the earth before man's creation, and the rising moon carved out black shadows of turreted cliffs, and showed him a dim path winding dizzily upward. A man-made trail that betokened human habitation somewhere.

He followed it; it wound up between sheer cliffs to a notch that showed a square of star-flecked sky. When he reached this he halted, panting from his exertions, and grunted with surprise. A heavy chain was stretched across the notch. With his hands resting on it, he gazed through the pass. It was narrow, and beyond it a long slope fell away into a valley where water gleamed in the moonlight among dense groves of trees. And something else gleamed among the trees—towers and walls, apparently of white marble.

Then the native tales were true, and there was a city among these hills. But what manner of men dwelt there? Even as the thought crossed his mind, something moved in the shadow of the cliffs. He caught a glimpse of a tall black figure with a curiously misshapen head, from which blazed eyes like balls of bale-fire. A choking cry escaped his lips. No human ever had eyes like that.

Gripping the chain to steady himself, he snatched at his revolver. And in that instant the universe burst around him, showering the sky with red sparks which were instantly quenched in the blackness of utter oblivion.

When Jim Brill regained his senses, his first impression was that he was lying on something soft and yielding to his rugged frame. There floated before him the soft pale oval of a face with dark, oblique eyes. A voice spoke somewhere, a familiar voice, but framed in an unfamiliar accent, and the face vanished. And then Jim Brill was fully conscious, and staring about him.

He lay on a satin divan in a chamber whose ceiling was a fretted dome. Satin hangings, worked with gilt dragons, adorned the walls, and thick carpets littered the floor.

This he saw in a sweeping glance, before his whole attention was riveted on the figure which sat before him. This was a heavily built man, whose incongruous robe of watered silk did not conceal the muscularity of his frame. A velvet cap was on his head, and from under this gleamed cold grey eyes, matching the rugged hardness of his features. It was the aggressive jut of the jaw that woke recognition in Brill.

"Barlow!"

He sat up, gripping the edge of the divan, glaring at the other as at one risen from the dead.

"Yes, it's me." The man's voice was sardonic. "Fancy *you* dropping in on me like this."

"I was hunting you, blast you!" bristled Brill; yes, this was Barlow, all right, with his gift of putting Brill's teeth on edge.

"Hunting me?" The surprise in Barlow's tone was genuine.

"Oh, it wasn't through any love of you," growled Brill. "I wasn't losing any sleep over you."

"Why, then?"

"Great Judas, man, can't you guess?" exclaimed Brill irritably. "Gloria—"

"Oh!" Barlow's expression was strange, as if he

had just had recalled to his mind something he had forgotten. "So my wife sent you?"

"Naturally. She waited four years. Nobody knew whether you were alive or dead. You'd simply vanished into inner Mongolia. No word ever came back. Gloria came to me, because she knew no one else to come to. She financed the expedition, and here I am."

"And disgusted to find me alive," bantered Barlow. Brill merely grunted; he was too straightforward for hypocrisy.

"What happened to me?" he demanded. "What was that devil-thing I glimpsed just before I went out?"

"Just one of my servants in a robe and hood, with phosphorescent eyes painted on it. A little trick to discourage our superstitious neighbors, the Mongols. This faithful servant knocked you out by merely doing as I have taught him to do. He's one of the guards of the pass. He pushed a little handle and sent some electricity shooting along the chain you were leaning against. If he hadn't seen you were white, you'd be dead now."

Brill glanced at his hand. He knew nothing about electricity, but he had a vague idea that a shock hard enough to knock him senseless would be enough to burn his hand off.

"No burns on you," Barlow assured him. "You've seen men knocked cold by lightning without being burnt, haven't you? Same principle. I can control electricity as easily as I write my name. I know more about it than any other man in the world."

"Modest as usual," grunted Brill.

Barlow smiled with contemptuous tolerance. He had changed subtly in four years. There was more poise about him, a greater air of superiority. And there was a dim difference in his face: in his complection, or the shape of his eyes—Brill could not place it, but it was there, somewhere. And his voice sounded almost unfamiliar at times.

"What is this dump, anyway?" Brill offered a strong contrast, in his dust-stained shirt, breeches and boots, to the exotic chamber and the figure in the embroidered silk. Brill was as tall and heavy as Barlow, a broad-shouldered, thick-chested man, with muscular arms and a nervous energy that could fire him to the quickness of a big cat.

"This is the city of Khor," said Barlow, as if that explained everything.

"Khor's a myth," grunted Brill. "I've heard the Mongols spinning their lies about it—"

Barlow smiled coldly. "You are in the position of the man who looked at a camel and refused to admit its existence. Khor exists and you are at this instant lying in its royal palace."

"Then where's the king?" demanded Brill sarcastically.

Barlow bowed with mock modesty, then folded his hands in his lap and looked at Brill with eyes that glinted between slitted lids. Brill was aware of a vague uneasiness. There was something wrong with his appearance.

"You mean you're the boss of this city?" he asked incredulously.

"And of this valley. Oh, it was not difficult. The people are grossly superstitious. I brought a whole laboratory on camels. My electrical devices alone convinced them that I was a mighty magician. I was the power behind the throne of their king, old Khitai Khan, until he was killed in a Mongol raid.

Then I stepped into his shoes without any trouble;
he had no heirs. I'm not only the big sorcerer of
Khor, I'm Ak Khan, the White King."

"Who are these people?"

"A mixed race, Mongolian and Turkish, originally,
with a strain of Chinese. Did you ever hear of Genghis Khan?"

"Who hasn't?" snapped Brill impatiently.

"Well, as you know, he conquered most of Asia
in the early thirteenth century. He destroyed many
cities, but he also built a few. This was his pleasure
city, and was erected by skilled Persian architects.
He filled it with slaves, both men and women.
When he died, the world forgot about Khor, far up
in these isolated mountains. The descendants of
those slaves have lived on here ever since, under
their own *khans*, raising their food in the valley,
getting other things they wanted from the few Mongol traders who visited the hills."

He clapped his hands. "I was forgetting. You'll
be hungry."

Brill's eyes widened as a slender silk-clad figure
glided lithely into the chamber. "Then she wasn't a
dream," he muttered.

"Scarcely!" Barlow laughed. "The Mongols stole
her from a Chinese caravan, and sold her to me.
Her name is Lala Tzu."

Chinese women held no attraction for Brill, but
this girl was undeniably beautiful. Her oblique eyes
glowed with a soft fire, her features were delicately
molded, and her slender body was a marvel of
suppleness.

"Dancing girl," decided Brill, as he set to work
ravenously on the food and wine she set before him.

From the corner of his eye, he saw her pass a slender arm about Barlow's shoulder and whisper some soft endearment into his ear. The man shrugged away from her with a show of impatience, and motioned her out of the room. Her slender shoulders drooped as if from a rebuke as she obeyed.

"Feel like seeing the city?" Barlow asked abruptly. Brill rose with a snort of disgust that such a question should be deemed necessary.

But as they left the chamber he realized that he had lain senseless for hours. Outside it was full daylight. Barlow led him through a series of hallways and out into a small open court, surrounded on three sides by galleries letting on to the palace, and on the fourth by a low wall. Over this wall Brill looked down into the city, in the midst of which the palace stood on a low hill. It was much like other Oriental towns, with market squares, open stalls with goods displayed, and flat-topped houses. The main differences were in the unusual cleanliness and the richness of the buildings. The houses were of marble instead of mud, and the streets were paved with the same material.

"Quarries of marble in these hills," grunted Barlow, as if reading Brill's thoughts. "Made them clean things up after I got to be *kahn*. Didn't want plagues breeding in filth."

Brill had a good view of the valley, which was walled in by sheer cliffs. Besides the pass through which he had been brought, and up to which a sort of natural ramp led, there was no break in the massive palisades. A stream flowed through the valley, and the vegetation which crowded its banks was relieving after the barren monotony of the outer desert. Gardens, with small huts, checkered the valley floor, and sheep and cattle grazed up to the very wall of the city, which was of no great extent, though rather densely populated.

The inhabitants moved indolently through the streets in their silk garments. Their skins were yellowish, their faces round and flat, their slanted eyes dreamy. They seemed to Brill the remnants of a race which had fulfilled their destiny and now waited drowsily for death.

Barlow's servants were of a different breed, lean, dark-skinned men from Tonkin, who seldom spoke but looked quick and dangerous as cats. Barlow said he had brought them with him to Khor.

"I suppose you're wondering why I came here in the first place," the scientist remarked. "Well, I was always cramped in America. Fools with their stupid laws were always interfering. I heard of this place and it sounded ideal for my purposes. It is. I've gone beyond the wildest dreams of western scientists. Nobody interferes with me. Here human life means nothing; the will of the ruler everything."

Brill scowled at the implication.

"You mean you experiment with human subjects?"

"Why not? These servants of mine live only to do my bidding, and the Khoranese consider me a priest of Erlik, the god they have worshipped since time immemorial. The subjects I demand of them are no more than offerings to the god, according to their way of thinking. I only sacrifice them to the cause of science."

"To the cause of the devil!" growled Brill, revolted. "Don't pull that stuff with me. You care nothing about the progress of humanity. All you've ever considered has been your own ambitions."

Barlow laughed without resentment.

"At any rate, my will is the only law there is in Khor—a fact you'll do well to remember. If I occasionally use one of these fat fools in an experiment from which he fails to recover, I also protect them. They used to suffer from the raids of the Mongols before I came. The only way into the valley is through that pass, but even so, the raiders often cut their way through and devastated everything outside the city walls. Sooner or later they'd have destroyed the city itself.

"I barred the pass with that electric chain, and have done other things that scared the Mongols so badly they seldom venture into the hills. I have a machine in a dome of this palace, for instance, that any world power would pay a fortune for if they knew of it."

"Those big spiders—" began Brill.

"More of my work. They were originally tiny creatures which inhabited caves in the hills. I used my science to make carnivorous monsters out of them. Good watch dogs. The Mongols fear them out of any proportion to their actual ability to do harm. Developing them was a triumph, but I've gone far beyond that now. I am now exploring the profoundest of all mysteries."

"What's that?"

"The human mind; the ego, spirit, soul. Call it what you will. It remains the primary essence of life. Too long men have dabbled in what they called the occult, after the fashion of witch-doctors. It's time the mystery was approached in a scientific manner. I have so approached it."

"Well, listen," said Brill abruptly. "I came a long way to find you, thinking you were a prisoner of a hill tribe. Now I find you master of the tribe, and here of your own free will. You might at least have sent word to Gloria."

"How?" demanded Barlow. "None of my servants could have got through alive, and I couldn't trust a Mongol trader to get a letter outside. Anyway, when a man is absorbed in his life's work, he can't worry himself about a woman."

"Not even his wife, eh?" sneered Brill, his resentment growing every minute. "Well, now I've found you, I want to know, are you coming back to America with me?"

"Certainly not."

"What shall I tell Gloria?"

"Tell her whatever you choose; you will anyway."

Brill's big fists clenched. The man's attitude was intolerable. But before he could make the savage reply which framed itself on his lips, Barlow said: "I'll show you my latest triumph. You won't understand it, and maybe you won't believe it. But it's too big for me to keep still about. I've got to show it to some white man, even you."

As Barlow led the way back through the corridors, Brill saw a slim hand draw aside a hanging, and the face of Lala Tzu was framed in the dark velvet. Her eyes rested meltingly on Barlow, then grew hard and bright with anger as they turned toward Brill. Evidently the girl resented his presence. Doubtless she understood English and had overheard enough of their conversation to fear that Brill was going to take her master back to America with him.

Barlow halted before an arched door of lacquered teak on which writhed a golden dragon. An antique lock was manipulated by an equally antique key, and Barlow led Brill into the chamber.

Above it rose a dome inlaid with gold and ivory. The walls, of a strange, softly glistening green stone, were not tapestried. The floor was of the same material. There were no windows, the dome being craftily pierced so as to let in enough light dimly to illuminate the interior. The only furniture was a satin divan.

"This is the meditation chamber of the great *khan*, Genghis," said Barlow. "He alone entered it during his life-time, and after his death none crossed the threshold until I came. Here he sat and dreamed the dreams induced by wine, opium and *bhang*. Here I first conceived my great discovery.

"Everything leaves its impression on its surroundings, sights, sounds, even thought, for thought is a tangible force, invisible only because on a different plane than visible substance. When a man occupies a room, he leaves the imprints of his personality on that room as surely as his fleshly feet leave their imprints in mud or sand. Wood, steel, stone, all are, in effect, potential camera films and phonograph whereon are imperishably recorded all sounds and scenes that have been in their vicinity. But, in the case of the man in the room, other people come and go, leaving their impressions too, and all these different impressions overlie each other and become hopelessly mixed and muddled.

"Naturally, some substances retain impressions longer and more clearly than others, just as mud retains a footprint more clearly than stone. These walls possess that quality to a phenomenal extent. There is no stone like this natural to the earth. I think it came from a meteorite which fell in this

valley long ago, and which was sawed up and used
for this purpose by the builders of Khor.

"These walls hold the thought-impressions of
Genghis Khan, overlaid by no others, except mine,
which are so few they scarcely count. They contain,
indelibly imprinted, all the thoughts and dreams
and ideas that made up the personality of the great
conqueror. Imagine these walls as a camera film.
On them I shall develop the pictures invisibly
recorded by them!"

Brill grunted scornfully.

"How? By waving a magic wand?"

"By processes I can no more make you understand than I can make a Congo savage understand
television," answered Barlow imperturbably. "I'll
tell you this much, that even you may be able to
understand: only a novice needs mechanical contriv-
ances to aid him in psychic experiments. A master
dispenses with artificial aids. He no more needs
them than an athlete needs crutches, to use an
example concrete enough for your low-grade mind
to grasp.

"I have developed my psychic energy—I use the
term for lack of a more explicit one. That energy is
the real power of life; the brain itself is but one of
its emanations, a machine through which it works.
It needs no mechanical devices. Mechanics are but
channels for its release. I have discovered how to
release its terrific energy naturally.

"I will admit that the experiment I am now about
to perform is made possible only by a strange series
of circumstances, depending, ultimately, upon the
marvelous quality of these walls. On this planet
some people are psychic; here is an inanimate substance which is definitely psychic."

"But an abstract thought—"

"What is any personality but a material appearance embodying myriad abstractions? The universe is a giant chain, with each link inseparably interlocked with every other link. Some of these links we are cognizant of by our external senses, others only through our psychic powers, and then only when these are specially developed. I merely frame an unseen link into a form recognizable by our external faculties.

"It is merely a matter of transmutation, of reduction to basic principles. Thoughts deal, ultimately, with material things. Emanations of the mentality which leave their impressions on material things, are transmutable into forms recognizable by the external senses. Watch!"

Barlow sank upon the divan and resting his elbows on his knees, dropped his chin in his hands and stared hypnotically at the opposite wall. A peculiar change passed over the atmosphere of the room; the light faded to a twilight grey. The even hue of the green walls altered with interchanging shades, like clouds passing over a dusky sky. Brill stared about uneasily. He saw only the bare, changing walls, the dim grey dome above them, and that cryptic figure sitting statue-like on the divan.

He looked again at the walls. Shadows flowed across them in endless procession; shapeless, nebulous, swiftly they passed. Sometimes a distortion of the dim light lent them the appearance of misshapen human figures. All converged upon the spot on which Barlow's mesmeric gaze was rivetted. And at that point the green substance began to glow, to deepen, to take on the appearance of translucency. In its depths there was movement and unrest, a

merging of dim anthropomorphic shapes. As the
shadows flowed into it, this amalgamation took on
more distinct outlines. Brill smothered a cry. It was
as if he looked into a deep green lake, and in its
depths, mistily, he saw a human figure, a squat giant
in silk robes. The outlines of the garments and body
were vague and unstable, but the face stood out
more distinctly beneath the velvet skull-cap. It was
a broad, immobile face, with slanted grey eyes, and
a wisp of a moustache drooping over wide thin lips.
It was—

The cry escaped Brill in spite of himself. He was
on his feet, shaking like a leaf. Abruptly the image
vanished. The shadows faded, leaving the smooth
green surface of the walls unclouded. Barlow was
watching him cynically.

"Well?" inquired the scientist.

"It's a trick," snapped Brill. "You've got a picture
projector hidden somewhere. I've seen Genghis
Khan's face on old Chinese coins, and so have you.
It wouldn't be hard for you to fake up something."
But as he spoke he was uncomfortably aware of the
cold sweat pouring off his skin.

"I didn't expect you to believe it," retorted Barlow, sitting like a silk-clad Buddha. In the dim light
the unpleasant change in his countenance was more
noticeable. It almost amounted to a deformity, and
still Brill could not place it.

"What you believe matters little," said Barlow
placidly. "I *know* the figure was Genghis Khan. No,
not his ghost; not a phantom resurrected from the
dead. But the combined total of his thoughts,
dreams and memories, which together make up a
sum as real and vital as the man himself. It *is* the

man; for what is a man besides the total of his feelings, emotions, sensations and thoughts? Genghis Khan's body has been dust for centuries; but the immortal parts of him slumber in these walls. When they are materialized upon a visible plane, naturally they take on the aspect of the physical man from which they emanated.

"I have sat here for hours and watched the great *khan* grow more and more distinct until walls and chamber and time seemed to fade, until only he and my own mind seemed the only realities in the universe—until he seemed to flow into and merge with my own ego! I understand his dreams, conceptions, the secret of his power.

"To all great conquerors, to Caesar, Alexander, Napoleon, Genghis Khan, nature gave powers not possessed by other men. And I am acquiring the uncanny genius by which Genghis Khan, who was born in a nomad's horse-hide tent, overthrew armies, kings, cities, empires!"

He had risen to his feet in his excitement, and now strode out into a curtained corridor, closing the lacquered door behind him.

"And what of it?" demanded Brill, who had naturally followed him.

"I too will become a conqueror! My ego absorbs all the impressions left by his. I shall be emperor of Asia!"

"Bunkum!" snorted Brill. "I'm sick of listening to your pipe dreams. What I want to know is, are you ever coming back to America, and Gloria?"

"No; you are going to bring Gloria to me."

"What!" exclaimed Brill.

"Yes, I've decided. She'll fit very nicely into my

schemes. She'll come if I send her a message, for she is a dutiful wife."

"Entirely too much so," snarled Brill. "Otherwise she'd have gotten a divorce long ago. Yes, she'd come. Not because she loves you. Her parents forced her into marrying you when she was only a child, and you've treated her like a dog; but she has an overdeveloped sense of duty. That's why she sent me looking for you. She and I have always loved one another. I hoped I'd find you dead. I'm sorry you're alive. But I'm not going to bring Gloria into this God-forsaken valley. What about that Chinese girl, Lala Tzu? You have the nerve to—"

"Silence!" roared Barlow imperiously. "You shall bring my wife to me!"

"Why, you—!" Brill was on his feet, his big fists clenched. But before either could move, a slim figure darted into the scene from behind a hanging. It was Lala Tzu, her beautiful features contorted with fury.

"I heard!" she shrilled at Barlow. "You shall not bring another woman here! You shall not put me aside for a white woman! I will kill—"

With his face convulsed with passion, Barlow struck her savagely in the face with his open hand, ripping out a volley of staccato gutturals Brill did not understand. Three lean silent Tonkinese glided into the hallway, laid hands on Lala Tzu and dragged her, kicking and screaming, through a curtained archway. There was the sound of a blow, a shriek of pain, then her passionate sobs dwindled as she was carried away.

Barlow stood posed like an image of imperial Oriental wrath, and Brill glared at him, his hair bristling with incredulous horror.

King of the Forgotten People 145

"I know now!" the explorer roared. "I've sensed a change in you, from the beginning! Your accent—it's Mongol! Your eyes have begun to slant; there's a copperish cast to your skin. Those impressions you've raved about—you've absorbed them until they're changing you! *Changing you!* You damned devil—*you're changing into a Mongol!*"

A wild flood of devilish exultation lit Barlow's countenance.

"*Yes!*" he bellowed. "I said I was absorbing the mental emanations of Genghis Khan. *I will be Genghis Khan!* His personality will replace mine, because his is the stronger. Like him I will conquer the world. I will fight the Mongols no longer, because I am becoming one of them. They will be my people; all Asians will be my people! I will make a gift to the chief of the Mongols and win his friendship. You shall return to America and bring me the little fool I married in a moment of weakness; she is beautiful; she shall be my gift to Togrukh Khan, the Mongol chief—"

With a maddened roar Brill drove at him, every nerve of his big muscular body straining with a primitive passion to smash and break and rip. With a guttural snarl the powerful scientist met him breast to breast.

Brill scarcely felt the blows that rained on his face and body. In a red mist of berserk fury he drove Barlow backward, smashing his iron fists again and again into the hated features of his enemy, until the scientist crashed over backwards among the ruins of a table, and Brill fell on him and sank his fingers into Barlow's bull throat. A worrying, wordless mouthing snarled from Brill's lips as he drove all the power of heavy shoulder and corded arms into his strangling hands. Blood from Barlow's torn throat trickled over Brill's fingers; the scientist's tongue protruded between blue lips; his eyes were glazing.

Men were swarming into the corridor, but Brill, in the fog of his wrath, was scarcely aware of their shouts, or of the hands which tore vainly at his corded forearms. Then a gun butt, swung with desperate force, crashed on his head and the lights went out.

Brill came to himself with a clear understanding of all that had occurred, and a fervent desire to renew the combat. But he was bound into a chair, hand and foot. Blood trickled into his eyes from a wound in his scalp. He shook his head to clear his vision, and saw Barlow facing him. Brill grinned wolfishly when he saw the damage he had done to the scientist's features. He knew that Barlow's nose was broken, and at least one of his ribs cracked. His face looked like a mask of raw beef, and his one good eye blazed fiendishly.

"Get out!" he croaked, choking with passion, and the impassive Tonkinese glided from the chamber. Twisting his head to stare about, Brill decided that he had been brought to Barlow's laboratory. Scientific appliances of all kinds littered the large room, and huge glass jars contained grisly relics at which Brill did not care to look twice. He glanced back at Barlow, from whom all sanity seemed to have departed.

"You hoped to find me dead," the man was raving, "so you could go back and marry my wife! Well, I'm going to send you back to her. Do you see that thing there? That stuffed ape? Well, that's what you're going to look like within the hour. Laugh, you ignorant fool! Less than a month ago that ape was a man, as intelligent and well developed as you are. I have discovered a process of degeneration that retrogrades the human into the beast which was his progenitor. I could go still further, and revert him to the protozoa which fathered us all.

"But I will leave you an ape. That specimen died, but you shall live—to prance and gibber in some zoo or circus!" His voice rose to a scream. "You fool, do you realize what I'm saying? You'll be a beast! A filthy, hairy, verminous anthropoid! I'll send you back to my loving wife with my compliments—*aaah!*"

It happened so quickly it blurred Brill's sight. From a curtained arch a lithe, tigerish figure had sprung, wielding a gleaming shard of steel. He heard the impact of the blow, the scientist's grunt of agony. Then Barlow, his face a death-mask, took one reeling step and crumpled. His hands, emerging from the wide silk sleeves, worked spasmodically and were still. And Brill shuddered, for those hands were yellow-tinted and the nails were not those of a white man. Barlow's dead features were scarcely recognizable; their aspect was alien and unnatural.

Lala Tzu stood over the man she had killed, grasping her dagger, and staring with a fixed, wide-eyed stare at Brill. He gave back her stare in fascinated dread; this lovely, soulless young animal was just as likely to kill him as she had killed the man she once had loved. Creatures of whims, these dancing girls, beautiful, vagrant, cruel and passionate. Then he cried out an instinctive warning. Over her shoulder a yellow face peered through parted hangings. One of the Tonkinese servants glared at the body of his master. Lala Tzu cried out shrilly and sprang at him, lifting her dagger, but the face vanished, and in the corridor outside sounded a strident screaming. Lala Tzu stood uncertainly.

"Cut me loose, girl!" Brill roared, tearing at his bonds. "I'll help you!"

In an instant she had reached him and slashed his cords. Casting about for a weapon, he saw a great Mongol scimitar hanging on the wall. He tore it free just as the Tonkinese rushed in, daggers in their hands. Gripping the ponderous weapon with both hands, he heaved it above his head and flailed right and left. The razor edge sheared through flesh and bone, severing a yellow man's head and shoulder from his body. Another screamed as his arm jumped from his shoulder on a spurting fountain of blood. The others gave back, appalled, then ran shrieking from the chamber. Brill glared after them, sickened at the havoc he had wrought, but fighting mad. Lala Tzu tugged at his arm.

"They have gone for guns!" she cried shrilly. "They will shoot us down like dogs! We can not escape from the palace, but there is a place where we can take refuge!"

He followed her out of the chamber and along a corridor. Behind them the palace was in an uproar, and somewhere sounded a popping like that of many fire-crackers. It seemed to come from outside the palace, but the din within was so furious Brill could not be certain. The girl's little feet pattered swiftly along the marble tiles ahead of him, until she came to a winding stair. Up this she went without hesitation. It wound up and up into a lofty dome. Brill's breath came in gasps before he reached the top. Their pursuers were closer on their heels than he realized. Just as he reached the head of the stair and turned, a howling Tonkinese charged up and around the last turn with such headlong reckless-ness that he was thrusting a pistol into Brill's face

before the American could move. The scimitar fell
as the gun cracked; powder burnt Brill's face, and
the Oriental's head caved in like an egg shell
beneath the shearing blade. The impact of the
stroke knocked the body backward down the stair
where it demoralized the men storming up it.

Guns spat and bullets spattered against the wall,
but Brill and the girl were out of sight around the
last bend of the stair, and the natives dared not
charge up around it in the teeth of those terrible
sword-strokes. As he waited, sweat dripping from
his face and both hands gripping the long hilt, Brill
heard a sudden uproar beyond the palace walls.
Those below heard it, and a sudden silence fell
upon the stair. In the hush Brill heard a rising
clamor of yells, and the cracking of many rifles. Lala
Tzu cried out to him, and he risked his life by
whirling and looking where she pointed.

There were under the arch of a lofty dome which
was the pinnacle of the palace. On a platform was
set what seemed to be a huge telescope, its muzzle
protruding through a kind of loop-hole. Looking
through a small window beside it, Brill could see the
city streets below him, and the walls and the valley
beyond. And he saw that doom had fallen on Khor.

Down the ramp that led from the pass swarmed
chanting riders, and others raced around the valley,
firing huts and shooting cattle in pure wantonness.
Several hundred more were thronged outside the
great gate. Swinging a huge log between their
horses like a battering ram, some were assailing the
portal, while others kept up a withering fire at the
defenders on the walls who strove to return their
volleys. The Mongols were in the valley at last,
despite all Barlow's barriers!

In the palace below the clamor burst out afresh, and Brill wheeled toward the stair, sword lifted. But the attack did not come. A strident voice screamed in desperate urgency, and Lala Tzu, listening, turned to Brill.

"They say the Mongols will break down the gate and cut all their throats," she said. "They beg you to save them. You, too, are a white magician, they think. They say a Mongol climbed the cliffs and shot the watcher at the pass before he could push the handle and make the chain impassable. They came in such numbers they did not fear the spiders. They are led by Togrukh Khan, who does not fear the white man's magic. They swear they will obey you if you save them from the Mongols."

"How can I?" he asked helplessly.

"I will show you!" She caught his hand and drew him toward the great machine on the platform. "*He* always said he would use this if the Mongols reached the wall. See, it is aimed like a gun at the gate. He showed me—hold it so and pull this trigger!"

"Make them swear first they won't harm us," said Brill, and she called to the terrified Khoranese below. There was an answering babble, wild shouts, the sudden sound of heavy blows, then one voice shouting triumphantly.

"What was that?" he demanded nervously.

"The Tonkinese wished to kill us," she answered. "The men of Khor have slain them, and swear to obey you. Fear not. They will keep their word. Haste, the gate begins to buckle!"

It was true. The wretched Khoranese who had been trying to hold the portal scattered screaming. The gate crashed inward and the riders began swarming through, howling like wolves as they saw their helpless prey before them. Brill sighted along the great barrel and pulled the trigger. He expected some kind of a report, an explosion accompanied by a recoil. There was nothing of the sort. But from the flaring muzzle a long beam of blue light shot to the gate and the horde which thronged it. The result was hideous.

For an instant there was a blurring in which nothing was distinct. Then an awful cry arose. The gate was choked with a blackened mass of disintegrated flesh and blackened bone that had been a hundred men and horses. That ray had neither burned nor shattered, by some awful force it had blasted into Eternity all that were crowded in the gate, and had cut a wide swath through the hordes massed outside. An instant the survivors sat stunned, then with mad screams they wheeled and flogged their steeds toward the hills, fighting like madmen to gain the pass. Brill watched, his soul revolted, until Lala Tzu touched his arm. On the stair below rose a paean of exultation.

"The people of Khor give thanks for their deliverance," said Lala Tzu, "and beg you mount the throne of Khitai Khan, which was the throne of Ak Khan, whom you have slain."

"Whom *I* have slain?" grunted Brill. "That's a good one! Well, you tell the people of Khor that I thank them kindly, but all I want is horses and food and canteens of water. I want to get out of this country while the Mongols are still running in another direction, and I want to get back to America as quick as I can. Somebody's waiting for me there."

This tale is told in the first person, but not by a sympathetic narrator. Even the strong-willed Kirowan demurs this time. . . .

THE CHILDREN OF THE NIGHT

There were, I remember, six of us in Conrad's bizarrely fashioned study, with its queer relics from all over the world and its long rows of books which ranged from the Mandrake Press edition of Boccaccio to a *Missale Romanum*, bound in clasped oak boards and printed in Venice, 1740. Clemants and Professor Kirowan had just engaged in a somewhat testy anthropoligical argument: Clements upholding the theory of a separate, distinct Alpine race, while the professor maintained that this so-called race was merely a deviation from an original Aryan stock— possibly the result of an admixture between the southern or Mediterranean races and the Nordic people.

"And how," asked Clemants, "do you account for their brachycephalicism? The Mediterraneans were as long-headed as the Aryans: would admixture between these dolichocephalic peoples produce a broad-headed intermediate type?"

"Special conditions might bring about a change in an originally long-headed race," snapped Kirowan. "Boaz has demonstrated, for instance, that in the case of immigrants to America, skull formations often change in one generation. And Flinders Petrie has shown that the Lombards changed from a long-headed to a round-headed race in a few centuries."

"But what caused these changes?"

"Much is yet unknown to science," answered Kirowan, "and we need not be dogmatic. No one knows, as yet, why people of British and Irish ancestry tend to grow unusually tall in the Darling district of Australia—Cornstalks, as they are called—or why people of such descent generally have thinner jaw-structures after a few generations in New England. The universe is full of the unexplainable."

"And therefore the uninteresting, according to Machen," laughed Taveral.

Conrad shook his head. "I must disagree. To me the unknowable is most tantalizingly fascinating."

"Which accounts, no doubt, for all the works on witchcraft and demonology I see on your shelves," said Ketrick, with a wave of his hand toward the rows of books.

And let me speak of Ketrick. Each of the six of us was of the same breed—that is to say, a Briton or an American of British descent. By British, I include all natural inhabitants of the British Isles. We represented various strains of English and Celtic blood, but basically, these strains are the same after all. But Ketrick: to me the man always seemed strangely alien. It was in his eyes that this difference showed externally. They were a sort of amber, almost yellow, and slightly oblique. At times, when one looked at his face from certain angles, they seemed to slant like a Chinaman's.

Others than I had noticed this feature, so unusual in a man of pure Anglo-Saxon descent. The usual myths ascribing his slanted eyes to some pre-natal influence had been mooted about, and I remember Professor Hendrik Brooler once remarked that Ketrick was undoubtedly an atavism, representing a reversion of type to some dim and distant ancestor of Mongolian blood—a sort of freak reversion, since none of his family showed such traces.

But Ketrick comes of the Welsh branch of the Cetrics of Sussex, and his lineage is set down in the Book of Peers. There you may read the line of his ancestry, which extends unbroken to the days of Canute. No slightest trace of Mongoloid inter-mixture appears in the genealogy, and how could there have been such intermixture in old Saxon England? For Ketrick is the modern form of Cedric, and though that branch fled into Wales before the invasion of the Danes, its male heirs consistently married with English families on the border marches, and it remains a pure line of the powerful Sussex Cedrics—almost pure Saxon. As for the man himself, this defect of his eyes, if it can be called a defect, is his only abnormality, except for a slight and occasional lisping of speech. He is highly intellectual and a good companion except for a slight aloofness and a rather callous indifference which may serve to mask an extremely sensitive nature.

Referring to his remark, I said with a laugh: "Conrad pursues the obscure and mystic as some men pursue romance; his shelves throng with delightful nightmares of every variety."

Our host nodded. "You'll find there a number of delectable dishes—Machen, Poe, Blackwood, Maturin—look, there's a rare feast—*Horrid Mysteries*, by the Marquis of Grosse—the real Eighteenth Century edition."

Taverel scanned the shelves. "Weird fiction seems to vie with works on witchcraft, voodoo and dark magic."

True; historians and chronicles are often dull; tale-weavers never—the masters, I mean. A voodoo sacrifice can be described in such a dull manner as to take all the real fantasy out of it, and leave it merely a sordid murder. I will admit that few writers of fiction touch the true heights of horror—most of their stuff is too concrete, given too much earthly shape and dimensions. But in such tales as Poe's *Fall of the House of Usher*, Machen's *Black Seal* and Lovecraft's *Call of Cthulhu*—the three master horror-tales, to my mind—the reader is borne into dark and *outer* realms of imagination.

"But look there," he continued, "there, sandwiched between that nightmare of Huysmans', and Walpole's *Castle of Otranto*—Von Junzt's *Nameless Cults*. There's a book to keep you awake at night!"

"I've read it," said Taverel, "and I'm convinced the man is mad. His work is like the conversation of a maniac—it runs with startling clarity for awhile, then suddenly merges into vagueness and disconnected ramblings."

Conrad shook his head. "Have you ever thought that perhaps it is his very sanity that causes him to write in that fashion? What if he dares not put on paper all he knows? What if his vague suppositions are dark and mysterious hints, keys to the puzzle, to those who know?"

"Bosh!" This from Kirowan. "Are you intimating

that any of the nightmare cults referred to by Von Junzt survive to this day—if they ever existed save in the hap-ridden brain of a lunatic poet and philosopher?"

"Not he alone used hidden meanings," answered Conrad. "If you will scan various works of certain great poets you may find double meanings. Men have stumbled on to cosmic secrets in the past and given a hint of them to the world in cryptic words. Do you remember Von Junzt's hints of 'a city in the waste'? What do you think of Flecker's line:

"Pass not beneath! Men say there blows in stony-deserts still a rose
" 'But with no scarlet to her leaf—and from whose heart no perfume flows.'

"Men may stumble upon secret things, but Von Junzt dipped deep into forbidden mysteries. He was one of the few men, for instance, who could read the *Necronomicon* in the original Greek translation."

Taverel shrugged his shoulders, and Professor Kirowan, though he snorted and puffed viciously at his pipe, made no direct reply; for he, as well as Conrad, had delved into the Latin version of the book, and had found there things not even a cold-blooded scientist could answer or refute.

"Well," he said presently, "suppose we admit the former existence of cults revolving about such nameless and ghastly gods and entities as Cthulhu, Yog Sothoth, Tsathoggua, Gol-Goroth, and the like, I can not find it in my mind to believe that survivals of such cults lurk in the dark corners of the world today."

To our surprise Clemants answered. He was a

tall, lean man, silent almost to the point of taciturnity, and his fierce struggles with poverty in his youth had lined his face beyond his years. Like many another artist, he lived a distinctly dual literary life, his swashbuckling novels furnishing him a generous income, and his editorial position on *The Cloven Hoof* affording him full artistic expression. *The Cloven Hoof* was a poetry magazine whose bizarre contents had often aroused the shocked interest of the conservative critics.

"You remember Von Junzt makes mention of a so-called Bran cult," said Clemants, stuffing his pipe-bowl with a peculiarly villainous brand of shag tobacco. "I think I heard you and Taverel discussing it once."

"As I gather from his hints," snapped Kirowan, "Von Junzt includes this particular cult among those still in existence. Absurd."

Again Clemants shook his head. "When I was a boy working my way through a certain university, I had for roommate a lad as poor and ambitious as I. If I told you his name, it would startle you. Though he came of an old Scotch line of Galloway, he was obviously a non-Aryan type.

"This is in strictest confidence, you understand. But my roommate talked in his sleep. I began to listen and put his disjointed mumbling together. And in his mutterings I first heard of the ancient cult hinted at by Von Junzt; of the king who rules the Dark Empire, which was a revival of an older, darker empire dating back into the Stone Age; and of the great, nameless cavern where stands the Dark Man—the image of Bran Mak Morn, carved in his likeness by a master-hand while the great king yet lived, and to which each worshipper of Bran makes a pilgrimage once in his or her lifetime. Yes, that cult lives today in the descendants of Bran's people—a silent, unknown current it flows on in the great ocean of life, waiting for the stone image of the great Bran to breathe and move with sudden life, and come from the great cavern to rebuild their lost empire."

"And who were the people of that empire?" asked Ketrick.

"Picts," answered Taverel, "doubtless the people known later as the wild Picts of Galloway were predominantly Celtic—a mixture of Gaelic, Cymric, aboriginal and possibly Teutonic elements. Whether they took their name from the older race or lent their own name to that race, is a matter yet to be decided. But when Von Junzt speaks of Picts, he refers specifically to the small, dark, garlic-eating peoples of Mediterranean blood who brought the Neolithic culture into Britain. The first settlers of that country, in fact, who gave rise to the tales of earth spirits and goblins."

"I can not agree to that last statement," said Conrad. "These legends ascribe a deformity and inhumanness of appearances to the characters. There was nothing about the Picts to excite such horror and repulsion in the Aryan peoples. I believe that the Mediterraneans were preceded by a Mongoloid type, very low, in the scale of development, whence these tales—"

"Quite true," broke in Kirowan, "but I hardly think they preceded the Picts, as you call them, into Britain. We find troll and dwarf legends all over the continent, and I am inclined to think that both the Mediterranean and Aryan people brought these tales with them from the Continent. They must have been of extremely inhuman aspect, those early Mongoloids."

"At least," said Conrad, "here is a flint mallet a miner found in the Welsh hills and gave to me, which has never been fully explained. It is obviously of no ordinary Neolithic make. See how small it is, compared to most implements of that age; almost like a child's toy; yet is surprisingly heavy and no doubt a deadly blow could be dealt with it. I fitted the handle to it, myself, and you would be surprised to know how difficult it was to carve it into a shape and balance corresponding with the head."

We looked at the thing. It was well made, polished somewhat like the other remnants of the Neolithic I had seen, yet as Conrad said, it was strangely different. Its small size was oddly disquieting, for it had no appearance of a toy, otherwise. It was as sinister in suggestion as an Aztec sacrificial dagger. Conrad had fashioned the oaken handle with rare skill, and in carving it to fit the head, had managed to give it the same unnatural appearance as the mallet itself had. He had even copied the workmanship of primal times, fixing the head into the cleft of the haft with rawhide.

"My word!" Taverel made a clumsy pass at an imaginary antagonist and nearly shattered a costly Shang vase. "The balance of the thing is all off center; I'd have to readjust all my mechanics of poise and equilibrium to handle it."

"Let me see it," Ketrick took the thing and fumbled with it, trying to strike the secret of its proper handling. At length, somewhat irritated, he swung it up and struck a heavy blow at a shield which hung on the wall near by. I was standing near it; I saw the hellish mallet twist in his hand like a live serpent, and his arm wrenched out of line; I heard a shout of alarmed warning—then darkness came with the impact of the mallet against my head.

Slowly I drifted back to consciousness. First there was dull sensation with blindness and total lack of knowledge as to where I was or what I was; then vague realization of life and being, and a hard something pressing into my ribs. Then the mists cleared and I came to myself completely.

I lay on my back half beneath some underbrush and my head throbbed fiercely. Also my hair was caked and clotted with blood, for the scalp had been laid open. But my eyes traveled down my body and limbs, naked but for a deerskin loincloth and sandals of the same material, and found no other wound. That which pressed so uncomfortably into my ribs was my ax, on which I had fallen.

Now an abhorrent babble reached my ears and stung me into clear consciousness. The noise was faintly like language, but not such language as men are accustomed to. It sounded much like the repeated hissing of many great snakes.

I stared. I lay in a great, gloomy forest. The glade was overshadowed, so that even in the daytime it was very dark. Aye—that forest was dark, cold, silent, gigantic and utterly grisly. And I looked into the glade.

I saw a shambles. Five men lay there—at least, what had been five men. Now as I marked the abhorrent mutilations my soul sickened. And about clustered the—Things. Humans they were, of a sort, though I did not consider them so. They were short and stocky, with broad heads too large for their scrawny bodies. Their hair was snaky and stringy, their faces broad and square, with flat noses, hideously slanted eyes, a thin gash for a mouth, and pointed ears. They wore the skins of beasts, as did I, but these hides were but crudely dressed. They bore small bows and flint-tipped arrows, flint knives and cudgels. And they conversed in a speech as hideous as themselves, a hissing, reptilian speech that filled me with dread and loathing.

Oh, I hated them as I lay there; my brain flamed with white-hot fury. And now I remembered. We had hunted, we six youths of the Sword People, and wandered far into the grim forest which our people generally shunned. Weary of the chase, we had paused to rest; to me had been given the first watch, for in those days, no sleep was safe without a sentry. Now shame and revulsion shook my whole being. I had slept—I had betrayed my comrades. And now they lay gashed and mangled—butchered while they slept, by vermin who had never dared to stand before them on equal terms. I, Aryara, had betrayed my trust.

Aye—I remembered. I had slept and in the midst of a dream of the hunt, fire and sparks had exploded in my head and I had plunged into a deeper darkness where there were no dreams. And now the penalty. They who had stolen through the dense forest and smitten me senseless, had not paused to mutilate me. Thinking me dead they had hastened swiftly to their grisly work. Now perhaps they had forgotten me for a time. I had sat somewhat apart from the others, and when struck, had fallen half under some bushes. But soon they would remember me. I would hunt no more, dance no more in the dances of hunt and love and war, see no more the wattle huts of the Sword People.

But I had no wish to escape back to my people. Should I slink back with my tale of infamy and disgrace? Should I hear the words of scorn my tribe would fling at me, see the girls point their contemptuous fingers at the youth who slept and betrayed his comrades to the knives of vermin?

Tears stung my eyes, and slow hate heaved up in my bosom, and my brain. I would never bear the sword that marked the warrior. I would never triumph over worthy foes and die gloriously beneath the arrows of the Picts or the axes of the Wolf People or the River People. I would go down to death beneath a nauseous rabble, whom the Picts had long ago driven into forest dens like rats.

And mad rage gripped me and dried my tears, giving in their stead a berserk blaze of wrath. If such reptiles were to bring about my downfall, I would make it a fall long remembered—if such beasts had memories.

Moving cautiously, I shifted until my hand was on the haft of my ax; then I called on Il-marinen and bounded up as a tiger springs. And as a tiger springs I was among my enemies and smashed a flat skull as a man crushes the head of a snake. A sudden wild clamor of fear broke from my victims and for an instant they closed round me, hacking and stabbing. A knife gashed my chest but I gave no heed. A red mist waved before my eyes, and my body and limbs moved in perfect accord with my fighting brain. Snarling, hacking and smiting, I was a tiger among reptiles. In an instant they gave way and fled, leaving me bestriding half a dozen stunted bodies. But I was not satiated.

I was close on the heels of the tallest one, whose head would perhaps come to my shoulder, and who seemed to be their chief. He fled down a sort of runway, squealing like a monstrous lizard, and when I was close at his shoulder, he dived, snake-like, into the bushes. But I was too swift for him, and I dragged him forth and butchered him in a most gory fashion.

And through the bushes I saw the trail he was striving to reach—a path winding in and out among the trees, almost too narrow to allow the traversing of it by a man of normal size. I hacked off my victim's hideous head, and carrying it in my left hand, went up the serpent-path, with my red ax in my right.

Now as I strode swiftly along the path and blood splashed beside my feet at every step from the severed jugular of my foe, I thought of those I hunted. Aye—we held them in so little esteem, we hunted by day in the forest they haunted. What they called themselves, we never knew; for none of our tribe ever learned the accursed hissing sibilances they used as speech; but we called them Children of the Night. And night-things they were indeed, for they slunk in the depths of the dark forests, and in subterraneous dwellings, venturing forth into the hills only when their conquerors slept. It was at night that they did their foul deeds—the quick flight of a flint-tipped arrow to the snatching of a child that had wandered from the village.

But it was for more than this we gave them their name; they were, in truth, people of night and darkness and the ancient horror-ridden shadows of bygone ages. For these creatures were very old, and they represented an outworn age. They had once overrun and possessed this land, and they had been driven into hiding and obscurity by the dark, fierce little Picts with whom we contested now, and who hated and loathed them as savagely as did we.

The Picts were different from us in general appearance, being shorter of stature and dark of hair, eyes and skin, whereas we were tall and powerful, with yellow hair and light eyes. But they were cast in the same mold, for all of that. These Children of the Night seemed not human to us, with their deformed dwarfish bodies, yellow skin and hideous faces. Aye—they were reptiles—vermin.

And my brain was like to burst with fury when I thought that it was these vermin on whom I was to glut my ax and perish. Bah! There is no glory slaying snakes or dying from their bites. All this rage and fierce disappointment turned on the objects of my hatred, and with the old red mist waving in front of me I swore by all the gods I knew, to wreak such red havoc before I died as to leave a dread memory in the minds of the survivors.

My people would not honor me, in such contempt they held the Children. But those Children that I left alive would remember me and shudder. So I swore, gripping savagely my ax, which was of bronze, set in a cleft of the oaken haft and fastened securely with rawhide.

Now I heard ahead a sibilant, abhorrent murmur, and a vile stench filtered to me through the trees, human, yet less than human. A few moments more and I emerged from the deep shadows into a wide open space. I had never before seen a village of the Children. There was a cluster of earthen domes, with low doorways sunk into the ground; squalid dwelling-places, half above and half below the earth. And I knew from the talk of the old warriors that these dwelling-places were connected by underground corridors, so the whole village was like an ant-bed, or a system of snake holes. And I wondered if other tunnels did not run off under the ground and emerge long distances from the villages.

Before the domes clustered a vast group of the creatures, hissing and jabbering at a great rate.

I had quickened my pace, and now I burst from cover, I was running with the fleetness of my race. A wild clamor went up from the rabble as they saw the avenger, tall, blood-stained and blazing-eyed leap from the forest, and I cried out fiercely, flung the dripping head among them and bounded like a wounded tiger into the thick of them.

Oh, there was no escape for them now! They might have taken to their tunnels but I would have followed, even to the guts of hell. They knew they must slay me, and they closed around, a hundred strong, to do it.

There was no wild blaze of glory in my brain as there had been against worthy foes. But the old berserk madness of my race was in my blood and the smell of blood and destruction in my nostrils.

I know not how many I slew. I only know that they thronged about me in a writhing, slashing mass, like serpents about a wolf, and I smote until the ax-edge turned and bent and the ax became no more than a bludgeon; and I smashed skulls, split heads, splintered bones, scattered blood and brains in one red sacrifice to Il-marinen, god of the Sword People.

Bleeding from half a hundred wounds, blinded by a slash across the eyes, I felt a flint knife sink deep into my groin and at the same instant a cudgel laid my scalp open. I went to my knees but reeled up again, and saw in a thick red fog a ring of leering, slant-eyed faces. I lashed out as a dying tiger strikes, and the faces broke in red ruin.

And as I sagged, overbalanced by the fury of my stroke, a taloned hand clutched my throat and a flint blade was driven into my ribs and twisted venomously. Beneath a shower of blows I went down again, but the man with the knife was beneath me, and with my left hand I found him and broke his neck before he could writhe away.

Life was waning swiftly; through the hissing and howling of the Children I could hear the voice of Il-marinen. Yet once again I rose stubbornly, through a very whirlwind of cudgels and spears. I could no longer see my foes, even in a red mist. But I could feel their blows and knew they surged about me. I braced my feet, gripped my slippery ax-haft with both hands, and calling once more on Il-marinen I heaved up the ax and struck one last terrific blow. And I must have died on my feet, for there was no sensation of falling; even as I knew, with a last thrill of savagery, that I slew, even as I felt the splintering of skulls beneath my ax, darkness came with oblivion.

I came suddenly to myself. I was half reclining in a big armchair and Conrad was pouring water on me. My head ached and a trickle of blood had half dried on my face. Kirowan, Taverel and Clemants were hovering about, anxiously, while Ketrick stood just in front of me, still holding the mallet, his face schooled to a polite perturbation which his eyes did not show. And at the sight of those cursed eyes a red madness surged up in me.

"There," Conrad was saying, "I told you he'd come out of it in a moment; just a light crack. He's taken harder than that. All right now, aren't you, O'Donnel?"

At that I swept them aside, and with a single low snarl of hatred launched myself at Ketrick. Taken utterly by surprise he had no opportunity to defend himself. My hands locked on his throat and we crashed together on the ruins of a divan. The others cried out in amazement and horror and sprang to separate us—or rather, to tear me from my victim, for already Ketrick's slant eyes were beginning to start from their sockets.

"For God's sake, O'Donnel," exclaimed Conrad, seeking to break my grip, "what's come over you? Ketrick didn't mean to hit you—let go, you idiot!"

A fierce wrath almost overcame me at these men who were my friends, men of my own tribe, and I swore at them and their blindness, as they finally managed to tear my strangling fingers from Ketrick's throat. He sat up and choked and explored the blue marks my fingers had left, while I raged and cursed, nearly defeating the combined efforts of the four to hold me.

"You fools!" I screamed. "Let me go! Let me do my duty as a tribesman! You blind fools! I care nothing for the paltry blow he dealt me—he and his dealt stronger blows than that against me, in bygone ages. You fools, he is marked with the brand of the beast—the reptile—the vermin we exterminated centuries ago! I must crush him, stamp him out, rid the clean earth of his accursed pollution!"

So I raved and struggled and Conrad gasped to Ketrick over his shoulder: "Get out, quick! He's out of his head! His mind is unhinged! Get away from him."

Now I look out over the ancient dreaming downs

and the hills and deep forests beyond and I ponder. Somehow that blow from that ancient accursed mallet knocked me back into another age and another life. While I was Aryara I had no cognizance of any other life. It was no dream; it was a stray bit of reality wherein I, John O'Donnel, once lived and died. And back into which I was snatched across the voids of time and space by a chance blow. Time and times are but cog-wheels, unmatched, grinding and oblivious to one another. Occasionally—oh, very rarely!—the cogs fit; the pieces of the plot snap together momentarily and give men faint glimpses beyond the veil of this everyday blindness we call reality.

I am John O'Donnel and I was Aryara, who dreamed dreams of war-glory and hunt-glory and feast-glory and who died on a red heap of his victims in some lost age. But in what age and where?

The last I can answer for you. Mountains and rivers change their contours; the landscapes alter; but the downs least of all. I look out upon them now and I remember them, not only with John O'Donnel's eyes, but with the eyes of Aryara. They are but little changed. Only the great forest has shrunk and dwindled and in many, many places vanished utterly. But here on these very downs Aryara lived and fought and loved and in yonder forest he died. Kirowan was wrong. The little, fierce, dark Picts were not the first men in the Isles. There were beings before them—aye, the Children of the Night. Legends—why, the Children were not unknown to us when we came into what is now the isle of Britain. We had encountered them before, ages before. Already we had our myths of them.

But we found them in Britain. Nor had the Picts totally exterminated them.

Nor had the Picts, as so many believe, preceded us by many centuries. We drove them before us as we came, in that long drift from the East. I, Aryara, knew old men who had marched on that century-long trek; who had been borne in the arms of yellow-haired women over countless miles of forest and plain, and who as youths had walked in the vanguard of the invaders.

As to the age—that I cannot say. But I, Aryara, was surely an Aryan and my people were Aryans—members of one of the thousand unknown and unrecorded drifts that scattered yellow-haired blue-eyed tribes all over the world. The Celts were not the first to come into western Europe. I, Aryara, was of the same blood and appearance as the men who sacked Rome, but mine was a much older strain. Of the language I spoke, no echo remains in the waking mind of John O'Donnel, but I knew that Aryara's tongue was to ancient Celtic what ancient Celtic is to modern Gaelic.

Il-marinen! I remember the god I called upon, the ancient, ancient god who worked in metals—in bronze then. For Il-marinen was one of the base gods of the Aryans from whom many gods grew; and he was Wieland and Vulcan in the ages of iron. But to Aryara he was Il-marinen.

And Aryara—he was one of many tribes and many drifts. Not alone did the Sword People come or dwell in Britain. The River People were before us and the Wolf People came later. But they were Aryans like us, light-eyed and tall and blond. We fought them, for the reason that the various drifts of Aryans have always fought each other, just as the

Achaeans fought the Dorians, just as the Celts and Germans cut each other's throats; aye, just as the Hellenes and the Persians, who were once one people and of the same drift, split in two different ways on the long trek and centuries later met and flooded Greece and Asia Minor with blood.

Now understand, all this I did not know as Aryara. I, Aryara, knew nothing of all these world-wide drifts of my race. I knew only that my people were conquerors, that a century ago my ancestors had dwelt in the great plains far to the east, plains populous with fierce, yellow-haired, light-eyed people, of older or newer drifts, they fought savagely and mercilessly, according to the old, illogical custom of the Aryan people. This Aryara knew, and I, John O'Donnel, who know much more and much less than I, Aryara, knew, have combined the knowledge of these separate selves and have come to conclusions that would startle many noted scientists and historians.

Yet this fact is well known: Aryans deteriorate swiftly in sedentary and peaceful lives. Their proper existence is a nomadic one; when they settle down to an agricultural existence, they pave the way for their downfall; and when they pen themselves with city walls, they seal their doom. Why, I, Aryara, remember the tales of the old men—how the Sons of the Sword, on that long drift, found villages of white-skinned yellow-haired people who had drifted into the west centuries before and had quit the wandering life to dwell among the dark, garlic-eating people and gain their sustenance from the soil. And the old men told how soft and weak they were, and how easily they fell before the bronze blades of the Sword People.

Look—is not the whole history of the Sons of Aryan laid on those lines? Look—how swiftly has Persian followed Mede; Greek, Persian; Roman, Greek; and German, Roman. Aye, and the Norseman followed the Germanic tribes when they had grown flabby from a century or so of peace and idleness, and despoiled the spoils they had taken in the southland.

But let me speak of Ketrick. Ha—the short hairs at the back of my neck bristle at the very mention of his name. A reversion to type—but not to the type of some cleanly Chinaman or Mongol of recent times. The Danes drove his ancestors into the hills of Wales; and there, in what medieval century, and in what foul way did that cursed aboriginal taint creep into the clean Saxon blood of the Celtic line, there to lie dormant so long! The Celtic Welsh never mated with the Children anymore than the Picts did. But there must have been survivals—vermin lurking in those grim hills, that had outlasted their time and age. In Aryara's day they were scarcely human. What must a thousand years of retrogression have done to the breed?

What foul shape stole into the Ketrick castle on some forgotten night, or rose out of the dusk to grip some woman of the line, straying in the hills?

The mind shrinks from such an image. But this I know: there must have been survivals of that foul, reptilian epoch when the Ketricks went into Wales. There still may be. But this changeling, this waif of darkness, this horror who bears the noble name of Ketrick, the brand of the serpent is upon him, and until he is destroyed there is no rest for me. Now that I know him for what he is, he pollutes the clean air and leaves the slime of the snake on the green earth. The sound of his lisping, hissing voice fills me with crawling horror and the sight of his slanted eyes inspires me with madness.

For I come of a royal race, and such as he is a continual insult and a threat, like a serpent under foot. Mine is a regal race, though now it is become degraded and falls into decay by continual admixture with conquered races. The waves of alien blood have washed my hair black and my skin dark, but I still have the lordly stature and the blue eyes of a royal Aryan.

And as my ancestors—as I, Aryara, destroyed the scum that writhed beneath our heels, so shall I, John O'Donnel, exterminate the reptilian thing, the monster bred of the snaky taint that slumbered so long unguessed in clean Saxon veins, the vestigial serpent-things left to taunt the Sons of Aryan. They say the blow I received affected my mind; I know it but opened my eyes. Mine ancient enemy walks often on the moors alone, attracted, though he may not know it, by ancestral urgings. And on one of these lonely walks I shall meet him, and when I meet him, I will break his foul neck with my hands, as I, Aryara, broke the necks of foul-night-things in the long, long ago.

Then they may take me and break ny neck at the end of a rope if they will. I am not blind, if my friends are. And in the sight of the old Aryan god, if not in the blinded eyes of men, I will have kept faith with my tribe.

As in "The Voice of El-Lil" and "Cassonetto's Last Song," Howard tells of the power of music, the power of men's minds—a fatal power, sometimes.

THE DREAM SNAKE

The night was strangely still. As we sat upon the wide veranda, gazing out over the broad, shadowy lawns, the silence of the hour entered our spirits and for a long while no one spoke.

Then far across the dim mountains that fringed the eastern skyline, a faint haze began to glow, and presently a great golden moon came up, making a ghostly radiance over the land and etching boldly the dark clumps of shadows that were trees. A light breeze came whispering out of the east, and the unmowed grass swayed before it in long, sinuous waves, dimly visible in the moonlight; and from among the group upon the veranda there came a swift gasp, a sharp intake of breath that caused us all to turn and gaze.

Faming was leaning forward, clutching the arms of his chair, his face strange and pallid in the spectral light; a thin trickle of blood seeping from the lip in which he had set his teeth. Amazed, we looked at him, and suddenly he jerked about with a short, snarling laugh.

"There's no need of gawking at me like a flock of sheep!" he said irritably and stopped short. We sat bewildered, scarcely knowing what sort of reply to make, and suddenly he burst out again.

"Now I guess I'd better tell the whole thing or you'll be going off and putting me down as a lunatic. Don't interrupt me, any of you! I want to get this thing off my mind. You all know that I'm not a very imaginative man; but there's a thing, purely a figment of imagination, that has haunted me since babyhood. A dream!" he fairly cringed back in his chair as he muttered, "A dream! and God, what a dream! The first time—no, I can't remember the first time I ever dreamed it—I've been dreaming the hellish thing ever since I can remember. Now it's this way: there is a sort of bungalow, set upon a hill in the midst of wide grasslands—not unlike this estate; but this scene is in Africa. And I am living there with a sort of servant, a Hindoo. Just why I am there is never clear to my waking mind, though I am always aware of the reason in my dreams. As a man of a dream, I remember my past life (a life which in no way corresponds with my waking life), but when I am awake my subconscious mind fails to transmit these impressions. However, I think that I am a fugitive from justice and the Hindoo is also a fugitive. How the bungalow came to be there I can never remember, nor do I know in what part of Africa it is, though all these things are known to my dream self. But the bungalow is a small one of a very few rooms, and it situated upon the top of the hill, as I said. There are no other hills about and the grasslands stretch to the horizon in every direction; knee-high in some places, waist-high in others.

"Now the dream always opens as I am coming up the hill, just as the sun is beginning to set. I am carrying a broken rifle and I have been on a hunting trip, I clearly remember—dreaming. But never upon waking. It is just as if a curtain were suddenly raised and a drama began; or just as if I were suddenly transferred to another man's body and life, remembering past years of that life, and not cognizant of any other existence. And that is the hellish part of it! As you know, most of us, dreaming, are, at the back of our consciousness, aware that we are dreaming. No matter how horrible the dream may become, we know that it is a dream, and thus insanity or possible death is staved off. But in this particular dream, there is no such knowledge. I tell you it is so vivid, so complete in every detail, that I wonder sometimes if that is not my real existence and this a dream! But no; for then I should have been dead years ago.

"As I was saying, I come up the hill and the first thing I am cognizant of that it is out of the ordinary, it is a sort of track leading up the hill in an irregular way; that is, the grass is mashed down as if something heavy had been dragged over it. But I pay no especial attention to it, for I am thinking with some irritation, that the broken rifle I carry is my only arm and that now I must forego hunting until I can send for another.

"You see, I remember thoughts and impressions of the dream itself, of the occurrences of the dream; it is the memories that the dream 'I' had, of that other dream existence that I cannot remember. So.

I come up the hill and enter the bungalow. The doors are open and the Hindoo is not there. But the main room is in confusion; chairs are broken, a table is overturned. The Hindoo's dagger is lying upon the floor, but there is no blood anywhere.

"Now, in my dreams, I never remember the other dreams, as sometimes one does. Always it is the first dream, the first time. I always experience the same sensations, in my dreams, with as vivid a force as the first time I ever dreamed. So. I am not able to understand this. The Hindoo is gone, but (thus I ruminate, standing in the center of the disordered room) what did away with him? Had it been a raiding party of negroes they would have looted the bungalow and probably burned it. Had it been a lion, the place would have been smeared with blood. Then suddenly I remember the track I saw going up the hill, and a cold hand touches my spine; for instantly the whole thing is clear: the thing that came up from the grasslands and wrought havoc in the little bungalow could be naught else except a giant serpent. And as I think of the size of the spoor, cold sweat beads my forehead and the broken rifle shakes in my hand.

"Then I rush to the door in a wild panic, my only thought to make a dash for the coast. But the sun has set and dusk is stealing across the grasslands. And out there somewhere, lurking in the tall grass is that grisly thing—that horror. God!" The ejaculation broke from his lips with such feeling that all of us started, not realizing the tension we had reached. There was a second's silence, then he continued:

"So I bolt the doors and windows, light the lamp I have and take my stand in the middle of the room.

And I stand like a statue—waiting—listening. After a while the moon comes up and her haggard light drifts though the windows. And I stand still in the center of the room; the night is very still—something like this night; the breeze occasionally whispers through the grass, and each time I start and clench my hands until the nails bite into the flesh and the blood trickles down my wrists—and I stand there and wait and listen but it does not come that night!" The sentence came suddenly and explosively, and an involuntary sigh came from the rest; a relaxing of tension.

"I am determined, if I live the night through, to start for the coast early the next morning, taking my chance out there in the grim grasslands—with it. But with morning, I dare not. I do not know in which direction the monster went; and I dare not risk coming upon him in the open, unarmed as I am. So, as in a maze, I remain at the bungalow, and ever my eyes turn toward the sun, lurching relentless down the sky toward the horizon. Ah, God! if I could but halt the sun in the sky!"

The man was in the clutch of some terrific power; his words fairly leaped at us.

"Then the sun rocks down the sky and the long gray shadows come stalking across the grasslands. Dizzy with fear, I have bolted the doors and windows and lighted the lamp long before the last faint glow of twilight fades. The light from the windows may attract the monster, but I dare not stay in the dark. And again I take my stand in the center of the room—waiting."

There was a shuddersome halt. Then he continued, barely above a whisper, moistening his lips: "There is no knowing how long I stand there; Time has ceased to be and each second is an eon; each minute is an eternity, stretching into endless eternities. Then, God! but what is that?" He leaned forward, the moonlight etching his face into such a mask of horrified listening that each of us shivered and flung a hasty glance over our shoulders.

"Not the night breeze this time," he whispered. "Something makes the grasses swish-swish—as if a great, long, plaint weight were being dragged through them. Above the bungalow it swishes and then ceases—in front of the door; then the hinges creak—creak! the door begins to bulge inward—a small bit—then some more!" The man's arms were held in front of him, as if braced strongly against something, and his breath came in quick gasps. "And I know I should lean against the door and hold it shut, but I do not, I cannot move. I stand there, like a sheep waiting to be slaughtered—but the door holds!" Again that sigh expressive of pent-up feeling.

He drew a shaky hand across his brow. "And all night I stand in the center of that room, as motionless as an image, except to turn slowly, as the swish-swish of the grass marks the fiend's course about the house. Ever I keep my eyes in the direction of the soft, sinister sound. Sometimes it ceases for an instant, or for several minutes, and then I stand scarcely breathing, for a horrible obsession has it that the serpent has in some way made entrance into the bungalow, and I start and whirl this way and that, frightfully fearful of making a noise, though I know not why, but ever with the feeling that the thing is at my back. Then the sounds commence again and I freeze motionless.

"Now here is the only time that my consciousness, which guides my waking hours, ever in any way pierces the veil of dreams. I am, in the dream, in no way conscious that it is a dream, but, in a detached sort of way, my other mind recognizes certain facts and passes them on to my sleeping—shall I say 'ego'? That is to say, my personality is for an instant truly dual and separate to an extent, as the right and left arms are separate, while making up parts in the same entity. My dreaming mind has no cognizance of my higher mind; for the time being the other mind is subordinated and the subconscious mind is in full control, to such an extent that it does not even recognize the existence of the other. But the conscious mind, now sleeping, is cognizant of dim thought-waves emanating from the dream mind. I know that I have not made this entirely clear, but the fact remains that I know that my mind, conscious and subconscious, is near to ruin. My obsession of fear, as I stand there in my dream, is that the serpent will raise itself and peer into the window at me. And I know, in my dream, that if this occurs I shall go insane. And so vivid is the impression imparted to my conscious, now sleeping mind that the thought-waves stir the dim seas of sleep, and somehow I can feel my sanity rocking as my sanity rocks in my dream. Back and forth it totters and sways until the motion takes on a physical aspect and I in my dream am swaying from side to side. Not always is the sensation the same, but I tell you, if that horror ever raises it terrible shape and leers at me, if I ever see the fearful thing in my dream, I shall become stark, wild insane." There was a restless movement among the rest.

"God! but what a prospect!" he muttered. "To be insane and forever dreaming that same dream, night and day! But there I stand, and centuries go by, but at last a dim gray light begins to steal through the windows, the swishing dies away in the distance and presently a red, haggard sun climbs the eastern sky. Then I turn about and gaze into a mirror—and my hair has become perfectly white. I stagger to the door and fling it wide. There is nothing in sight but a wide track leading away down the hill through the grasslands—in the opposite direction from that which I would take toward the coast. And with a shriek of maniacal laughter, I dash down the hill and race across the grasslands. I race until I drop from exhaustion, then I lie until I can stagger up and go on.

"All day I keep this up, with superhuman effort, spurred on by the horror behind me. And ever as I hurl myself forward on weakening legs, ever as I lie gasping for breath, I watch the sun with a terrible eagerness. How swiftly the sun travels when a man races it for life! A losing race it is, as I know when I watch the sun sinking toward the skyline, and the hills which I had to gain ere sundown seemingly as far away as ever."

His voice was lowered and instinctively we leaned toward him; he was gripping the chair arms and the blood was seeping from his lip.

"Then the sun sets and the shadows come and I stagger on and fall and rise and reel on again. And I laugh, laugh, laugh! Then I cease, for the moon comes up and throws the grasslands in ghostly and silvery relief. The light is white across the land, though the moon itself is like blood. And I look back the way I have come—and far—back"—all of us leaned farther toward him, our hair a-prickle; his voice came like a ghostly whisper—"far back—I—

see—the—grass—waving. There is no breeze, but the tall grass parts and sways in the moonlight, in a narrow, sinuous line—far away, but nearing every instant." His voice died away.

Somebody broke the ensuing stillness: "And then—?"

"Then I awake. Never yet have I seen the foul monster. But that is the dream that haunts me, and from which I have wakened, in my childhood screaming, in my manhood in cold sweat. At irregular intervals I dream it, and each time, lately"—he hesitated and then went on—"each time lately, the thing has been getting closer—closer—the waving of the grass marks his progress and he nears me with each dream; and when he reaches me, then—"

He stopped short, then without a word rose abruptly and entered the house. The rest of us sat silent for awhile, then followed him, for it was late.

How long I slept I do not know, but I woke suddenly with the impression that somewhere in the house someone had laughed long, loud and hideously, as a maniac laughs. Starting up, wondering if I had been dreaming, I rushed from my room, just as a truly horrible shriek echoed through the house. The place was now alive with other people who had been awakened, and all of us rushed to Famings's room, whence the sounds had seemed to come.

Faming lay dead upon the floor, where it seemed he had fallen in some terrific struggle. There was no mark upon him, but his face was terribly distorted; as the face of a man who had been crushed by some superhuman force—such as some gigantic snake.

A young man, new to the wild, takes the adventure to Africa. But a tenderfoot and a tender heart both can get you into trouble.

THE HYENA

From the time when I first saw Senecoza, the fetish-man, I distrusted him, and from vague distrust the idea eventually grew into hatred.

I was but newly come to the East Coast, new to African ways, somewhat inclined to follow my impulses, and possessed of a large amount of curiosity.

Because I came from Virginia, race instinct and prejudice were strong in me, and doubtless the feeling of inferiority which Senecoza constantly inspired in me had a great deal to do with my antipathy for him.

He was surprisingly tall, and lankly built. Six inches above six feet he stood, and so muscular was his spare frame that he weighed a good two hundred pounds. His weight seemed incredible when

one looked at his lanky build, but he was all mus-
cle—a lean, black giant. His features were not pure
negro. They more resembled Berber than Bantu,
with the high, bulging forehead, thin nose and thin,
straight lips, but his hair was as kinky as a Bushman's and his color was blacker even than the
Masai. In fact, his glossy hide had a different hue
from those of the native tribesmen, and I believe
that he was of a different tribe.

It was seldom that we of the ranch saw him. Then
without warning he would be among us, or we
would see him striding through the shoulder-high
grass of the veldt, sometimes alone, sometimes followed at a respectful distance by several of the wilder Masai, who bunched up at a distance from the
buildings, grasping their spears nervously and eyeing everyone suspiciously.

He would make his greetings with a courtly grace;
his manner was deferentially courteous, but somehow it "rubbed me the wrong way," so to speak. I
always had a vague feeling that the black was mocking us. He would stand before us, a naked bronze
giant; make trade for a few simple articles, such as
a copper kettle, beads or a trade musket; repeat
words of some chief, and take his departure.

I did not like him. And being young and impetu-
ous, I spoke my opinion to Ludtvik Strolvaus, a very
distant relative, tenth cousin or suchlike, on whose
trading-post ranch I was staying.

But Ludtvik chuckled in his blond beard and said
that the fetish-man was all right.

"A power he is among the natives, true. They all
fear him. But a friend he is to the whites. *Ja.*"

Ludtvik was long a resident on the East Coast;

he knew natives and he knew the fat Australian cattle he raised, but he had little imagination.

The ranch buildings were in the midst of a stockade, on a kind of slope, overlooking countless miles on miles of the finest grazing land in Africa. The stockade was large, well suited for defense. Most of the thousand cattle could be driven inside in case of an uprising of the Masai. Ludtvik was inordinately proud of his cattle.

"One thousand now," he would tell me, his round face beaming, "one thousand now. But later, ah! ten thousand and another ten thousand. This is a good beginning, but only a beginning. *Ja.*"

I must confess that I got little thrill out of the cattle. Natives herded and corralled them; all Ludtvik and I had to do was to ride about and give orders. That was the work he liked best, and I left it mostly to him.

My chief sport was in riding away across the veldt, alone or attended by a gun-bearer, with a rifle. Not that I ever bagged much game. In the first place I was an execrable marksman; I could hardly have hit an elephant at close range. In the second place, it seemed to me a shame to shoot so many things. A bush-antelope would bound up in front of me and race away, and I would sit watching him, admiring the slim, lithe figure, thrilled with the graceful beauty of the creature, my rifle lying idle across my saddle-horn.

The native boy who served as my gun-bearer began to suspect that I was deliberately refraining from shooting, and he began in a covert way to throw sneering hints about my womanishness. I was young and valued even the opinion of a native; which is very foolish. His remarks stung my pride, and one day I hauled him off his horse and pounded him until he yelled for mercy. Thereafter my doings were not questioned.

But still I felt inferior when in the presence of the fetish-man. I could not get the other natives to talk about him. All I could get out of them was a scared rolling of the eyeballs, gesticulation indicative of fear, and vague information that the fetish-man dwelt among the tribes some distance in the interior. General opinion seemed to be that Senecoza was a good man to let alone.

One incident made the mystery about the fetish-man take on, it seemed, a rather sinister form.

In the mysterious way that news travels in Africa, and which white men so seldom hear of, we learned that Senecoza and a minor chief had had a falling out of some kind. It was vague and seemed to have no special basis of fact. But shortly afterward that chief was found half-devoured by hyenas. That, in itself, was not unusual, but the fright with which the natives heard the news was. The chief was nothing to them; in fact he was something of a villain, but his killing seemed to inspire them with a fright that was little short of homicidal. When the black reaches a certain stage of fear, he is as dangerous as a cornered panther. The next time Senecoza called, they rose and fled en masse and did not return until he had taken his departure.

Between the fear of the blacks, the tearing to pieces of the chief of the hyenas, and the fetish-man, I seemed to sense vaguely a connection of some kind. But I could not grasp the intangible thought.

Not long thereafter, that thought was intensified by another incident. I had ridden far out on the veldt, accompanied by my servant. As we paused to rest our horses close to a kopje, I saw, upon the top, a hyena eyeing us. Rather surprised, for the beasts are not in the habit of thus boldly approaching man in the daytime, I raised my rifle and was taking a steady aim, for I always hated the things, when my servant caught my arm.

"No shoot, *bwana!* No shoot!" he exclaimed hastily, jabbering a great deal in his own language, with which I was not familiar.

"What's up?" I asked impatiently.

He kept on jabbering and pulling my arm, until I gathered that the hyena was a fetish-beast of some kind.

"Oh, all right," I conceded, lowering my rifle just as the hyena turned and sauntered out of sight.

Something about the lank, repulsive beast and his shambling yet gracefully lithe walk struck my sense of humor with a ludicrous comparison.

Laughing, I pointed toward the beast and said, "That fellow looks like a hyena-imitation of Senecoza, the fetish-man." My simple statement seemed to throw the native into a more abject fear than ever.

He turned his pony and dashed off in the general direction of the ranch, looking back at me with a scared face.

I followed, annoyed. And as I rode I pondered. Hyenas, a fetish-man, a chief torn to pieces, a countryside of natives in fear; what was the connection? I puzzled and puzzled, but I was new to Africa; I was young and impatient, and presently with a shrug of annoyance I discarded the whole problem.

The next time Senecoza came to the ranch, he

managed to stop directly in front of me. For a fleeting instant his glittering eyes looked into mine. And in spite of myself, I shuddered and stepped back, involuntarily, feeling much as a man feels who looks unaware into the eyes of a serpent. There was nothing tangible, nothing on which I could base a quarrel, but there was a distinct threat. Before my Nordic pugnacity could reassert itself, he was gone. I said nothing. But I knew that Senecoza hated me for some reason and that he plotted my killing. Why, I did not know.

As for me, my distrust grew into bewildered rage, which in turn became hate.

And then Ellen Farel came to the ranch. Why she should choose a trading-ranch in East Africa for a place to rest from the society life of New York, I do not know. Africa is no place for a woman. That is what Ludtvik, also a cousin of hers, told her, but he was overjoyed to see her. As for me, girls never interested me much; usually I felt like a fool in their presence and was glad to be out. But there were few whites in the vicinity and I tired of the company of Ludtvik.

Ellen was standing on the wide veranda when I first saw her, a slim, pretty young thing, with rosy cheeks and hair like gold and large gray eyes. She was surprisingly winsome in her costume of riding-breeches, puttees, jacket and light helmet.

I felt extremely awkward, dusty and stupid as I sat on my wiry African pony and stared at her.

She saw a stocky youth of medium height, with sandy hair, eyes in which a kind of gray predominated; an ordinary, unhandsome youth, clad in dusty riding-clothes and a cartridge belt on one side of which was slung an ancient Colt of big caliber, and on the other a long, wicked hunting-knife.

I dismounted, and she came forward, hand outstretched.

"I'm Ellen," she said, "and I know you're Steve. Cousin Ludtvik has been telling me about you."

I shook hands, surprised at the thrill the mere touch of her hand gave me.

She was enthusiastic about the ranch. She was enthusiastic about everything. Seldom have I seen anyone who had more vigor and vim, more enjoyment of everything done. She fairly scintillated with mirth and gaiety.

Ludtvik gave her the best horse on the place, and we rode much about the ranch and over the veldt.

The blacks interested her much. They were afraid of her, not being used to white women. She would have been off her horse and playing with the pickaninnies if I had let her. She couldn't understand why she should treat the black people as dust beneath her feet. We had long arguments about it. I could not convince her, so I told her bluntly that she didn't know anything about it and she must do as I told her.

She pouted her pretty lips and called me a tyrant, and then was off over the veldt like an antelope, laughing at me over her shoulder, her hair blowing free in the breeze.

Tyrant! I was her slave from the first. Somehow the idea of becoming a lover never entered my mind. It was not the fact that she was several years older than I, or that she had a sweetheart (several of them, I think) back in New York. Simply, I worshipped her; her presence intoxicated me, and I could think of no more enjoyable existence than serving her as a devoted slave.

I was mending a saddle one day when she came running in.

"Oh, Steve!" she called; "there's the most romantic-looking savage! Come quick and tell me what his name is."

She led me out of the veranda.

"There he is," she said, naively pointing. Arms folded, haughty head thrown back, stood Senecoza.

Ludtvik, who was talking to him, paid no attention to the girl until he had completed his business with the fetish-man; and then, turning, he took her arm and they went into the house together.

Again I was face to face with the savage; but this time he was not looking at me. With a rage amounting almost to madness, I saw that he was gazing after the girl. There was an expression in his serpentlike eyes—

On the instant my gun was out and leveled. My hand shook like a leaf with the intensity of my fury. Surely I must shoot Senecoza down like the snake he was, shoot him down and riddle him, shoot him into a shredded heap!

The fleeting expression left his eyes and they were fixed on me. Detached they seemed, inhuman in their sardonic calm. And I could not pull the trigger.

For a moment we stood, and then he turned and strode away, a magnificent figure, while I glared after him and snarled with helpless fury.

I sat down on the veranda. What a man of mystery was that savage! What strange power did he possess? Was I right, I wondered, in interpreting the fleeting expression as he gazed after the girl? It seemed to me, in my youth and folly, incredible that a black man, no matter what his rank, should look at a white woman as he did. Most astonishing of all, why could I not shoot him down?

I started as a hand touched my arm.

"What are thinking about, Steve?" asked Ellen, laughing. Then before I could say anything. "Wasn't that chief, or whatever he was, a fine specimen of a savage? He invited us to come to his kraal; is that what you call it? It's away off in the veldt somewhere, and we're going."

"No!" I exclaimed violently, springing up.

"Why Steve," she gasped, recoiling, "how rude! He's a perfect gentleman, isn't he, Cousin Ludtvik?"

"Ja," nodded Ludtvik, placidly, "we go to his kraal sometime soon, maybe. A strong chief, that savage. His chief has perhaps good trade."

"No!" I repeated furiously. "I'll go if somebody has to! Ellen's not going near that beast!"

"Well, that's nice!" remarked Ellen, somewhat indignantly. "I guess you're my boss, mister man?"

With all her sweetness, she had a mind of her own. In spite of all I could do, they arranged to go to the fetish-man's village the next day.

That night the girl came out to me, where I sat on the veranda in the moonlight, and she sat down on the arm of my chair.

"You're not angry at me, are you, Steve?" she said, wistfully, putting her arm around my shoulders. "Not mad, are you?"

Mad? Yes, maddened by the touch of her soft body—such mad devotion as a slave feels. I wanted to grovel in the dust at her feet and kiss her dainty shoes. Will women never learn the effect they have on men?

I took her hand hesitantly and pressed it to my lips. I think she must have sensed some of my devotion.

"Dear Steve," she murmured, and the words were like a caress, "come, let's walk in the moonlight."

We walked outside the stockade. I should have known better, for I had no weapon but the big Turkish dagger I carried and used for a hunting-knife, but she wished to.

"Tell me about this Senecoza," she asked, and I welcomed the opportunity. And then I thought: what could I tell her? That hyenas had eaten a small chief of the Masai? That the natives feared the fetish-man? That he had looked at her?

And then the girl screamed as out of the tall grass leaped a vague shape, half-seen in the moonlight.

I felt a heavy, hairy form crash against my shoulders; keen fangs ripped my upflung arm. I went to the earth, fighting with frenzied horror. My jacket was slit to ribbons and the fangs were at my throat before I found and drew my knife and stabbed, blindly and savagely. I felt my blade rip into my foe, and then, like a shadow, it was gone. I staggered to my feet somewhat shaken. The girl caught and steadied me.

"What was it?" she gasped, leading me toward the stockade.

"A hyena," I answered. "I could tell by the scent. But I never heard of one attacking like that."

She shuddered. Later on, after my torn arm had been bandaged, she came close to me and said in a wondrously subdued voice, "Steve, I've decided not to go to the village, if you don't want me to."

After the wounds on my arm had become scars Ellen and I resumed our rides, as might be expected. One day we had wandered rather far out on the veldt, and she challenged me to a race. Her horse easily distanced mine, and she stopped and waited for me, laughing.

She had stopped on a sort of kopje, and she pointed to a clump of trees some distance away.

"Trees!" she said gleefully. "Let's ride down there. There are so few trees on the veldt."

And as she dashed away. I followed some instinctive caution, loosening my pistol in its holster, and, drawing my knife, I thrust it down in my boot so that it was entirely concealed.

We were perhaps half-way to the trees when from the tall grass about us leaped Senecoza and some twenty warriors.

One seized the girl's bridle and the others rushed me. The one who caught at Ellen went down with a bullet between his eyes, and another crumpled at my second shot. Then a thrown war-club hurled me from the saddle, half senseless, and as the blacks closed in on me I saw Ellen's horse, driven frantic by the prick of a carelessly handled spear, scream and rear, scattering the blacks who held her, and dash away at headlong speed, the bit in her teeth.

I saw Senecoza leap on my horse and give chase, flinging a savage command over his shoulder; and both vanished over the kopje.

The warriors bound me hand and foot and carried me into the trees. A hut stood among them— a native hut of thatch and bark. Somehow the sight of it set me shuddering. It seemed to lurk, repellent and indescribably malevolent amongst the trees; to hint of horrid and obscene rites, of voodoo.

I know not why it is, but the sight of a native hut, alone and hidden, far from a village or tribe, always has to me a suggestion of nameless horror. Perhaps that is because only a black who is crazed or one who is so criminal that he has been exiled by his tribe will dwell that way.

In front of the hut they threw me down.

"When Senecoza returns with the girl," said they, "you will enter." And they laughed like fiends. Then, leaving one black to see that I did not escape, they left.

The black who remained kicked me viciously; he was a bestial-looking Negro, armed with a trade-musket.

"They go to kill white men, fool!" he mocked me. "They go to the ranches and trading-posts, first to that fool of an Englishman." Meaning Smith, the owner of a neighboring ranch.

And he went on giving details. Senecoza had made the plot, he boasted. They would chase all the white men to the coast.

"Senecoza is more than a man," he boasted. "You shall see, white man," lowering his voice and glancing about him, from beneath his low, beetling brows; "you shall see the magic of Senecoza." And he grinned, disclosing teeth filed to points.

"Cannibal! A man of Senecoza," he answered.

"Who will kill no white men," I jeered.

He scowled savagely. "I will kill you, white man."

"You dare not."

"That is true," he admitted, and added angrily, "Senecoza will kill you himself."

And meantime Ellen was riding like mad, gaining

on the fetish-man, but unable to ride toward the ranch, for he had gotten between and was forcing her steadily out upon the veldt.

The black unfastened my bonds. His line of reasoning was easy to see; absurdly easy. He could not kill a prisoner of the fetish-man, but he could kill him to prevent his escape. And he was maddened with blood-lust. Stepping back, he half-raised his trade-musket, watching me as a snake watches a rabbit.

It must have been about that time, as she afterward told me, that Ellen's horse stumbled and threw her. Before she could rise, the black had leaped from his horse and seized her in his arms. She screamed and fought, but he gripped her, held her helpless and laughed at her. Tearing her jacket to pieces, he bound her arms and legs, remounted and started back, carrying the half-fainting girl in front of him.

Back in front of the hut I rose slowly. I rubbed my arms where the ropes had been, moved a little closer to the black, stretched, stooped and rubbed my legs; then with a catlike bound I was on him, my knife flashing from my boot. The trade-musket crashed and the charge whizzed above my head as I knocked up the barrel and closed with him. Hand to hand, I would have been no match for the black giant; but I had the knife. Clinched close together we were too close for him to use the trade musket for a club. He wasted time trying to do that, and with a desperate effort I threw him off his balance and drove the dagger to the hilt in his black chest.

I wrenched it out again; I had no other weapon, for I could find no more ammunition for the trade-musket.

I had no idea which way Ellen had fled. I assumed she had gone toward the ranch, and in that direction I took my way. Smith must be warned. The warriors were far ahead of me. Even then they might be creeping up about the unsuspecting ranch.

I had not covered a fourth of the distance, when a drumming of hoofs behind me caused me to turn my head. Ellen's horse was thundering toward me, riderless. I caught her as she raced past me, and managed to stop her. The story was plain. The girl had either reached a place of safety and had turned the horse loose, or what was much more likely, had been captured, the horse escaping and fleeing toward the ranch, as a horse will do. I gripped the saddle, leaped on the horse and sent her flying toward Smith's ranch. It was not many miles; Smith must not be massacred by those black devils, and I must find a gun if I escaped to rescue the girl from Senecoza.

A half-mile from Smith's I overtook the raiders and went through them like drifting smoke. The workers at Smith's place were startled by a wild-riding horseman charging headlong into the stockade, shouting, "Masai! Masai! A raid, you fools!" snatching a gun and flying out again.

So when the savages arrived they found everybody ready for them, and they got such a warm reception that after one attempt they turned tail and fled back across the veldt.

And I was riding as I never rode before. The mare was almost exhausted, but I pushed her mercilessly. On, on!

I aimed for the only place I knew likely. The hut among the trees. I assumed that the fetish-man would return there.

And long before the hut came into sight, a horse-man dashed from the grass, going at right angles to my course, and our horses, colliding, sent both tired animals to the ground.

"Steve!" It was a cry of joy mingled with fear. Ellen lay, tied hand and foot, gazing up at me wildly as I regained my feet.

Senecoza came with a rush, his long knife flashing in the sunlight. Back and forth we fought—slash, ward and parry, my ferocity and agility matching his savagery and skill.

A terrific lunge which he aimed at me, I caught on my point, laying his arm open, and then with a quick engage and wrench, disarmed him. But before I could use my advantage, he sprang away into the grass and vanished.

I caught up the girl, slashing her bonds, and she clung to me, poor child, until I lifted her and car-ried her toward the horses. But we were not yet through with Senecoza. He must have had a rifle cached away somewhere in the bush, for the first I knew of him was when a bullet spat within a foot above my head.

I caught at the bridles, and then I saw that the mare had done all she could, temporarily. She was exhausted. I swung Ellen up on the horse.

"Ride for our ranch," I ordered her. "The raiders are out, but you can get through. Ride low and ride fast!"

"But you, Steve!"

"Go, go!" I ordered, swinging her horse around and starting it. She dashed away, looking at me wist-fully over her shoulder. Then I snatched the rifle and a handful of cartridges I had gotten at Smith's, and took to the bush. And through the hot African day, Senecoza and I played a game of hide-and-seek. Crawling, slipping in and out of the scanty veldt-bushes, crouching in the tall grass, we traded shots back and forth. A movement of the grass, a snapping twig, the rasp of grass-blades, and a bullet came questing, another answering it.

I had but a few cartridges and I fired carefully, but presently I pushed my one remaining cartridge into the rifle—a big, six-bore, single-barrel breech-loader, for I had not had time to pick when I snatched it up.

I crouched in my covert and watched for the black to betray himself by a careless movement. Not a sound, not a whisper among the grasses. Away off over the veldt a hyena sounded his fiendish laugh and another answered, closer at hand. The cold sweat broke out on my brow.

What was that? A drumming of many horses' hoofs! Raiders returning? I ventured a look and could have shouted for joy. At least twenty men were sweeping toward me, white men and ranch-boys, and ahead of them all rode Ellen! They were still some distance away. I darted behind a tall bush and rose, waving my hand to attract their attention.

They shouted and pointed to something beyond me. I whirled and saw, some thirty yards away, a huge hyena slinking toward me, rapidly. I glanced carefully across the veldt. Somewhere out there, hidden by the billowing grasses, lurked Senecoza. A shot would betray to him my position—and I had but one cartridge. The rescue party was still out of range.

I looked again at the hyena. He was still rushing toward me. There was no doubt as to his intentions. His eyes glittered like a fiend's from hell, and a scar on his shoulder showed him to be the same beast that had once before attacked me. Then a kind of horror took hold of me, and resting the old elephant rifle over my elbow, I sent my last bullet crashing through the bestial thing. With a scream that seemed to have a horribly human note in it, the hyena turned and fled back into the bush, reeling as it ran.

And the rescue party swept up around me.

A fusillade of bullets crashed through the bush from which Senecoza had sent his last shot. There was no reply.

"Ve hunt ter snake down," quoth Cousin Ludtvik, his Boer accent increasing with his excitement. And we scattered through the veldt in a skirmish line, combing every inch of it warily.

Not a trace of the fetish-man did we find. A rifle we found, empty, with empty shells scattered about, and (which was very strange) *hyena tracks leading away from the rifle.*

I felt the short hairs of my neck bristle with intangible horror. We looked at each other, and said not a word, as with a tacit agreement we took up the trail of the hyena.

We followed it as it wound in and out in the shoulder-high grass, showing how it had slipped up on me, stalking me as a tiger stalks its victim. We struck the trail the thing had made, returning to the bush after I had shot it. Splashes of blood marked the way it had taken. We followed.

"It leads toward the fetish-hut," muttered an Englishman. "Here, sirs, is a damnable mystery."

And Cousin Ludtvik ordered Ellen to stay back, leaving two men with her.

We followed the trail over the kopje and into the

clump of trees. Straight to the door of the hut it led. We circled the hut cautiously, but no tracks led away. It was inside the hut. Rifles ready, we forced the rude door.

No tracks led away from the hut and no tracks led to it except the tracks of the hyena. Yet there was no hyena within that hut; and on the dirt floor, a bullet through his black breast, lay Senecoza, the fetish-man.

Amelia Earhart was lost in 1937—a year after Howard died. This story seems strangely prophetic. Here Howard changes the tables on the reader. We come to the shocked realization along with the hero that I am the wild beast, they are the civilized scientists.

PEOPLE OF THE BLACK COAST

This comes of idle pleasure seeking and—now what prompted that thought? Some Puritanical atavism lurking in my crumbling brain, I suppose. Certainly, in my past life I never gave much heed to such teachings. At any rate, let me scribble down here my short and hideous history, before the red hour breaks and death shouts across the beaches.

There were two of us, at the start. Myself, of course, and Gloria, who was to have been my bride. Gloria had an airplane, and she loved to fly the thing—that was the beginning of the whole horror. I tried to dissuade her that day—I swear I did!— but she insisted, and we took off from Manila with Guam as our destination. Why? The whim of a reckless girl who feared nothing and always burned with the zest for some new adventure—some untried sport.

Of our coming to the Black Coast there is little to tell. One of those rare fogs rose; we soared above it and lost our way among thick billowing clouds. We struggled along, how far out of our course God alone knows, and finally fell into the sea just as we sighted land through the lifting fog.

We swam ashore from the sinking craft, unhurt, and found ourselves in a strange and forbidding land. Broad beaches sloped up from the lazy waves to end at the foot of vast cliffs. These cliffs seemed to be of solid rock and were—are—hundreds of feet high. The material was basalt or something similar. As we descended in the falling aircraft, I had had time for a quick glance shoreward, and it had seemed to me that beyond these cliffs, rose other, higher cliffs, as if in tiers, rampart above rampart. But of course, standing directly beneath the first, we could not tell. As far as we looked in either direction, we could see the narrow strip of beach running along at the foot of the black cliffs, in silent monotony.

"Now that we're here," said Gloria, somewhat shaken by our recent experience, "what are we to do? Where are we?"

"There isn't any telling," I answered. "The Pacific is full of unexplored islands. We're probably on one. I only hope that we haven't a gang of cannibals for neighbors."

I wished then that I had not mentioned cannibals, but Gloria did not seem frightened—at that.

"I'm not afraid of natives," she said uneasily. "I don't think there are any here."

I smiled to myself, reflecting how women's opinions merely reflected their wishes. But there was something deeper, as I soon learned in a hideous manner, and I believe now in feminine intuition. Their brain fibers are more delicate than ours— more readily disturbed and reached by psychic influences. But I had no time to theorize.

"Let's stroll along the beach and see if we can find some way of getting up these cliffs and back on the island."

"But the island is all cliffs, isn't it?" she asked.

Somehow I was startled. "Why do you say that?"

"I don't know," she answered rather confusedly. "That was the impression I had, that this island is just a series of high cliffs, like stairs, one on top of the other, all bare black rock."

"If that's the case," said I, "we're out of luck, for we can't live on seaweed and crabs—"

"Oh!" Her exclamation was sharp and sudden.

I caught her in my arms, rather roughly in my alarm, I fear.

"Gloria! What is it?"

"I don't know." Her eyes stared at me rather bewilderedly, as if she were emerging from some sort of nightmare.

"Did you see or hear anything?"

"No." She seemed to be averse to leaving my sheltering arms. "It was something you said—no, that wasn't it. I don't know. People have daydreams. This must have been a nightmare."

God help me; I laughed in my masculine complacency and said:

"You girls are a queer lot in some ways. Let's go up the beach a way—"

"No!" she exclaimed emphatically.

"Then let's go down the beach—"

"No, no!"

I lost patience.

"Gloria, what's come over you? We can't stay here all day. We've got to find a way to go up those cliffs and find what's on the other side. Don't be so foolish; it isn't like you."

"Don't scold me," she returned with a meekness strange to her. "Something seems to keep chasing at the outer edge of my mind, something that I can't translate—do you believe in transmission of thought waves?"

I stared at her. I'd never heard her talk in this manner before.

"Do you think somebody's trying to signal you by sending thought waves?"

"No, they're not thoughts," she murmured absently. "Not as I know thoughts, at least."

Then, like a person suddenly coming out of a trance, she said:

"You go on and look for a place to go up the cliffs, while I wait here."

"Gloria, I don't like the idea. You come along— or else I'll wait until you feel like going."

"I don't think I'll ever feel that way," she answered forlornly. "You don't need to go out of sight; one can see a long way here. Did you ever see such black cliffs; this is a black coast, sure enough? Did you ever read Tevis Clyde Smith's poem—'The long black coasts of death'—something? I can't remember exactly."

I felt a vague uneasiness at hearing her talk in this manner, but sought to dismiss the feeling with a shrug of my shoulders.

"I'll find a trail up," I said, "and maybe get something for our meal—clams or a crab—"

She shuddered violently.

"Don't mention crabs. I've hated them all my life,

but I didn't realize it until you spoke. They eat dead things, don't they? I know the Devil looks just like a monstrous crab."

"All right," said I, to humor her. "Stay right here; I won't be gone long."

"Kiss me before you go," she said with a wistfulness that caught at my heart, I knew not why. I drew her tenderly into my arms, joying in the feel of her slim young body so vibrant with life and loveliness. She closed her eyes as I kissed her, and I noted how strangely white she seemed.

"Don't go out of sight," she said as I released her. A number of rough boulders dotted the beach, fallen, no doubt, from the overhanging cliff face, and on one of these she sat down.

With some misgivings, I turned to go. I went along the beach close to the great black wall which rose into the blue like a monster against the sky, and at last came to a number of unusually large boulders. Before going among these I glanced back and saw Gloria sitting where I had left her. I know my eyes softened as I looked on that slim, brave little figure—for the last time.

I wandered in among the boulders and lost sight of the beach behind me. I often wonder why I so thoughtlessly ignored her last plea. A man's brain fabric is coarser than a woman's, not so susceptible to outer influences. Yet I wonder if even then, pressure was being brought to bear upon me—

At any rate, I wandered along, gazing up at the towering black mass until it seemed to have a sort of mesmeric effect upon me. One who has never seen these cliffs cannot possibly form any true conception of them, nor can I breathe into my description the invisible aura of malignity which seemed to emanate from them. I say, they rose so high above me that their edges seemed to cut through the sky—that I felt like an ant crawling beneath a Babylonian wall—that their monstrous serrated faces seemed like the breasts of dusty gods of unthinkable age—this I can say, this much I can impart to you. But if any man ever reads this, let him not think that I have given a true portrait of the Black Coast. The reality of the thing lay, not in sight and sense nor even in the thoughts which they induced; but in the things you know without thinking—the feelings and the stirrings of consciousness the faint clawings at the outer edge of the mind which are not thoughts at all—

But these things I discovered later. At the moment, I walked along like a man in a daze, almost mesmerized by the stark monotony of the black ramparts above me. At times I shook myself, blinked and looked out to sea to get rid of this mazy feeling, but even the sea seemed shadowed by the great walls. The further I went, the more threatening they seemed. My reason told me that they could not fall, but the instinct at the back of my brain whispered that they would suddenly hurtle down and crush me.

Then suddenly I found some fragments of driftwood which had washed ashore. I could have shouted my elation. The mere sight of them proved that man at least *existed* and that there was a world far removed from these dark and sullen cliffs, which seemed to fill the whole universe. I found a long fragment of iron attached to a piece of the wood and tore it off; if the necessity arose, it would make a very serviceable iron bludgeon. Rather heavy for the ordinary man, it is true, but in size and strength, I am no ordinary man.

At this moment, too, I decided I had gone far enough. Gloria was long out of sight and I retraced my steps hurriedly. As I went I noted a few tracks in the sand and reflected with amusement that if a spider crab, something larger than a horse, had crossed the beach here, it would make just such a track. Then I came in sight of the place where I had left Gloria and gazed along a bare and silent beach.

I had heard no scream, no cry. Utter silence had reigned as it reigned now, when I stood beside the boulder where she had sat and looked in the sand of the beach. Something small and slim and white lay there, and I dropped to my knees beside it. It was a woman's hand, severed at the wrist, and as I saw upon the second finger the engagement ring I had placed there myself, my heart withered in my breast and the sky became a black ocean which drowned the sun.

How long I crouched over that pitiful fragment like a wounded beast, I do not know. Time ceased to be for me, and from its dying minutes was born Eternity. What are days, hours, years, to a shattered heart, to whose empty hurt each instant is an Everlasting Forever? But when I rose and reeled down to the sea edge, holding that little hand close to my hollow bosom, the sun had set and the moon had set and the hard white stars looked scornfully at me across the immensity of space.

There I pressed my lips again and again to that pitiful cold flesh and laid the slim little hand on the flowing tide which carried it out to the clean, deep sea, as I trust, merciful God, the white flame of her soul found rest in the Everlasting Sea. And the sad and ancient waves that know all the sorrows of men seemed to weep for me, for I could not weep. But since, many have shed tears, oh God, and the tears were of blood!

I staggered along the mocking whiteness of the beach like a drunken man or a lunatic. And from the time that I rose from the sighing tide to the time that I dropped exhausted and became unconscious seems centuries on countless centuries, during which I raved and screamed and staggered along huge black ramparts which frowned down on me in cold inhuman disdain—which brooded above the squeaking ant at their feet.

The sun was up when I awoke, and I found I was not alone. I sat up. On every hand I was ringed in by a strange and horrible throng. If you can imagine spider crabs larger than a horse—yet they were not true spider crabs, outside the difference in the size. Leaving that difference out, I should say that there was as much variation in these monsters and the true spider crab as there is between a highly developed European and an African bushman. These were more highly developed, if you understand me.

They sat up and looked at me. I remained motionless, uncertain just what to expect—and a cold fear began to steal over me. This was not caused by any especial fear of the brutes killing me, for I felt somehow that they would do that, and did not shrink from the thought. But their eyes bored in on me and turned my blood to ice. For in them I recognized an intelligence infinitely higher than mine, yet terribly different. This is hard to conceive, harder to explain. But as I looked into those frightful eyes, I knew that keen, powerful brains lurked behind them, brains which worked in a higher sphere, a different dimension than mine.

There was neither friendliness nor favor in those eyes, no sympathy or understanding—not even fear or hate. It is a terrible thing for a human being to be looked at in that manner. Even the eyes of a human enemy who is going to kill us have understanding in them, and a certain acceptance of kindred. But these fiends gazed upon me in something of the manner in which cold-hearted scientists might look at a worm about to be stuck on a specimen board. They did not—they could not—understand me. My thoughts, sorrows, joys, ambitions, they never could fathom, any more than I could fathom theirs. We were of different species! And no wars of human kind can ever equal in cruelty the constant warfare that is waged between living things of diverging order. Is it possible that all life came from one stem? I cannot now believe it.

There was intelligence and power in the cold eyes which were fixed on me, but not intelligence as I knew it. They had progressed much further than mankind in their ways, but they progressed along different lines. Further than this, I cannot say. Their minds and reasoning faculties are closed doors to me and most of their actions seem absolutely meaningless; yet I know that these actions are guided by definite, though inhuman, thoughts, which in turn are the results of a higher stage of development than the human race may ever reach in *their way*.

But as I sat there and these thoughts were borne in on me—as I felt the terrific force of their inhuman intellect crashing against my brain and will power, I leaped up, cold with fear; a wild unreasoning fear which wild beasts must feel when first confronted by men. I knew that these things were of a higher order than myself, and I feared to even threaten them, yet with all my soul I hated them.

The average man feels no compunction in his dealings with the insects underfoot. He does not feel, as he does in his dealings with his brother man, that the Higher Powers will call upon him for an accounting—of the worms on which he treads, nor the fowls he eats. Nor does a lion devour a lion, yet feasts nobly on buffalo or man. I tell you, Nature is most cruel when she sets the species against each other.

These thinking-crabs, then, looking upon me as God only knows what sort of prey or specimen, were intending me God only knows what sort of evil, when I broke the chain of terror which held me. The largest one, whom I faced, was now eyeing me with a sort of grim disapproval, a sort of anger, as if he haughtily resented my threatening actions— as a scientist might resent the writhing of a worm beneath the dissecting knife. At that, fury blazed in me and the flames were fanned by my fear. With one leap I reached the largest crab and with one desperate smash I crushed and killed him. Then bounding over his writhing form, I fled.

But I did not flee far. The thought came to me as I ran that these were they whom I sought for vengeance. Gloria—no wonder she started when I spoke the accursed name of "crab" and conceived the Devil to be in the form of a crab, when even then those fiends must have been stealing about us, tingling her sensitive thoughts with the psychic waves that flowed from their horrid brains. I turned, then, and came back a few steps, my bludgeon lifted. But the throng had bunched together, as cattle do upon the approach of a lion. Their claws were

raised menacingly, and their cruel thought emanations struck me so like a power of physical force
that I staggered backward and was unable to proceed against it. I knew then that in their way they
feared me, for they backed slowly away toward the
cliffs, ever fronting me.

My history is long, but I must shortly draw it to
a close. Since that hour I have waged a fierce and
merciless warfare against a race I knew to be higher
in culture and intellect than I. Scientists, they are,
and in some horrid experiment of theirs, Gloria
must have perished. I cannot say.

This I have learned. Their city is high up among
those lofty tiers of cliffs which I cannot see because
of the overhanging crags of the first tier. I suppose
the whole island is like that, a mere base of basaltic
rock, rising to a high flung pinnacle, no doubt, this
pinnacle being the last tier of innumerable tiers of
rocky walls. The monsters descend by a secret way
which I have only just discovered. They have
hunted me, and I have hunted them.

I have found this, also: the one point in common
between these beasts and the human is that the
higher the race develops mentally, the less acute
become the physical faculties. I, who am as much
lower than they mentally as a gorilla is lower than
a human professor, am as deadly in single combat
with them as a gorilla would be with an unarmed
professor. I am quicker, stronger, of keener senses.
I possess coordinations which they do not. In a
word, there is a strange reversion here—I am the
wild beast and they are the civilized and developed
beings. I ask no mercy and I give none. What are
my wishes and desires to them? I would never have
molested them, any more than an eagle molests

men, had they not taken my mate. But to satisfy some selfish hunger or to evolve some useless scientific theory, they took her life and ruined mine.

And now I have been, and shall be, the wild beast with a vengeance. A wolf may wipe out a herd, a man-eating lion has destroyed a whole village of men, and I am a wolf, a lion, to the people—if I may call them that—of the Black Coast. I have lived on such clams as I have found, for I have never been able to bring myself to eat of crab flesh. And I have hunted my foes, along the beaches, by sunlight and by starlight, among the boulders, and high up in the cliffs as far as I could climb. It has not been easy, and I must shortly admit defeat. They have fought me with psychic weapons against which I have no defense, and the constant crashing of their wills against mine has weakened me terribly, mentally and physically. I have lain in wait for single enemies and have even attacked and destroyed several, but the strain has been terrific.

Their power is mainly mental, and far, far exceeds human mesmerism. At first it was easy to plunge through the enveloping thought-waves of one crab-man and kill him, but they have found weak places in my brain.

This I do not understand, but I know that of late I have gone through Hell with each battle. Their thought-tides have seemed to flow into my skull in waves of molten metal, freezing, burning, withering my brain and my soul. I lie hidden and when one crab-man approaches, I leap and I must kill quickly, as a lion must kill a man with a rifle before the victim can aim and fire.

Nor have I always escaped physically unscathed, for only yesterday the desperate stroke of a dying crab-man's claws tore off my left arm at the elbow. This would have killed me at one time, but now I shall live long enough to consumate my vengeance. Up there, in the higher tiers, up among the clouds where the crab city of horror broods, I must carry doom. I am a dying man—the wounds of my enemies' strange weapons have shown me my Fate, but my left arm is bound so that I shall not bleed to death, my crumbling brain will hold together long enough, and I still have my right hand and my iron bludgeon. I have noted that at dawn the crab-people keep closer to their high cliffs, and such as I have found at that time are very easy to kill. Why, I do not know, but my lower reason tells me that these Masters are at a low ebb of vitality at dawn, for some reason.

I am writing this by the light of a low-hanging moon. Soon dawn will come, and in the darkness before dawn, I shall go up the secret trail I have found which leads to the clouds—and above. I shall find the demon city and as the east begins to redden, I shall begin the slaughter. Oh, it will be a great battle! I will crush and crash and kill, and my foes will lie in a great shattered heap, and at last I, too, shall die. Good enough. I shall be content. I have scattered death like a lion. I have littered the beaches with their corpses. Before I die I shall slay many more.

Gloria, the moon swings low. Dawn will be here soon. I do not know if you look in approval, from shadowland, on my red work of vengeance, but it has to some extent brought ease to my frozen soul. After all, these creatures and I are of different species, and it is Nature's cruel custom that the diverging orders may never live in peace with each other. They took my mate; I take their lives.

We end our journey beyond the borders near the cradle of civilization. Again we hear a story within a story, of an old wrong and old enemies to be faced again. Two brave wanderers face curses from millennia ago, enmities from decades ago, together.

THE FIRE OF ASSHURBANIPAL

Yar Ali squinted carefully down the blue barrel of his Lee-Enfield, called devoutly on Allah and sent a bullet through the brain of a flying rider.

"Allaho akbar!"

The big Afghan shouted in glee, waving his weapon above his head, "God is great! By Allah, *sahib*, I have sent another one of the dogs to Hell!"

His companion peered cautiously over the rim of the sand-pit they had scooped with their hands. He was a lean and wiry American, Steve Clarney by name.

"Good work, old horse," said this person. "Four left. Look—they're drawing off."

The white-robed horsemen were indeed reining away, clustering together just out of accurate rifle-range, as if in council. There had been seven when they had first swooped down on the comrades, but

the fire from the two rifles in the sand-pit had
been deadly.

"Look, *sahib*—they abandon the fray!"

Yar Ali stood up boldly and shouted taunts at the
departing riders, one of whom whirled and sent a
bullet that kicked up sand thirty feet in front of
the pit.

"They shoot like the sons of dogs," said Yar Ali
in complacent self-esteem. "By Allah, did you see
that rogue plunge from his saddle as my lead went
home? Up, *sahib;* let us run after them and cut
them down!"

Paying no attention to this outrageous proposal—
for he knew it was but one of the gestures Afghan
nature continually demands—Steve rose, dusted off
his breeches and gazing after the riders, now white
specks far out on the desert, said musingly: "Those
fellows ride as if they had some purpose in mind—
not a bit like men running from a licking."

"Aye," agreed Yar Ali promptly and seeing nothing inconsistent with his present attitude and recent
blood-thirsty suggestion, "they ride after more of
their kind—they are hawks who give up their prey
not quickly. We had best move our position quickly,
Steve *sahib*. They will come back—maybe in a few
hours, maybe in a few days—it all depends on how
far away lies the oasis of their tribe. But they will
be back. We have guns and lives—they want both.
And behold."

The Afghan levered out the empty shell and
slipped a single cartridge into the breech of his rifle.

"My last bullet, *sahib*."

Steve nodded. "I've got three left."

The raiders whom their bullets had knocked from
the saddle had been looted by their own comrades.

No use searching the bodies which lay in the sand for ammunition. Steve lifted his canteen and shook it. Not much water remained. He knew that Yar Ali had only a little more than he, though the big Afridi, bred in a barren land, had used and needed less water than did the American; although the latter, judged from a white man's standards, was hard and tough as a wolf. As Steve unscrewed the canteen cap and drank very sparingly, he mentally reviewed the chain of events that had led them to their present position.

Wanderers, soldiers of fortune, thrown together by chance and attracted to each other by mutual admiration, he and Yar Ali had wandered from India up through Turkistan and down through Persia, an oddly assorted but highly capable pair. Driven by the restless urge of inherent wanderlust, their avowed purpose—which they swore to and sometimes believed themselves—was the accumulation of some vague and undiscovered treasure, some pot of gold at the foot of some yet unborn rainbow.

Then in ancient Shiraz they had heard of the Fire of Asshurbanipal. From the lips of an ancient Persian trader, who only half believed what he repeated to them, they heard the tale that he in turn had heard from the babbling lips of delirium, in his distant youth. He had been a member of a caravan, fifty years before, which, wandering far on the southern shore of the Persian Gulf trading for pearls, had followed the tale of a rare pearl far into the desert.

The pearl, rumored found by a diver and stolen by a shaykh of the interior, they did not find, but they did pick up a Turk who was dying of starvation, thirst and a bullet wound in the thigh. As he died in delirium, he babbled a wild tale of a silent dead city of black stone set in the drifting sands of the desert far to the westward, and of a flaming gem clutched in the bony fingers of a skeleton on an ancient throne.

He had not dared bring it away with him, because of an overpowering brooding horror that haunted the place, and thirst had driven him into the desert again, where Bedouins had pursued and wounded him. Yet he had escaped, riding hard until his horse fell under him. He died without telling how he had reached the mythical city in the first place, but the old trader thought he must have come from the northwest—a deserter from the Turkish army, making a desperate attempt to reach the Gulf.

The men of the caravan had made no attempt to plunge still further into the desert in search of the city; for, said the old trader, they believed it to be the ancient, ancient City of Evil spoken of in the *Necronomicon* of the mad Arab Alhazred—the city of the dead on which an ancient curse rested. Legends named it vaguely: the Arabs called it *Beled-el-Djinn*, the City of Devils, and the Turks, *Kara-Shehr*, the Black City. And the gem was that ancient and accursed jewel belonging to a king of long ago, whom the Grecians called Sardanapalus and the Semitic peoples Asshurbanipal.

Steve had been fascinated by the tale. Admitting to himself that it was doubtless one of the ten thousand cock-and-bull myths booted about the East, still there was a possibility that he and Yar Ali had stumbled onto a trace of that pot of rainbow gold for which they searched. And Yar Ali had heard hints before of a silent city of the sands; tales had followed the eastbound caravans over the high Persian uplands and across the sands of Turkistan, into the mountain country and beyond—vague tales, whispers of a black city of the djinn, deep in the hazes of a haunted desert.

So, following the trail of the legend, the companions had come from Shiraz to a village on the Arabian shore of the Persian Gulf, and there had heard more from an old man who had been a pearl-diver in his youth. The loquacity of age was on him and he told tales repeated to him by wandering tribesmen who had them in turn from the wild nomads of the deep interior; and again Steve and Yar Ali heard of the still black city with giant beasts carved of stone, and the skeleton sultan who held the blazing gem.

And so, mentally swearing at himself for a fool, Steve had made the plunge, and Yar Ali, secure in the knowledge that all things lay on the lap of Allah, had come with him. Their scanty supply of money had been just sufficient to provide riding-camels and provisions for a bold flying invasion of the unknown. Their only chart had been the vague rumors that placed the supposed location of Kara-Shehr.

There had been days of hard travel, pushing the beasts and conserving water and food. Then, deep in the desert they invaded, they had encountered a blinding sand-wind in which they had lost the camels. After that came long miles of staggering through the sands, battered by a flaming sun, subsisting on rapidly dwindling water from their canteens, and food Yar Ali had in a pouch. No thought of finding the mythical city now. They pushed on blindly, in hope of stumbling upon a spring; they knew that behind them no oases lay within a distance they could hope to cover on foot. It was a desperate chance, but their only one.

Then white-clad hawks had swooped down on them, out of the haze of the skyline, and from a shallow and hastily scooped trench the adventurers had exchanged shots with the wild riders who circled them at top speed. The bullets of the Bedouins had skipped through their makeshift fortifications, knocking dust into their eyes and flicking bits of cloth from their garments, but by good chance neither had been hit.

Their one bit of luck, reflected Clarney, as he cursed himself for a fool. What a mad venture it had been, anyway! To think that two men could so dare the desert and live, much less wrest from its abysmal bosom the secrets of the ages! And that crazy tale of a skeleton hand gripping a flaming jewel in a dead city—bosh! What utter rot! He must have been crazy himself to credit it, the American decided with the clarity of view that suffering and danger bring.

"Well, old horse," said Steve, lifting his rifle, "let's get going. It's a toss-up if we die of thirst or get sniped off by the desert-brothers. Anyway, we're doin' no good here."

"God gives," agreed Yar Ali cheerfully. "The sun sinks westward. Soon the coolness of night will be upon us. Perhaps we shall find water yet, *sahib*. Look, the terrain changes to the south."

Clarney shaded his eyes against the dying sun. Beyond a level, barren expanse of several miles width, the land did indeed become more broken; aborted hills were in evidence. The American slung his rifle over his arm and sighed.

"Heave ahead; we're food for the buzzards anyhow."

The sun sank and the moon rose, flooding the desert with weird silver light. Drifted sand glimmered in long ripples, as if a sea had suddenly been frozen into immobility. Steve, parched fiercely by a thirst he dared not fully quench, cursed beneath his breath. The desert was beautiful beneath the moon, with the beauty of a cold marble lorelei to lure men to destruction. What a mad quest! his weary brain reiterated; the Fire of Asshurbanipal retreated into the mazes of unreality with each dragging step. The desert became not merely a material wasteland, but the gray mists of the lost eons, in whose depths dreamed sunken things.

Clarney stumbled and swore; was he failing already? Yar Ali swung along with the easy, tireless stride of a mountain man, and Steve set his teeth, nerving himself to greater effort. They were entering the broken country at last, and the going became harder. Shallow gullies and narrow ravines knifed the earth with wavering patterns. Most of them were nearly filled with sand, and there was no trace of water.

"This country was once oasis country," commented Yar Ali. "Allah knows how many centuries ago the sand took it, as the sand has taken so many cities in Turkistan."

They swung on like dead men in a gray land of death. The moon grew red and sinister as she sank, and shadowy darkness settled over the desert before they had reached a point where they could see what lay beyond the broken belt. Even the big Afghan's feet began to drag, and Steve kept himself erect only by a savage effort of will. At last they toiled up a sort of ridge, on the southern side of which the land sloped downward.

"We rest," declared Steve. "There's no water in this hellish country. No use in goin' on for ever. My legs are stiff as gun-barrels. I couldn't take another step to save my neck. Here's a kind of stunted cliff, about as high as a man's shoulder, facing south. We'll sleep in the lee of it."

"And shall we not keep watch, Steve *sahib?*"

"We don't," answered Steve. "If the Arabs cut our throats while we're asleep, so much the better. We're goners anyhow."

With which optimistic observation Clarney lay down stiffly in the deep sand. But Yar Ali stood, leaning forward, straining his eyes into the elusive darkness that turned the star-flecked horizons to murky wells of shadow.

"Something lies on the skyline to the south," he muttered uneasily. "A hill? I cannot tell, or even be sure that I see anything at all."

"You're seeing mirages already," said Steve irritably. "Lie down and sleep."

And so saying Steve slumbered.

The sun in his eyes awoke him. He sat up, yawning, and his first sensation was that of thirst. He lifted his canteen and wet his lips. One drink left. Yar Ali still slept. Steve's eyes wandered over the southern horizon and he started. He kicked the recumbent Afghan.

"Hey, wake up, Ali. I reckon you weren't seeing things after all. There's your hill—and a queer-lookin' one, too."

The Afridi woke as a wild thing wakes, instantly and completely, his hand leaping to his long knife

as he glared about for enemies. His gaze followed
Steve's pointing fingers and his eyes widened.

"By Allah and by Allah!" he swore. "We have
come into a land of djinn! That is no hill—it is a
city of stone in the midst of the sands!"

Steve bounded to his feet like a steel spring
released. As he gazed with bated breath, a fierce
shout escaped his lips. At his feet the slope of the
ridge ran down into a wide and level expanse of
sand that stretched away southward. And far away,
across the sands, to his straining sight the "hill"
slowly took shape, like a mirage growing from the
drifting sands.

He saw great uneven walls, massive battlements;
all about crawled the sands like a living, sensate
thing, drifted high about the walls, softening the
rugged outlines. No wonder that at first glance the
whole had appeared like a hill.

"Kara-Shehr!" Clarney exclaimed fiercely. "Beled-
ed-Djinn! The city of the dead! It wasn't a pipe-
dream after all! We've found it—by Heaven, we've
found it! Come on! Let's go!"

Yar Ali shook his head uncertainly and muttered
something about evil djinn under his breath, but he
followed. The sight of the ruins had swept from
Steve his thirst and hunger, and the fatigue that a
few hours' sleep had not fully overcome. He
trudged on swiftly, oblivious to the rising heat, his
eyes gleaming with the lust of the explorer. It was
not altogether greed for the fabled gem that had
prompted Steve Clarney to risk his life in that grim
wilderness; deep in his soul lurked the age-old heritage of the white man, the urge to seek out the

hidden places of the world, and that urge had been stirred to the depths by the ancient tales.

Now as they crossed the level wastes that separated the broken land from the city, they saw the shattered walls take clearer form and shape, as if they grew out of the morning sky. The city seemed built of huge blocks of black stone, but how high the walls had been there was no telling because of the sand that drifted high about their base; in many places they had fallen away and the sand hid the fragments entirely.

The sun reached her zenith and thirst intruded itself in spite of zeal and enthusiasm, but Steve fiercely mastered his suffering. His lips were parched and swollen, but he would not take that last drink until he had reached the ruined city. Yar Ali wet his lips from his own canteen and tried to share the remainder with his friend. Steve shook his head and plodded on.

In the ferocious heat of the dessert afternoon they reached the ruin, and passing through a wide breach in the crumbling wall, gazed on the dead city. Sand choked the ancient streets and lent fantastic form to huge, fallen and half-hidden columns. So crumbled into decay and so covered with sand was the whole that the explorers could make out little of the original plan of the city; now it was but a waste of drifted sand and crumbling stone over which brooded, like an invisible cloud, an aura of unspeakable antiquity.

But directly in front of them ran a broad avenue, the outline of which not even the ravaging sands and winds of time had been able to efface. On either side of the wide way were ranged huge columns, not unusually tall, even allowing for the sand that hid their bases, but incredibly massive. On the top of each column stood a figure carved from solid stone—great, somber images, half human, half bestial, partaking of the brooding brutishness of the whole city. Steve cried out in amazement.

"The winged bulls of Nineveh! The bulls with men's heads! By the saints, Ali, the old tales are true! The Assyrians did build this city! The whole tale's true! They must have come here when the Babylonians destroyed Assyria—why, this scene's a dead ringer for pictures I've seen—reconstructed scenes of Old Nineveh! And look!"

He pointed down the broad street to the great building which reared at the other end, a colossal, brooding edifice whose columns and walls of solid black stone blocks defied the winds and sands of time. The drifting, obliterating sea washed about its foundations, overflowing into its doorways, but it would require a thousand years to inundate the whole structure.

"An abode of devils!" muttered Yar Ali, uneasily.

"The temple of Baal!" exclaimed Steve. "Come on! I was afraid we'd find all the palaces and temples hidden by the sand and have to dig for the gem."

"Little good it will do us," muttered Yar Ali. "Here we die."

"I reckon so." Steve unscrewed the cap of his canteen. "Let's take our last drink. Anyway, we're safe from the Arabs. They'd never dare come here, with their superstitions. We'll drink and then we'll die, I reckon, but first we'll find the jewel. When I pass out, I want to have it in my hand. Maybe a few centuries later some lucky son-of-a-gun will find

our skeletons—and the gem. Here's to him, whoever he is!"

With which grim jest Clarney drained his canteen
and Yar Ali followed suit. They had played their last
ace; the rest lay on the lap of Allah.

They strode up the broad way, and Yar Ali,
utterly fearless in the face of human foes, glanced
nervously to right and left, half expecting to see a
horned and fantastic face leering at him from
behind a column. Steve himself felt the somber
antiquity of the place, and almost found himself
fearing a rush of bronze war chariots down the forgotten streets, or to hear the sudden menacing flare
of bronze trumpets. The silence in dead cities was
so much more intense, he reflected, than that on
the open desert.

They came to the portals of the great temple.
Rows of immense columns flanked the wide doorway, which was ankle-deep in sand, and from which
sagged massive bronze frameworks that had once
braced mighty doors, whose polished woodwork had
rotted away centuries ago. They passed into a
mighty hall of misty twilight, whose shadowy stone
roof was upheld by columns like the trunks of forest
trees. The whole effect of the architecture was one
of awesome magnitude and sullen, breathtaking
splendor, like a temple built by somber giants for
the abode of dark gods.

Yar Ali walked fearfully, as if he expected to
awake sleeping gods, and Steve, without the Afridi's
superstitions, yet felt the gloomy majesty of the
place lay somber hands on his soul.

No trace of a footprint showed in the deep dust
on the floor; half a century had passed since the

affrighted and devil-ridden Turk had fled these silent halls. As for the Bedouins, it was easy to see why those superstitious sons of the desert shunned this haunted city—and haunted it was, not by actual ghosts, perhaps, but by the shadows of lost splendors.

As they trod the sands of the hall, which seemed endless, Steve pondered many questions: How did these fugitives from the wrath of frenzied rebels build this city? How did they pass through the country of their foes,—for Babylonia lay between Assyria and the Arabian desert. Yet there had been no other place for them to go; westward lay Syria and the sea, and north and east swarmed the "dangerous Medes," those fierce Aryans whose aid had stiffened the arm of Babylon to smite her foe to the dust.

Possibly, thought Steve, Kara-Shehr—whatever its name had been in those dim days—had been built as an outpost border city before the fall of the Assyrian empire, whither survivals of that overthrow fled. At any rate it was possible that Kara-Shehr had outlasted Nineveh by some centuries—a strange, hermit city, no doubt, cut off from the rest of the world.

Surely, as Yar Ali had said, this was once fertile country, watered by oases; and doubtless in the broken country they had passed over the night before, there had been quarries that furnished the stone for the building of the city.

Then what caused its downfall? Did the encroachment of the sands and the filling up of the springs cause the people to abandon it, or was Kara-Shehr a city of silence before the sands crept over the walls? Did the downfall come from within or without? Did civil war blot out the inhabitants, or were they slaughtered by some powerful foe from the desert? Clarney shook his head in baffled chagrin. The answers to those questions were lost in the maze of forgotten ages.

"*Allaho akbar!*" They had traversed the great shadowy hall and at its further end they came upon a hideous black stone altar, behind which loomed an ancient god, bestial and horrific. Steve shrugged his shoulders as he recognized the monstrous aspect of the image—aye, that was Baal, on which black altar in other ages many a screaming, writhing, naked victim had offered up its naked soul. The idol embodied in its utter, abysmal and sullen bestiality the whole soul of this demoniac city. Surely, thought Steve, the builders of Nineveh and Kara-Shehr were cast in another mold from the people of today. Their art and culture were too ponderous, too grimly barren of the lighter aspects of humanity, to be wholly human, as modern man understands humanity. Their architecture was repellent; of high skill, yet so massive, sullen and brutish in effect as to be almost beyond the comprehension of moderns.

The adventurers passed through a narrow door which opened in the end of the hall close to the idol, and came into a series of wide, dim, dusty chambers connected by column-flanked corridors. Along these they strode in the gray ghostly light, and came at last to a wide stair, whose massive stone steps led upward and vanished in the gloom. Here Yar Ali halted.

"We have dared much, *sahib*," he muttered. "Is it wise to dare more?"

Steve, aquiver with eagerness, yet understood the

Afghan's mind. "You mean we shouldn't go up those stairs?"

"They have an evil look. To what chambers of silence and horror may they lead? When djinn haunt deserted buildings, they lurk in the upper chambers. At any moment a demon may bite off our heads."

"We're dead men anyhow," grunted Steve. "But I tell you—you go on back through the hall and watch for the Arabs while I go upstairs."

"Watch for a wind on the horizon," responded the Afghan gloomily, shifting his rifle and loosening his long knife in its scabbard. "No Bedouin comes here. Lead on, *sahib*. Thou'rt mad after the manner of all Franks, but I would not leave thee to face the djinn alone."

So the companions mounted the massive stairs, their feet sinking deep into the accumulated dust of centuries at each step. Up and up they went, to an incredible height until the depths below emerged into a vague gloom.

"We walk blind to our doom, *sahib*," muttered Yar Ali. "*Allah il allah*—and Muhammad is his Prophet! Nevertheless, I feel the presence of slumbering Evil and never again shall I hear the wind blowing up the Khyber Pass."

Steve made no reply. He did not like the breathless silence that brooded over the ancient temple, nor the grisly gray light that filtered from some hidden source.

Now above them the gloom lightened somewhat and they emerged into a vast circular chamber, grayly illumined by light that filtered in through the high, pierced ceiling. But another radiance lent itself to the illumination. A cry burst from Steve's lips, echoed by Yar Ali.

Standing on the top step of the broad stone stair, they looked directly across the broad chamber, with its dust-covered heavy tile floor and bare black stone walls. From above the center of the chamber, massive steps led up to a stone dais, and on this dais stood a marble throne. About this throne glowed and shimmered an uncanny light, and the awe-struck adventurers gasped as they saw its source. On the throne slumped a human skeleton, an almost shapeless mass of moldering bones. A fleshless hand sagged outstretched upon the broad marble throne-arm, and in its grisly clasp there pulsed and throbbed like a living thing, a great crimson stone.

The Fire of Asshurbanipal! Even after they had found the lost city Steve had not really allowed himself to believe that they would find the gem, or that it even existed in reality. Yet he could not doubt the evidence of his eyes, dazzled by that evil, incredible glow. With a fierce shout he sprang across the chamber and up the steps. Yar Ali was at his heels, but when Steve would have seized the gem, the Afghan laid a hand on his arm.

"Wait!" exclaimed the big Muhammadan. "Touch it not yet, *sahib!* A curse lies on ancient things— and surely this is a thing triply accursed! Else why has it lain here untouched in a country of thieves for so many centuries? It is not well to disturb the possessions of the dead."

"Bosh!" snorted the American. "Superstitions! The Bedouins were scared by the tales that have come down to 'em from their ancestors. Being desert-dwellers they mistrust cities anyway, and no doubt this one had an evil reputation in its lifetime. And nobody except Bedouins have seen this place before, except that Turk, who was probably half demented with suffering.

"These bones may be those of the king mentioned in the legend—the dry desert air preserves such things indefinitely—but I doubt it. May be Assyrian—most likely Arab—some beggar that got the gem and then died on that throne for some reason or other."

The Afghan scarcely heard him. He was gazing in fearful fascination at the great stone, as a hypnotized bird stares into a serpent's eye.

"Look at it, *sahib!*" he whispered. "What is it? No such gem as this was ever cut by mortal hands! Look how it throbs and pulses like the heart of a cobra!"

Steve was looking, and he was aware of a strange undefined feeling of uneasiness. Well versed in the knowledge of precious stones, he had never seen a stone like this. At first glance he had supposed it to be a monster ruby, as told in the legends. Now he was not sure, and he had a nervous feeling that Yar Ali was right, that this was no natural, normal gem. He could not classify the style in which it was cut, and such was the power of its lurid radiance that he found it difficult to gaze at it closely for any length of time. The whole setting was not one calculated to soothe restless nerves. The deep dust on the floor suggested an unwholesome antiquity; the gray light evoked a sense of unreality, and the heavy black walls towered grimly, hinting at hidden things.

"Let's take the stone and go!" muttered Steve, an unaccustomed panicky dread rising in his bosom.

"Wait!" Yar Ali's eyes were blazing, and he gazed, not at the gem, but at the sullen stone walls. "We are flies in the lair of the spider! *Sahib*, as Allah lives, it is more than the ghosts of old fears that lurk over this city of horror! I feel the presence of peril, as I have felt it before—as I felt it in a jungle cavern where a python lurked unseen in the darkness—as I felt it in the temple of Thuggee where the hidden stranglers of Siva crouched to spring upon us—as I feel it now, tenfold!"

Steve's hair prickled. He knew that Yar Ali was a grim veteran, not to be stampeded by silly fear or senseless panic; he well remembered the incidents referred to by the Afghan, as he remembered other occasions upon which Yar Ali's Oriental telepathic instinct had warned him of danger before that danger was seen or heard.

"What is it, Ali?" he whispered.

The Afghan shook his head, his eyes filled with a weird mysterious light as he listened to the dim occult promptings of his subconsciousness.

"I know not; I know it is close to us, and that it is very ancient and very evil. I think—" Suddenly he halted and wheeled, the eery light vanishing from his eyes to be replaced by a glare of wolf-like fear and suspicion.

"Hark, *sahib!*" he snapped. "Ghosts or dead men mount the stair!"

Steve stiffened as the stealthy pad of soft sandals on stone reached his ear.

"By Judas, Ali!" he rapped; "something's out there—"

The ancient walls re-echoed to a chorus of wild yells as a horde of savage figures flooded the chamber. For one dazed insane instant Steve believed wildly that they were being attacked by re-embodied warriors of a vanished age; then the spiteful crack of a bullet past his ear and the acrid smell of powder told him that their foes were material enough. Clarney cursed; in their fancied security they had been caught like rats in a trap by the pursuing Arabs.

Even as the American threw up his rifle, Yar Ali fired point-blank from the hip with deadly effect, hurled his empty rifle into the horde and went down the steps like a hurricane, his three-foot Khyber knife shimmering in his hairy hand. Into his gusto for battle went real relief that his foes were human. A bullet ripped the turban from his head, but an Arab went down with a split skull beneath the hillman's first, shearing stroke.

A tall Bedouin clapped his gun-muzzle to the Afghan's side, but before he could pull the trigger, Clarney's bullet scattered his brains. The very number of the attackers hindered their onslaught on the big Afridi, whose tigerish quickness made shooting as dangerous to themselves as to him. The bulk of them swarmed about him, striking with scimitar and rifle-stock while others charged up the steps after Steve. At that range there was no missing; the American simply thrust his rifle muzzle into a bearded face and blasted it into a ghastly ruin. The others came on, screaming like panthers.

And now as he prepared to expend his last cartridge, Clarney saw two things in one flashing instant—a wild warrior who, with froth on his beard and a heavy scimitar uplifted, was almost upon him, and another who knelt on the floor drawing a careful bead on the plunging Yar Ali. Steve made an instant choice and fired over the shoulder of the charging swordsman, killing the rifleman—and voluntarily offering his own life for his friend's; for the scimitar was swinging at his own head. But even as the Arab swung, grunting with the force of the blow, his sandaled foot slipped on the marble steps and the curved blade, veering erratically from its arc, clashed on Steve's rifle-barrel. In an instant the American clubbed his rifle, and as the Bedouin recovered his balance and again heaved up the scimitar, Clarney struck with all his rangy power, and stock and skull shattered together.

Then a heavy ball smacked into his shoulder, sickening him with the shock.

As he staggered dizzily, a Bedouin whipped a turban-cloth about his feet and jerked viciously. Clarney pitched headlong down the steps, to strike with stunning force. A gun-stock in a brown hand went up to dash out his brains, but an imperious command halted the blow.

"Slay him not, but bind him hand and foot."

As Steve struggled dazedly against many gripping hands, it seemed to him that somewhere he had heard that imperious voice before.

The American's downfall had occurred in a matter of seconds. Even as Steve's second shot had cracked, Yar Ali had half severed a raider's arm and himself received a numbing blow from a rifle-stock on his left shoulder. His sheepskin coat, worn despite the desert heat, saved his hide from half a dozen slashing knives. A rifle was discharged so close to his face that the powder burnt him fiercely, bringing a bloodthirsty yell from the maddened Afghan. As Yar Ali swung up his dripping blade the rifleman, ashy-faced, lifted his rifle above his head in both hands to parry the downward blow, whereat the Afridi, with a yelp of ferocious exultation, shifted as a jungle-cat strikes and plunged his long knife into the Arab's belly. But at that instant a rifle-stock, swung with all the hardy ill-will its wielder could evoke, crashed against the giant's head, laying open the scalp and dashing him to his knees.

With the dogged and silent ferocity of his breed, Yar Ali staggered blindly up again, slashing at foes he could scarcely see, but a storm of blows battered him down again, nor did his attackers cease beating him until he lay still. They would have finished him in short order then but for another peremptory order from their chief; whereupon they bound the senseless knife-man and flung him down alongside Steve, who was fully conscious and aware of the savage hurt of the bullet in his shoulder.

He glared up at the tall Arab who stood looking down at him.

"Well, *sahib*," said this one—and Steve saw he was no Bedouin—"do you not remember me?"

Steve scowled; a bullet-wound is no aid to concentration.

"You look familiar—by Judas!—you are! Nureddin El Mekru!"

"I am honored! The *sahib* remembers!" Nureddin salaamed mockingly. "And you remember, no doubt, the occasion on which you made me a present of—this?"

The dark eyes shadowed with bitter menace and the shaykh indicated a thin white scar on the angle of his jaw.

"I remember," snarled Clarney, whom pain and

anger did not tend to make docile. "It was in Somaliland, years ago. You were in the slave-tarde then.
A wretch of a nigger escaped from you and took
refuge with me. You walked into my camp one night
in your high-handed way, started a row and in the
ensuing scrap you got a butcher-knife across your
face. I wish I'd cut your lousy throat."

"You had your chance," answered the Arab.
"Now the tables are turned."

"I thought your stamping-ground lay west,"
growled Clarney; "Yemen and the Somali country."

"I quit the slave-trade long ago," answered the
shaykh. "It is an outworn game. I led a band of
thieves in Yemen for a time; then again I was forced
to change my location. I came here with a few faithful followers, and by Allah, those wild men nearly
slit my throat at first. But I overcame their suspi-
cions, and now I lead more men than have followed
me in years.

"They whom you fought off yesterday were my
men—scouts I had sent out ahead. My oasis lies far
to the west. We have ridden for many days, for I was
on my way to this very city. When my scouts rode in
and told me of two wanderers, I did not alter my
course, for I had business first in Beled-el-Djinn. We
rode into the city from the west and saw your tracks
in the sand. We followed them, and you were blind
buffalo who heard not our coming."

Steve snarled. "You wouldn't have caught us so
easy, only we thought no Bedouin would dare come
into Kara-Shehr."

Nureddin nodded. "But I am no Bedouin. I have
traveled far and seen many lands and many races,
and I have read many books. I know that fear is
smoke, that the dead are dead, and that djinn and

ghosts and curses are mists that the wind blows away. It was because of the tales of the red stone that I came into this forsaken desert. But it has taken months to persuade my men to ride with me here.

"But—I am here! And your presence is a delightful surprise. Doubtless you have guessed why I had you taken alive; I have more elaborate entertainment planned for you and that Pathan swine. Now—I take the Fire of Asshurbanipal and we will go."

He turned toward the dais, and one of his men, a bearded one-eyed giant, exclaimed, "Hold, my lord! Ancient evil reigned here before the days of Muhammad! The djinn howl through these halls when the winds blow, and men have seen ghosts dancing on the walls beneath the moon. No man of mortals has dared this black city for a thousand years—save one, half a century ago, who fled shrieking.

"You have come here from Yemen; you do not know the ancient curse on this foul city, and this evil stone, which pulses like the red heart of Satan! We have followed you here against our judgement, because you have proven yourself a strong man, and have said you hold a charm against all evil beings. You said you but wished to look on this mysterious gem, but now we see it is your intention to take it for yourself. Do not offend the djinn!"

"Nay, Nureddin, do not offend the djinn!" chorused the other Bedouins. The shaykh's own hard-bitten ruffians, standing in a compact group somewhat apart from the Bedouins, said nothing; hardened to crimes and deeds of impiety, they were less affected by the superstitions of the desert men, to whom the dread tale of the accursed city had been repeated for centuries. Steve, even while hating Nureddin with concentrated venom, realized the magnetic power of the man, the innate leadership that had enabled him to overcome thus far the fears and traditions of ages.

"The curse is laid on infidels who invade the city," answered Nureddin, "not on the Faithful. See, in this chamber have we overcome our *kafar* foes!"

A white-bearded desert hawk shook his head.

"The curse is more ancient than Muhammad, and recks not of race or creed. Evil men reared this black city in the dawn of the Beginnings of Days. They oppressed our ancestors of the black tents, and warred among themselves; aye, the black walls of this foul city were stained with blood, and echoed to the shouts of unholy revel and the whispers of dark intrigues.

"Thus came the stone to the city; there dwelt a magician at the court of Asshurbanipal, and the black wisdom of ages was not denied to him. To gain honor and power for himself, he dared the horrors of a nameless vast cavern in a dark, untraveled land, and from those fiend-haunted depths he brought that blazing gem, which is carved of the frozen flames of Hell! By reason of his fearful power in black magic, he put a spell on the demon which guarded the ancient gem, and so stole away the stone. And the demon slept in the cavern unknowing.

"So this magician—Xuthltan by name—dwelt in the court of the sultan Asshurbanipal and did magic and forecast events by scanning the lurid deeps of the stone, into which no eyes but his could look unblinded. And men called the stone the Fire of Asshurbanipal, in honor of the king.

"But evil came upon the kingdom and men cried out that it was the curse of the djinn, and the sultan in great fear bade Xuthltan take the gem and cast it into the cavern from which he had taken it, lest worse ill befall them.

"Yet it was not the magician's will to give up the gem wherein he read strange secrets of pre-Adamite days, and he fled to the rebel city of Kara-Shehr, where soon civil war broke out and men strove with one another to possess the gem. Then the king who ruled the city, coveting the stone, seized the magician and put him to death by torture, and in this very room he watched him die; with the gem in his hand the king sat upon the throne—even as he has sat upon the throne—even as he has sat throughout the centuries—even as now he sits!"

The Arab's finger stabbed at the moldering bones on the marble throne, and the wild desert men blenched; even Nureddin's own scoundrels recoiled, catching their breath, but the shaykh showed no sign of perturbation.

"As Xuthltan died," continued the old Bedouin, "he cursed the stone whose magic had not saved him, and he shrieked aloud the fearful words which undid the spell he had put upon the demon in the cavern, and set the monster free. And crying out on the forgotten gods, Cthulhu and Koth and Yog-Sothoth, and all the pre-Adamite Dwellers in the black cities under the sea and the caverns of the earth, he called upon them to take back that which was theirs, and with his dying breath pronounced doom on the false king, and that doom was that the king should sit on his throne holding in his hand the Fire of Asshurbanipal until the thunder of Judgment Day.

"Thereat the great stone cried out as a live thing cries, and the king and his soldiers saw a black cloud spinning up from the floor, and out of the cloud blew a fetid wind, and out of the wind came a grisly shape which stretched forth fearsome paws and laid them on the king, who shriveled and died at their touch. And the soldiers fled screaming, and all the people of the city ran forth wailing into the desert, where they perished or gained through the wastes to the far oasis towns. Kara-Shehr lay silent and deserted, the haunt of the lizard and the jackal. And when some of the desert-people ventured into the city they found the king dead on his throne, clutching the blazing gem, but they dared not lay hand upon it, for they knew the demon lurked near to guard it through all the ages—as he lurks near even as we stand here."

The warriors shuddered involuntarily and glanced about, and Nureddin said, "Why did he not come forth when the Franks entered the chamber? Is he deaf, that the sound of the combat has not awakened him?"

"We have not touched the gem," answered the old Bedouin, "nor had the Franks molested it. Men have looked on it and lived; but no mortal may touch it and survive."

Nureddin started to speak, gazed at the stubborn, uneasy faces and realized the futility of argument. His attitude changed abruptly.

"I am master here," he snapped, dropping a hand to his holster. "I have not sweat and bled for this gem to be balked at the last by groundless fears!

Stand back, all! Let any man cross me at the peril of his head!"

He faced them, his eyes blazing, and they fell back, cowed up the force of his ruthless personality. He strode boldly by the marble steps, and the Arabs caught their breath, recoiling toward the door; Yar Ali, conscious at last, groaned dismally. God! thought Steve, what a barbaric scene!—bound captives on the dust-heaped floor, wild warriors clustered about, gripping their weapons, the raw acrid scent of blood and burnt powder still fouling the air, corpses strewn in a horrid welter of blood, brains and entrails—and on the dais, the hawk-faced shaykh, oblivious to all except the evil crimson glow in the skeleton fingers that rested on the marble throne.

A tense silence gripped all as Nureddin stretched forth his hand slowly, as if hypnotized by the throbbing crimson light. And in Steve's subconsciousness there shuddered a dim echo, as of something vast and loathsome waking suddenly from an age-long slumber. The American's eyes moved instinctively toward the grim cyclopean walls. The jewel's glow had altered strangely; it burned a deeper, darker red, angry and menacing.

"Heart of all evil," murmured the shaykh, "how many princes died for thee in the Beginnings of Happenings? Surely the blood of kings throbs in thee. The sultans and the princesses and the generals who wore thee, they are dust and are forgotten, but thou blazest with majesty undimmed, fire of the world—"

Nureddin seized the stone. A shuddery wail broke from the Arabs, cut through by a sharp inhuman cry. To Steve it seemed, horribly, that the great jewel had cried out like a living thing! The stone slipped from the shaykh's hand. Nureddin might have dropped it; to Steve it looked as though it leaped convulsively, as a live thing might leap. It rolled from the dais, bounding from step to step, with Nureddin springing after it, cursing as his clutching hand missed it. It struck the floor, veered sharply, and despite the deep dust, rolled like a revolving ball of fire toward the back wall. Nureddin was close upon it—it struck the wall—the shaykh's hand reached for it.

A scream of mortal fear ripped the tense silence. Without warning the solid wall had opened. Out of the black wall that gaped there, a tentacle shot and gripped the shaykh's body as a python girdles its victim, and jerked him headlong into the darkness. And then the wall showed blank and solid once more; only from within sounded a hideous, high-pitched, muffled screaming that chilled the blood of the listeners. Howling wordlessly, the Arabs stampeded, jammed in a battling, screeching mass in the doorway, tore through and raced madly down the wide stairs.

Steve and Yar Ali, lying helplessly, heard the frenzied clamor of their flight fade away into the distance, and gazed in dumb horror at the grim wall. The shrieks had faded into a more horrific silence. Holding their breath, they heard suddenly a sound that froze the blood in their veins—the soft sliding of metal or stone in a groove. At the same time the hidden door began to open, and Steve caught a glimmer in the blackness that might have been the glitter of monstrous eyes. He closed his own eyes; he dared not look upon whatever horror slunk from that hideous black well. He knew that there

are strains the human brain cannot stand, and every
primitive instinct in his soul cried out to him that
this thing was nightmare and lunacy. He sensed that
Yar Ali likewise closed his eyes, and the two lay like
dead men.

Clarney heard no sound, but he sensed the presence of a horrific evil too grisly for human comprehension—of an invader from Outer Gulfs and far
black reaches of cosmic being. A deadly cold per-
vaded the chamber, and Steve felt the glare of inhuman eyes sear through his closed lids and freeze his
consciousness. If he looked, if he opened his eyes,
he knew stark black madness would be his instant
lot.

He felt a soul-shakingly foul breath against his
face and knew that the monster was bending close
above him, but he lay like a man frozen in a nightmare. He clung to one thought: neither he nor Yar
Ali had touched the jewel this horror guarded.

Then he no longer smelled the foul odor, the
coldness in the air grew appreciably less, and he
heard again the secret door slide in its groove. The
fiend was returning to its hiding-place. Not all the
legions of Hell could have prevented Steve's eyes
from opening a trifle. He had only a glimpse as the
hidden door slid to—and that one glimpse was
enough to drive all consciousness from his brain.
Steve Clarney, iron-nerved adventurer, fainted for
the only time in his checkered life.

How long he lay there Steve never knew, but it
could not have been long, for he was roused by Yar
Ali's whisper, "Lie still, *sahib*, a little shifting of my
body and I can reach thy cords with my teeth."

Steve felt the Afghan's powerful teeth at work on

his bonds, and as he lay with his face jammed into the thick dust, and his wounded shoulder began to throb agonizingly—he had forgotten it until now—he began to gather the wandering threads of his consciousness, and it all came back to him. How much, he wondered dazedly, had been the nightmares of delirium, born from suffering and the thirst that caked his throat? The fight with the Arabs had been real—the bonds and the wounds showed that—but the grisly doom of the shaykh—the thing that had crept out of the black entrance in the wall—surely that had been a figment of delirium. Nureddin had fallen into a well or pit of some sort—Steve felt his hands were free and he rose to a sitting posture, fumbling for a pocket-knife the Arabs had overlooked. He did not look up or about the chamber as he slashed the cords that bound his ankles, and then freed Yar Ali, working awkwardly because his left arm was stiff and useless.

"Where are the Bedouins?" he asked, as the Afghan rose, lifting him to his feet.

"Allah, *sahib,*" whispered Yar Ali, "are you mad? Have you forgotten? Let us go quickly before the djinn returns!"

"It was a nightmare," muttered Steve. "Look—the jewel is back on the throne—" His voice died out. Again that red glow throbbed about the ancient throne, reflecting from the moldering skull; again in the outstretched finger-bones pulsed the Fire of Asshurbanipal. But at the foot of the throne lay another object that had not been there before—the severed head of Nureddin el Mekru stared sightlessly up at the gray light filtering through the stone ceiling. The bloodless lips were drawn back from the teeth in a ghastly grin, the staring eyes mirrored an intolerable horror. In the thick dust of the floor three spoors showed—one of the shaykh's where he had followed the red jewel as it rolled to the wall, and above it two other sets of tracks, coming to the throne and returning to the wall—vast, shapeless tracks, as of splayed feet, taloned and gigantic, neither human nor animal.

"My God!" choked Steve. "It was true—and the Thing—the Thing I saw—"

Steve remembered the flight from that chamber as a rushing nightmare, in which he and his companion hurtled headlong down an endless stair that was a gray well of fear, raced blindly through dusty silent chambers, past the glowering idol in the mighty hall and into the blazing light of the desert sun, where they fell slavering, fighting for breath.

Again Steve was roused by the Afridi's voice: "*Sahib, sahib,* in the Name of Allah the Compassionate, our luck has turned!"

Steve looked at his companion as a man might look in a trance. The big Afghan's garments were in tatters, and blood-soaked. He was stained with dust and caked with blood, and his voice was a croak. But his eyes were alight with hope and he pointed with a trembling finger.

"In the shade of yon ruined wall!" he croaked, striving to moisten his blackened lips. "*Allah il allah!* The horses of the men we killed! With canteens and food-pouches at the saddle-horns! Those dogs fled without halting for the steeds of their comrades!"

New life surged up into Steve's bosom and he rose, staggering.

"Out of here," he mumbled. "Out of here, quick!"

Like dying men they stumbled to the horses, tore them loose and climbed fumblingly into the saddles.

"We'll lead the spare mounts," croaked Steve, and Yar Ali nodded emphatic agreement.

"Belike we shall need them ere we sight the coast."

Though their tortured nerves screamed for the water that swung in canteens at the saddle-horns, they turned the mounts aside and, swaying in the saddle, rode like flying corpses down the long sandy street of Kara-Shehr, between the ruined palaces and the crumbling columns, crossed the fallen wall and swept out into the desert. Not once did either glance back toward that black pile of ancient horror, nor did either speak until the ruins faded into the hazy distance. Then and only then did they draw rein and ease their thirst.

"*Allah il allah!*" said Yar Ali piously. "Those dogs have beaten me until it is as though every bone in my body were broken. Dismount, I beg thee, *sahib*, and let me probe for that accursed bullet, and dress they shoulder to the best of my meager ability."

While this was going on, Yar Ali spoke, avoiding his friend's eye. "You said, *sahib*, you said something about—about seeing? What saw ye, in Allah's name?"

A strong shudder shook the American's steely frame.

"You didn't look when—when the—the Thing put back the jewel in the skeleton's hand and left Nureddin's head on the dais?"

"By Allah, not I!" swore Yar Ali. "My eyes were

as closed as if they had been welded together by the molten irons of Satan!"

Steve made no reply until the comrades had once more swung into the saddle and started on their long trek for the coast, which, with spare horses, food, water and weapons, they had a good chance to reach.

"I looked," the American said somberly. "I wish I had not; I know I'll dream about it for the rest of my life. I had only a glance; I couldn't describe it as a man describes an earthly thing. God help me, it wasn't earthly or sane either. Mankind isn't the first owner of the earth; there were Beings here before his coming—and now, survivals of hideously ancient epochs. Maybe spheres of alien dimensions press unseen on this material universe today. Sorcerers have called up sleeping devils before now and controlled them with magic. It is not unreasonable to suppose an Assyrian magician could invoke an elemental demon out of the earth to avenge him and guard something that must have come out of Hell in the first place.

"I'll try to tell you what I glimpsed; then we'll never speak of it again. It was gigantic and black and shadowy; it was a hulking monstrosity that walked upright like a man, but it was like a toad, too, and it was winged and tentacled. I saw only its back; if I'd seen the front of it—its face—I'd have undoubtedly lost my mind. The old Arab was right; God help us, it was the monster that Xuthltan called up out of the dark blind caverns of the earth to guard the Fire of Asshurbanipal!"